ARCANA
THE DEVIL'S MANDRAKE

JOSHUA FENNER

Arcana
The Devil's Mandrake

Copyright © Joshua Fenner, 2012

All characters in this book are fictitious. Any resemblance to actual persons, living or dead, is purely coincidental.

ISBN: 978-0-9856271-0-2

For mom and dad

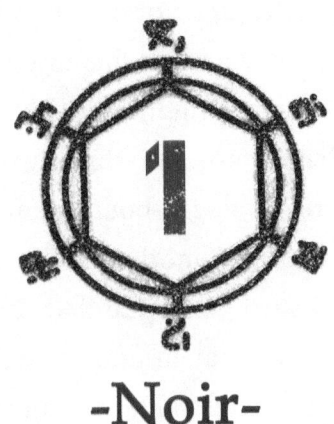

-Noir-

It was a starless Thursday night, but most of them are when you live in a big city. Clouds that were gray enough to be black spat the occasional raindrop to the ground, into an asphalt crater in the road, or at the dusty panes of my apartment's windows. The tempo that thudded after was persistent but slow, pattering out a song that made you long for something just beyond memory, like an event that hadn't happened yet. It was the perfect night to plan for a jewel heist.

To that end, I had invited a couple of mooks over. I guess you could call them friends, or maybe business associates. They had both been to my apartment a few times, usually to plan out some kind of job. This time they sat in the living room, where the feeble light of a forty dollar floor lamp spread shadows across the dirty beige carpet. Their faces were obscured under the brims of two very different hats.

I mean that literally. No metaphor there. The first was in a top hat straight out of a Dickens novel. He was seated in a wooden chair, wearing a black Victorian suit, his arms wrapped around his chest with a steadily increasing tightness. That was Lucas Worthing. Stuffy, uppity, and British are the three words I would use to describe him if we were playing a board game where you have to choose three words to describe another player within a time limit. I think there might be a board game like that. If there is, it's the sort of thing Lucas would play. That in and of itself tells you as much about him as you probably need to know. I mentioned that he wears a top hat, right?

Then there was Kurt. He was situated on the couch with his hands crammed behind his head, the brim of a torn baseball cap completely overshadowing his rounded, stubbly features. Kurt was a friend of mine from high school. He didn't talk much, but he was a good guy. Where Lucas was irritable, edgy, and the textbook definition of proper, Kurt was on the opposite end of the spectrum. His emotions didn't boil over often, but when they did, it meant trouble for everyone in a mile radius. And when he bothered to open his mouth, you knew to shut up and listen, because it was important.

I kept up my watch from the kitchen, leaning on a wall at the threshold between rooms. Mother nature's quiet sonata had caught me off-guard, so I stopped to listen for a while. She was one talented dame, playing on my heartstrings like that.

It couldn't last forever, though. I had business to discuss with the gents in the living room. Business about a hunk of rock like nothing you've ever seen. I cleared my throat before walking into the smoky room.

"Here's the thing, boys," I said, working the words around in my mouth like flat cola, "We've got another caper on our hands. It's not going to be easy, and it sure isn't going to be pretty, but I've got my eyes on something real nice for our private collection."

Neither of them said anything. I'd have to take that as my cue to explain our future misdeed further.

"It's called the Rouen Diamond. A great big gem, the size of my fist, understand? It's in a museum right now, the Ecotarium." I dropped a brochure for the place on the coffee table. It prominently featured a bunch of smiling kids at the base of a big telescope. I'd probably be smiling too, looking up at all those stars.

"Long story short, I think it'd look a lot nicer here. The cops probably won't agree, but hey, creative differences like those have never stopped us before." I smirked at the two, but still got nothing in response. "What do you say, gentlemen?"

"Foster, why on Earth are you speaking in that ridiculous manner?"

Of course, leave it to Lucas to ruin everything forever. Also, let me just say that he had no right to criticize my 50s gangster voice, especially with his pronounced English accent. At least I was making an effort, y'know?

"And why are we sitting here in the dark? Are you swearing off light bulbs for lent? Because I regret to inform you that it doesn't work that way."

"It's for the atmosphere, Lucas. What's so hard to understand about that? When you're planning to steal a gem from a museum, it's absolutely essential to have a film noir environment, and that includes dramatic lighting!"

3

"And that is the reason for the fine mist, I take it." The shadows that filled his tall, clean-shaven cheekbones shifted with each spoken word.

"Do you have something against fog machines?" I lifted a pretzel rod to my mouth and bit down on one end to simulate a cigar. "It took Kurt like twenty minutes to set that thing up."

"It would've taken five if you hadn't jammed a pencil in one end of it," Kurt noted.

"Regardless, who are you trying to impress? You already know that I have naught but disdain for literally everything about you." Lucas swirled his hands in the air a bit before going back to crossing his arms.

"C'mon. If that was true, you wouldn't even be here." I wasn't pleased to hear Lucas scoff at that sentiment, but I wasn't exactly surprised, either.

"Foster, if you believe that I am here because I enjoy your company or these criminal activities you thrust us into, you are even more delusional than I had thought. I am here because you told me months ago that you would be able to find a safeguard against my unique affliction as soon as you had the appropriate equipment!"

"Lucas, hey, don't worry about it! I promised I'd find you a cure, and I totally will. But you guys have to work with me, here. If I'm going to find you something that rare, I need the right stuff. And if we're going to steal the right stuff, we need a plan. And if we're planning, we need it to look like 1950s New York in here."

"We're going to need a lot more rats," Kurt said. He had a point, though I didn't know where we would find an open pet store at that hour.

"Sean!" A loud whisper came from the shadows of the

kitchen, "Sean, should I go in now?" That was my little sister, Zoe, who had been standing by the fridge with a few bottles of cream soda balanced on a white ceramic plate.

"Yeah! Go ahead!" I gave her a smile and a subtle thumbs up, and the little basket of energy and blonde hair bounced into the room. The drinks skittered on their porcelain tray like sailors on a capsizing ship, yet somehow she kept them aloft. Not bad for a five-year-old.

"Foster, really? Conscripting your younger sibling into the work force already?" Lucas shook his head disapprovingly, but my little sister didn't miss a beat.

"Nuh-uh! I told Sean I wanted to be a waitress or a princess for the meeting, and he said he didn't mind either way, but I wanted to wear my apron so I did." She nodded firmly and reached up to stick a bottle between Lucas' arms and his chest. "Enjoy your soda!"

He sighed, but even Lucas wasn't frigid enough to say no to her. When she came around the coffee table to Kurt, he smiled and accepted his drink a little more graciously, including a playful noogie as a tip. Zoe squealed and ran to me with the last bottle of cream soda.

"Thanks, doll," I said in my best gangster impersonation, "You done good, y'see? I'll talk to those guys at the mills and make sure you've got enough sugary cereal to last you a lifetime, yeah?"

"Myaah, y'see! Sounds good, boss!" Zoe held the plate against her embroidered apron with one hand and saluted me with the other. I could hear Lucas facepalming in the corner.

"Now you go get in the bath, y'see? Kaitlin's coming over to watch you while we case the joint, and I told her we didn't want no dirty rats in here." For some reason, my accent was quickly becoming more JFK-like by the second. Zoe didn't seem to notice. She just nodded, wrapped my legs in a hug, and skipped down the hallway to go wash up.

"She's a sweet kid," Kurt said after Zoe had gone. The moment she was out of sight, he pulled an old, rust-colored backpack up from the floor and into his lap. There was a zip, and then a pile of electronics and tools poured out next to him on the couch.

"You really don't waste time with that stuff, huh?" I grinned and moved closer to examine the tangle of wires. He was already fiddling with a circuit board and some kind of round metal casing by that point.

"Y'know what they say. Early bird blows up the worm."

"That is almost certainly not what any person says," Lucas sighed. "Can we just get on with this plan of yours? We will be here until you are both dead of old age at this rate."

"I don't know if I'm physically capable of talking for eighty years straight. That might be a feat, even for me." I said with a broad smile. "But I've never been one to shy away from a challenge!"

Lucas just sat and glowered at me. Tough crowd.

"The street entrance to the museum is surrounded by a concrete wall, and the woods surrounding it are protected by a chain-link fence. For anyone else, these would be problems, but it's nothing my book can't handle." I leaned over the coffee table to take up my messenger bag, which contained the book in question. It was a huge tome with binding the color of natural clay and pages that were made of thinner, ivory-colored leather. The symbols and diagrams inside had been burned there a long time ago, but they were still black and crisp somehow.

"I'm going to set up a chalk array on the street, which should be able to get us inside the perimeter. Once we're there, it's just a matter of breaking in and finding the diamond."

"What about security cameras?" Kurt asked, looking up from some wires he had been stripping.

"I'll take care of that when we get there, no worries." My book didn't just depict methods of teleportation. It also contained arrays that produced explosions, illusions, and probably hamsters if you used the right ingredients. Unfortunately, I had yet to find a way to make that last one useful.

"Why do I find that to be less than reassuring?" Lucas groaned.

"Probably because you're a negative Nellie. Or maybe your hat's on too tight. Either way, you don't need to worry. I've got this."

"My hat was crafted specifically for my head, I will have you know. I think it more likely that you have yet to display any tactical ability whatsoever, and there is no reason to assume it will be any different for this particular heist." He picked the brochure up off of the coffee table like it was covered in radioactive waste, pinching one corner and holding it far from his face. "What is it that we are stealing, exactly?"

"The Rouen Diamond," I repeated. "It's a huge, cut stone that was imbued with arcane powers by the legendary wizard Bernart Guizan. The enchantment he put on it still serves as inspiration for arcanists today. Without the legacy of his work, half the arrays in my book wouldn't exist."

"Yes, and that is all supremely interesting, I assure you, but I would like to know what the diamond itself does."

"You'll find out when we steal it," I stated, reaching over to nab the brochure from his gloved hand.

"What? Why?"

"Because it'll be better if it's a surprise." I said with a nod. "It'll be like your birthday, except we won't be in England and you'll get something other than fish and chips. Or monocles. Actually, do you own any monocles? I have this theory about British peoples' eyes I've never been able to decidedly prove."

"For the love of..." Lucas rubbed at one of his temples, undoubtedly trying to massage some frustration out of his head. "No, I do not! And if you refuse to explain the exact function of this rock, can we please just be on with it? The sooner we finish this task, the fewer brain hemorrhages I will develop in trying to comprehend the exact depths of your idiocy."

"That's the spirit!" I searched the pockets of my messenger bag for one of the simple visitor's maps you get when you go to the Ecotarium. It was folded up in the front pocket, next to my cell phone charger and a pack of stale gum. I flattened the map out and put it down on the coffee table for reference. "The plan is simple. We drive up, park at the high school down the road, and then walk up to the front gates. Like I said, a translocation rune will get us inside."

I placed my fingertip on the map where we'd end up, in front of a stegosaurus statue near the entrance. "It's a short walk up this path, staying as far as we can from any animal exhibits. We go in through this door," I said, pointing to the lower entrance of the museum's main building. "The whole wall is glass, so Kurt's got that one covered. Once we're inside, the mineral exhibit is right up the stairs."

I tossed the brochure down on top of the map, open to the

part that showed the Rouen Diamond. "We get up there, steal the gem, and run back to the entrance, where I set up a second translocation array to get us back over the wall."

"Why can't you just use an array to get us into the building?" Kurt asked. He had paused momentarily in the middle of attaching some wires to a green chip board. "And is there a reason we have to run back to the gate? Couldn't you just draw the second array inside the museum?"

"They don't have that kind of range. After 10 or 15 feet, they get pretty unreliable. You might end up with your arm stuck in a wall or something. Also, the stuff I draw the runes with is pretty expensive. I don't have that much of it, so I need to use it sparingly."

"Gotcha." With that, he went back to working on the mess of wires, batteries, and metal. It was hard to say exactly what he was making.

"Is there security of any description?" Lucas asked. "There must be guards at night." I shook my head in response, though it was a reasonable assumption to make.

"The last time I went, they had a couple of video feeds set up on different exhibits so you could cycle through and watch how they changed over time. I watched them pretty carefully and didn't see a single flashlight or any movement outside the main building after 9 PM." I also got to watch a starfish scuttle across an indoor tidepool on one of those video feeds. It was neat, but I had an inkling that the guys wouldn't be as interested in it as I was.

"The only things we really need to worry about are the otters," I added, mostly as an afterthought.

"Excuse me?" Lucas asked.

"Otters. Y'know, they're like giant weasels but adorable.

9

They swim around in rivers, crack open clams on their bellies, that kind of thing." When I first saw otters as a kid, I thought they were cute and that it was my right as an American to have one as a pet. Then I found out about the size of their teeth and the strength of their jaws, and I gained a healthy appreciation for their status as carnivores. Along with my status as being made of meat.

"Yes, I know what an otter is! I mean why do we need to be concerned about them? Or is that another of your pointless surprises?"

"Oh, the museum has a few otters in a little habitat, but one of them escaped a while ago and they never found him. So more likely than not, there's a maladjusted feral otter running around in the woods outside the museum. I can't say whether or not he's developed a taste for human flesh."

Lucas slowly nodded as he mulled that over. Fortunately, an electronic chirp came on through the apartment's intercom-thing before he had the chance to poke any holes in the plan.

"That's Kaitlin," I said, walking over to the metal panel next to the door. I stuck my thumb down on the button that would let her inside the building. "Which means it's time for The Lemurs to go steal another piece of arcana."

"Wait, stop." Lucas said. "Are you actually referring to us as The Lemurs?"

"Well, yeah. I thought it would be cool if we had a team name and a mascot. Except it'd really be three lemurs, and they'd all have different hats."

"No. Absolutely not. I was willing to go along with your insipid machinations until this point, but I refuse to assist you any further if you do not immediately retract that simian moniker."

"Okay, what about Sean and the Lemurs? Then it's like we're in a band!" A band from the 70s, yeah, but that wasn't the point.

"That is infinitely worse."

"Guys," Kurt said with a thin screwdriver between his teeth, "We can do this on the way to the museum." He looked to be about finished with his big robot eyeball-looking creation, using both hands to force the two sides of the casing together.

"Good point!" I unlocked the door for Kaitlin before running back to my room to grab my sword and the simple baldric I had recently made out of thrift store belts. The first one I had made was crafted out of duct tape, which apparently wasn't designed to hold up civil war sabers. From my bedroom, I careened over to the bathroom to let Zoe know what was going on.

"Hey, Zoe!" I called through the closed door. "Kaitlin's here! We're heading out, so be good!"

"Okay!" She yelled back. "Say bye to Lucas for me!"

"I will," I said. I also planned to call him a doofus, but she didn't need to know that. Upon my return to the living room, Lucas and Kurt were both up and ready to go.

"This is going to be awesome," I said with an adventurous smile.

"Or we are all going to be arrested and shot," Lucas replied.

"Well, yeah. Maybe. But if we don't, it'll be awesome."

"If we do, we will be dead."

"C'mon, Lucas. Lighten up! They'll never be able to catch Sean and the Legion of Lemurs!" I purposefully started heading for the door at that point in an attempt to outrun Lucas' death glare. Just then, in another stupendous display of luck, a knock came at the door. Lucas was a little less likely to strangle me with a lady in the room.

"Hey, Mister Foster." Kaitlin said as she walked into the apartment. She was somewhere in her mid-teens, with a brown ponytail and relatively preppy fashion sense. As of that point, she was the only babysitter I had been able to convince that I was an astronaut doing night training down at the YMCA. Or maybe she just didn't care where I was going at night. Either way, she was my babysitter of choice.

"Hey, Kaitlin! There's pizza in the fridge, sandwich stuff also in the fridge, help yourself."

"I know the drill." She strode past me and flopped down on the couch where Kurt's pile of stuff had been. "Zoe needs to be in bed by nine, no scary movies, and only one glass of strawberry milk a night." Zoe would drink gallons of the stuff if I let her. It's hard to say whether it's because she likes the taste or the fact that it's pink. Probably both.

"Exactly right," I nodded, grabbing my brown coat off of the hook in the corner of the room. "Zoe'll probably be getting out of her bath soon. We should be back around ten, anyway."

Kaitlin nodded and made a shooing motion at me with her hand. "Good luck on your barf training or whatever."

"Uh, thanks," I replied. Lucas and Kurt were obviously a little confused by that comment. I motioned for them to follow me out, since I wasn't about to blow my cover in front of the babysitter. The three of us shuffled into the hallway outside the apartment and onto the creaking wooden stairs leading down.

"Barf training?" Lucas asked. "Do I even want to know?"

"I'm an astronaut." I said.

"Excuse me?"

It hadn't occurred to me that Lucas might not know what those were. He was a little behind on the times, as his clothing might suggest. Not sure if all English people are like that, or if Lucas was just a few hundred years old. Again, maybe both.

"Y'know what, let's get to the car and I'll explain it on the way."

The three of us stepped out into the last of the rain and moved as a group to Kurt's car. It was a black, homemade monstrosity with the body of an old muscle car, wheels that looked more appropriate for a backhoe, and an interior that had more speakers than seating. I decided to take the cramped back seat this time, leaving Lucas to duck into shotgun. Kurt fired up the engine, which sounded a hundred times bigger than it probably was. The pleasant smell of a resting storm accompanied us as we began the newest in a growing line of capers.

Lucas hates it when I call them capers.

-The Diamond-

I barely had the chance to adequately explain the idea of space travel before we were pulling up to the school that neighbored the museum. The Ecotarium was only a couple of miles from my apartment, tucked into a cozy spot between a high school and a surprisingly spacious Worcester suburb. It's the kind of place you'd never know existed if you weren't looking for it. Heck, I only knew about it because my parents had taken me there a few years before Zoe was born. Ever since then, the place has stuck out in my head like a brain-hernia. In a good way, though.

"Yes, I understand the conflict between Russian communism and the philosophy of the United States after the second World War. I simply do not understand why that translated into a competition to reach the moon."

"Because it's the moon?" I replied. Seemed like a good enough reason to me.

"Sorry to interrupt, but we're here." Kurt turned off the car's lights as he pulled into the school's expansive parking lot. "I don't see anything we can park behind."

"That's unfortunate," I grumbled. Looking around, the area had been rendered pretty barren by some recent construction. There was a big pile of dirt left over to one side, though, and that was enough to give me an idea. "Can you pull over near that mound? I've got a spell I think I can work with."

Kurt did as I asked, steering his car off the asphalt and parking beside the pile of sandy earth. I jumped out from the back seat and crouched down next to the miniature hill. It was more than tall enough for what I needed, though the width might not be sufficient. Still, it was worth a shot. With one fluid, super impressive movement, I unsheathed my saber from its metal scabbard and plunged the tip into the dirt at the base of the pile.

"Are you planning to stab the ground until it cooperates, then? Because that may be even more stupid than your usual behavior." Lucas had clambered all the way out of the car just to insult me. How touching.

"Sarcastic laughter, sarcastic laughter," I responded, dragging the sword through the dirt and around the pile. "I'm setting up an array, thank you very much."

"Ah, of course. More of your chalk drawings. Or dirt drawings, in this case." Well, happy snoot-day to you too, Mr. Worthing. "I will admit, it is slightly impressive that you actually manage to memorize these things, considering their complexity."

"I'll choose to take that as a compliment," I said with a grunt. I finished connecting the circle that I had started around the base of the mound. All that remained for that half of the spell was to draw

16

specific symbols all around the outside of the ring.

"That is rather disappointing, since my intention was to point out the limited capacity of your brain." Lucas said with the slightest grin. While I was toiling to make this mission a success, he was taking the time to slip off his gloves and examine his cuticles. I turned around to squint an eye at the uppity Brit, resting an arm on the handle of my sword as I did so.

"What's going to be really disappointing is when the next full moon comes up and you're stuck at home without your cure because I decided not to find it for you," I stated, only a little vindictive.

"You are an idiot, Foster. Especially when you confuse mythology for fact."

"Said the guy who still thinks neckerchiefs are in style."

"This is a silk cravat, you simpleton!"

"I'm gonna run you both over in about three seconds if you don't shut up," Kurt said from inside the car.

"Point taken." I went back to drawing symbols in the dirt, and to his credit, Lucas held his tongue until I was finished. I cut a line over to the side of the car and made another circle of similar size in the ground. After a few minutes of rune drawing, crickets chirping, and Lucas standing around awkwardly, the second part of the array was done. Another swooping line between the two, and I'd made a sort of bloated figure eight around the pile and the car.

"And now for the fun part," I said, reaching into my backpack for a plastic baggie full of tiny opalescent shards. It was surprisingly heavy, even if the glossy flecks inside didn't look it. I glanced over to Lucas, expecting some sort of questioning from him. Nothing. "Don't you want to know what this is?"

"No, not really," He said, leaning against the car as he had been for a while now. His arms were crossed. "A new American snack food of some description? Crunchy High-Fructose Clusters or something equally appalling to the senses?"

"What? No! Not even close." I shook my head and went about sprinkling a handful of the stuff around each of the circles. "They're thin quartz flakes. Although that does sound like a breakfast cereal, now that I think about it."

Lucas rolled his eyes. "Regardless, does this mean that you are almost done with this rock gardening project you have so passionately taken up?"

"Yes, actually." I smiled as the last inch of the array came to shimmer under the orange lights of the parking lot. Dusting my hands off, I spoke the ancient words that would give the whole thing power. "Korusath aderim! Mordanres hatan!"

With the last syllable off of my tongue and into the cool night air, the lines I had drawn in the dirt began to glow with a blue aura. It made for a stark contrast to the warm light from the school's lamp posts. The blue glow quickly ballooned and became a cloud of emerald dust that danced in a wind that wasn't there. The particles spun, and in the blur that was created, a mound of dirt appeared in the second circle that was identical in every way to the original. Kurt's car sat in the middle of the illusionary hill, rendered effectively invisible. The sound of a car door shutting came from within the earthy pile, heralding Kurt's approach. The illusion offered no resistance as he stepped out, melting back into place immediately after he passed through it. He came to stand next to Lucas and I before turning to look at the effects of the spell.

"Works for me," he said, nodding in approval. It was about then that the glittering quartz flakes settled down, leaving the mound of false dirt looking completely normal next to its twin.

"Then there's just one more thing to do before we break into this museum," I replied. Replacing my sword in its sheath, I hopped back onto the asphalt of the school's empty parking lot. "I just need to make us a little less conspicuous."

I set my messenger bag on the ground and pulled out my book, flipping to the page of a spell that would do the trick. All I needed were depictions of what we were going to look like, some human hair, and a small vial of tears. I came prepared with those components just about every time we were out hunting for arcana, since it was just so useful when breaking into places. Hair and tears were pretty easy to acquire, too, as I could harvest those from myself with a pair of scissors and a recording of that one ASPCA commercial. The pictures of what the illusion would look like came from magazines, old textbooks, or the internet. The most important part was to make sure the images were in color. I had found that out the hard way a caper or two ago, resulting in a black and white Curly, Larry, and Moe running down the street and away from a bunch of cops. That one actually got on the local news as some kind of publicity stunt, which would have been hilarious except that I almost lost my shoe in the ditch we had to duck into.

"Alright, guys, stand still!" I had arranged the bits and pieces on the asphalt in a triangle with the hair and a small vial of tears in the middle. All that remained was to say more of the magic words. "Korusath antremor! Bororus avren trenarium!"

There was a flash of blue light, and then a blue-green mist shot up from the basic array. I definitely didn't feel different, but when I looked over at Lucas, I could see the illusion gradually forming over him. It was like turning on a projector, where it takes a minute for the image to fully appear. Lucas was getting a beard, whereas Kurt's long-sleeved tee was flickering into a suit. A glance down at my hands showed wrinkles that weren't there before.

"Foster, what exactly did you choose for us to become with your spell?" Lucas seemed a little wary, because he's actually a giant wuss. It wasn't even a transformative spell. Illusions are like masks in that they sit over your actual features, but they're awesome because they don't have those two centimeter wide eye holes no one can possibly see through.

"Well, last time I did characters from *The Princess Bride*."

"Yes, I remember," Lucas winced. "You had a mask and Kurt was a short version of André the Giant." It was a blast explaining who that was to Lucas, let me tell you.

"Yep! This time, I thought I'd go with something of a classic when it comes to robberies," I scooped up and presented the three history book clippings I had gathered a few days ago. "The presidents!"

Lucas, or rather Abe Lincoln, scowled until I thought the vein in his forehead would pop.

"You said you would make us less conspicuous, you idiot! Now we'll appear to be dead historical figures robbing a sodding museum!"

"Hey, hey! Bill Clinton isn't dead." I pointed at Kurt, who didn't seem the least bit concerned about the effects of the spell. He looked pretty snazzy in a suit, or at least his proportions did, if that makes any sense. Kurt shrugged and gave a Clintonesque thumbs up.

"How!" Lucas growled, "How do you manage to be so infuriatingly stupid!"

"I think it's pronounced 'awesome,' actually." I packed my bag back up and started over to the road. "C'mon, the museum's this way. These spells don't last forever!"

The way up to the museum was surrounded on both sides by trees, which made the walk over a little spookier than it might have been otherwise. But soon enough, the three of us were standing in front of a tall concrete wall separated into two parts by big, metal bars. I situated myself in front of the left gate and pulled an oddly-shaped hunk of chalk from my backpack. With it, I drew another circle on the asphalt, this one big enough for us all to stand in. The outside ring would contain an octagon with lines streaming from each corner of the shape and a few basic symbols in the center. Once it was done, I clapped my hands together to get rid of the excess chalk and stepped within the boundaries of the array.

"Everybody on. This is the Larceny Express, making stops at the other side of this gate, Albuquerque, and Istanbul."

"Is there even a point to me commenting on your idiocy anymore?" Lucas muttered, resigning himself to join me inside the chalk circle. Kurt stepped in behind him.

"A better question might be whether there was ever a point to it. I'm pretty sure the first thing you ever said to me was, 'Are you dense?!'" I did my best to contort my face into one of Lucas' patented scowls.

"Yes, fair enough," he sighed. "Your antics have only become more idiotic and childish, if anything. Forgive me. Go ahead with your thing." He said the last word with as much disdain as humanly possible, gesturing with his gloved hand toward the circle.

"I will, thank you." I cleared my throat to make way for more of the language I had only ever seen in my leather tome and on other pieces of arcana. "Ventrus ardeas, cororum villisentra." There was a whoosh, a sudden whirling of blue smoke, and a moment of pressure on every inch of my body. It was over as quickly as it started, and like that we were on the other side of the gate, standing in a column of azure mist.

"There we go," I said with a nod. "Right next to Siegfried, just like I'd planned." I stepped out of the arcane fog and over to a grassy area where the museum had set up a life-sized stegosaurus statue, petting it on the head.

"Good lord, you are actually on a first-name basis with plastic dinosaurs." Lucas sputtered a bit, waving a hand to dispel some of the bluish fog.

"Hey!" I turned and pointed at him, then back to my eyes, then to him again. "You can say whatever you want about me, but you hurt Siggy's feelings and we're going to have words."

Lucas just stared at me, apparently unafraid of the threat. He shook his head before turning to the asphalt paths before us. "Which way are we going, Foster?" The various paved walkways snaked between the grass and trees like rivers, one path pooling at the base of the museum in a big swath of darkness.

"To the left," I said, giving Siegfried one last pat before sprinting in that direction. "Down to that pavilion, then up the stairs. That's the side with the glass wall and the mineral exhibit!"

Lucas and Kurt had to jog to catch up to my initial lead. We breezed past a big white tent that must have been for some kind of special event, and then we were on the rocky stairs, scurrying up toward the entrance to the museum. That whole side of the building was made up of glass panes, including the alcove that housed the glass doors to get inside. We were standing on a big patio-looking thing, with a raised section that was full of dirt. One could assume that plants would eventually go in there. To our side was the housing for a porcupine, some skunks, a couple of snakes, and an eagle of some kind. From the outside, it looked more like a huge tool shed, but I guess that was part of its charm.

We moved as a group to the glass wall in front of us, with Kurt taking the lead. He dug around in his backpack and pulled out a little two-armed contraption that kind of reminded me of those compasses you use in high school math classes. Y'know, where everyone in the class is really just trying to deal with the fact that a teacher gave them something sharp to do math with. That might be the one time in history where geometry piqued the interest of my squishy teenage mind.

The difference between those things and what Kurt had was that a suction cup was stuck on the end of one of the arms, which he affixed to the surface of a glass pane. He drew the tiny metal blade on the other side of the tool across the glass in a perfect circle, making a brief but painful screech that tore through the night air.

"Ah! C'mon, Kurt," I said, looking back at the trees just beyond the habitat-shed. "I told you, I can get us more of those glass-cutty things. Whatever they're called."

"Glasscutters," Kurt muttered. He went back to work, and soon had a fist-sized circle cut into the window. He pulled back on the suction cup, which simply popped off of the glass. The window still looked whole to me, but what did I know.

"Alright, good, so now we-" I looked back to Kurt. He was just staring ahead blankly. "What? What's wrong?"

"Didn't go through," Kurt said.

"What?" My eyes went from Kurt to the scratch in the wall.

"Didn't go through," he repeated. He stepped back from the pane and tossed me the glasscutter. "Blade's too short."

"Friggin' crap," I looked out to the vacant museum grounds one last time before focusing up at the window, tapping on the white scratch mark with my finger. Surprisingly sturdy, considering that Kurt had just gone to town on it with that little contraption. It was going to be one of those times when having an authentic, alchemically-hardened civil war saber would come in handy. Brawn over brains, as it were.

I tossed the glasscutter over my shoulder, drew my sword as quietly as possible, and went to smack the pommel against the glass wall when Kurt grabbed me by the shoulder.

"What the hell are you doing?"

"Uh, y'know. Getting us into the museum? Smashy-smashy, breaky-inny?"

"Yeah, that'd be a great way to set off every alarm they've got. But how about we try this first?" Kurt held up the thing he had been working on in the apartment. It was a dented metal sphere with a seam going down the middle where he'd forced the casing together. Set into one part was a black circle that looked like a speaker, except with segmented metal plates reaching into the middle like fingers. Additionally, he had attached handles to either side of the sphere. They looked like they might have come out of the interior of a car.

"Yes. I have no idea what that thing is, but I like the cut of its jib." I reined my sword arm back in and followed Kurt over to the main doors of the building. They were the kind with push bars going across, which probably meant they were locked with magnets.

"It's a localized EMP generator," Kurt stated simply.

"Emp?" Lucas asked, clearly lost. "What is an emp?"

"It stands for electromagnetic pulse," Kurt explained. "It's a short blast of energy that messes up anything that runs on electricity."

"Like those locks," I added.

"Yep." Kurt pointed the front of the device at the doors and pushed a button on one of the handles with his thumb. The crease down the middle of the thing glowed a yellow hue which quickly turned white, and then a huge blast of sound shot out from its center. I was honestly surprised it didn't shatter the glass on the doors, because it sure as heck destroyed the crap out of my ears.

"Jesus, Kurt!" I said, though all I heard was a high-pitched whine from within my own head. It looked like he mouthed an apology before offering me a pair of earplugs.

"Yeah, friggin' thanks." I just had to hope that my tone came across as super sarcastic on that one. I pressed my palms to my ears and moved forward, shouldering one of the doors open. For what it was worth, the metal eyeball had done its job perfectly. We huddled into the museum, specifically in front of a huge, taxidermied bear, where I decided to wait until I could hear again.

"Man. Okay, wow." I shook my head around to dislodge the last of my temporary deafness. "Let's not ever do that again."

"I concur," Lucas snarled. He seemed to be in about as much pain as I was, maybe more. I'm not sure if he had really sensitive hearing, or if he just heard notes that were out of the range of a normal person. Either way, the explosion of noise couldn't have been fun for him.

"Or you guys could cover your ears when somebody says they're gonna set off an EMP right next to you," Kurt muttered.

"We'll save this argument for later. I'll be amazed if we didn't get somebody to call the cops with that thing." I glanced around to get my bearings. The place hadn't changed any since I scouted it out, which was a good thing. "The minerals are up the stairs, just past a bunch of interactive exhibits. Come on."

I hustled up the stairs and did my best to ignore the fact that we were rushing past the best part of the museum: The kids' section. I wouldn't even get the chance to beat Lucas over the head with a giant chess piece or anything. I was disappointed, but focused. I would power through anything that came between me and the Rouen Diamond. No more distractions!

Then we hit the top of the stairs, where I spotted something I hadn't seen before: A new display on the second floor. It was an exhibit on the variations of bird species in New England. Stuffed geese and seagulls stood frozen on man-made beaches. Placards described the species in complete scientific detail, and each bird had a corresponding red button. Buttons that triggered the birds' noises.

I stopped, staring at a weird-looking quail of some kind. It stared back with its beady, black eyes. My eyes went to the button. Then back to the bird. Then the button again. My hand, almost of its own volition, slowly reached for the circle of red plastic.

"Foster!"

"What." My eyes were fixated on the button. It was hypnotizing. How could I not press it? That's why it was there!

"I will not hesitate to rip your spine out through your chest."

My hand dropped. It's not like I was afraid of Lucas. He wouldn't actually do that, for fear of getting his fancy white gloves covered in my dirty, Yankee blood. That said, he probably would pick up a car and throw it at me. Lucas can do that, and it's really cool to watch it happen to someone else. Not so much from the first-person, I'd imagine.

We kept moving, but I watched that button. When it was daytime again, I was going to pay the twenty bucks for Zoe and I to get in and I was going to press every single one. Zoe wouldn't threaten to pull my spine out, either, which is why she gets to come to the museum and Lucas doesn't. That policy also goes for the movies, the mall, the park, and most furniture stores. There was a situation with Lucas and an ottoman that I don't really like to talk about.

After the brief lapse with the button of ultimate temptation, we made it through the bird room and came back into the main section of the building. Clouded moonlight splashed down onto the floor from the glass wall, leaving things just bright enough where we could read the signs to each exhibit. Kurt tapped me on the shoulder and pointed to my left, toward the mineral section. I readied my book, pulling it from the spacious back pocket of my messenger bag and motioning for them to follow. I'm not positive why we got quiet all of a sudden, considering the sound Kurt's machine had unleashed a few minutes ago. Maybe there's just something about a late night jewel heist and sneaking around like ninjas. Or maybe panthers. Ninja-panthers.

The mineral exhibit was mostly a bunch of rocks and crystals in glass cases, which was a little underwhelming when you compared it to the other awesome stuff they had set up in the museum. There was a man-made tunnel with more formations stuck behind lighted panes of plexiglass, but our quarry wouldn't be found there. It was on the other side of the cave in its own display case. It was actually something of a pedestal, with the gigantic cut

27

gem resting on a black velvet cushion that put it around chest height. The grayish light that echoed through the room refracted beautifully within its faces.

"The Rouen Diamond," I said with a grin. "From the town Joan of Arc was burned in. Of course, the diamond was enchanted more than a hundred years before she was born."

"There really isn't much in the way of security," Lucas observed from behind me. "And that is easily the largest diamond I have ever seen."

"Well, it's not actually a diamond," I said, catching on to where he was going with that. "It's a freaking huge quartz crystal, but because of its beauty, people in the renaissance just started calling it a diamond. It's not worth much, y'know, monetarily, but it's priceless in the eyes of those who know its true value."

"Of course," Lucas said, his tone flat. "And what is its true value, exactly? What does it do?" Lucas has a way of always putting a damper on any situation. We're looking at one of the most incredible pieces of arcana in the United States, and he wants to know what it does.

"What do you mean, what does it do?"

"What does it do, why are we stealing it, the question is pretty well straightforward!"

"I told you, it'll be better if it's a surprise!"

"I think we have had just about enough of your foolishness mucking things up already, Foster!"

"Your *mom's* had enough of my foolishness mucking things up already!" Oh, burn.

"What? What does that even mean?!"

"There are cops outside," Kurt said, catching us both by

surprise. He was standing over on the balcony, overlooking the kids' section and the big glass wall. Telltale red and blue lights alternated from the top of a police car, which also had its high beams and a few insanely bright lights focused inside the building.

"Crap!" I yelled, losing my cool for a moment. I drew my sword again, charged the display case, and smacked it with the butt of the weapon. The glass dented in, and a spiderweb of cracks appeared. Bulletproof.

"Are you frickin'-" It was then that the cop's siren started going off. I assaulted the glass with abandon, creating more cracks but no hole. Having no other recourse, I kicked the base of the pedestal in frustration. Stubbing my toe just then put museum display cases on my list of most hated inanimate objects, just after dental floss.

"Spare us the theatrics, Foster, and stand aside." Lucas stepped forward, staring purposefully at the crater in the display. He removed his hat, handing it to me as he passed. Honest Abe's stovepipe remained on his head, thanks to the illusion.

"What am I, your butler?" Despite my objection, I took the hat as I limped to the side.

"My butler was well-dressed, polite, and could do basic arithmetic without a calculator." Lucas removed the glove from his right hand and rolled the sleeve of his overcoat up. "So, no."

Before I could posit my counter-insult, Lucas punched the display case. A shower of glass splinters fell on the diamond as the entire bulletproof pane shattered. Lucas slowly retracted his fist, holding it away from his body. Shards of glass stuck out from between his knuckles, coaxing his blood to spatter down onto the waxed floors. Lucas can be an uptight jerk about things, but he

29

occasionally does hardcore stuff like that which pretty much makes up for it.

"Do not concern yourself with the blood, Foster," Lucas stated with a handful of extra snoot. "It responds terribly to scientific apparatuses. Just concentrate on getting us somewhere safe."

"I'm working on it. Kurt, grab the gem and a weapon, I'm going to try something. It's probably going to be pretty risky."

Kurt stepped up to the ruined display and slid his hand further into the sleeve of his shirt, dusting the glass bits from the top of the gem. Once it was clear, he grabbed the diamond and stuck it in his backpack. With his other hand he reached for one of the paintball guns he kept in the bag's front pocket. Its nonlethal payload rattled around in the hopper as he aimed for the door.

"This is the police," a man's voice called from outside the museum. "We have you surrounded. Come out with your hands up." So, yeah, I guess they do actually say that at the scene of a crime.

"You have what you wanted," Lucas said through clenched teeth, staring at the wounds in his hand. "Now, we need to leave!" Over the course of that statement, the cuts started to disappear, healing with unnatural speed. Another advantage to that ailment of his, I guess. Once the blood stopped flowing from his knuckles and through the illusion, Lucas replaced his glove, jogged over to me to nab his hat, and placed it back on his head. It sat under the illusionary one nicely, just as I had planned.

"I know, I know." I pulled out my book and flipped through the leather pages until I spotted the translocation spell that got us through the gates. "Got it. I'm going to need you to help me draw this array, fast."

I dug through my bag and produced the hunk of white chalk from before, breaking it into two pieces and tossing one to Lucas. As soon as he had that, I shoved my book at him as well. I already knew what the circle looked like, but Lucas would need to copy it directly from the page. I shifted down on one knee and started drawing a circle.

"This is your last warning," the police called. I hated working under time limits.

Lucas examined the page for a moment, and then sniffed his chalk with a hint of disgust. "What is this made of, dead fish?"

"Vitriol and calcium sulfate," I said. "Now draw!"

Kurt had retaken his spot at the top of the stairs, vigilantly watching the entrance. He hadn't fired anything yet, which I was glad for. I really didn't want anyone to get hurt. Well, maybe Lucas, but only a little bit.

I quickly finished drawing the outer circle of the large rune, and started on the inside. Lucas was struggling with all the symbols, meaning that the majority of the work was up to me.

"We don't have time, we don't have- Kurt, get over here!" I called as I rushed to finish the last line, nabbing the leather tome from Lucas. With all three of us standing in the arcane circle, I spouted the words that would take us as far away from that spot as I could get us. "Ventrus ardeas, cororum villisentra!"

Arcane smoke shot up around us once again, and then we were standing outside the museum. I looked up through the eye of the blue storm to gaze contentedly at the cloudy night sky.

"That was way too close," I chuckled, sliding my book back in its bag.

"Foster," Lucas said.

"Lucas, don't. We're out, and that's all that-"

"Foster."

The smoke had dissipated, and we were standing just in front of the building, a few feet away from the police car. What I had assumed would be a small army of cops was really just one guy with a megaphone. The single officer stared at us, and we stared back. As Abe Lincoln, Bill Clinton, and George Washington.

"What?" He said, completely baffled by everything about the situation unfolding before him.

"You had us surrounded, huh?" I leaned over to look around the building as best I could from where I was standing.

"You... You're under-" Before he could finish that statement, Lucas socked him across the face. The man crumpled against the hood of his car like so many floppy accordions. There was a brief pause as we all stared at the fallen policeman.

"Dude! Lucas!" I thrust both of my hands out toward the cop.

"What?" He asked, slightly indignant.

"You just punched out a cop! You can't do that!"

"I believe I have quite a lot of evidence to the contrary!" He said, also gesturing at the unconscious man.

"No, I mean you aren't supposed to punch people unless you really have to! That guy probably has a broken nose now! What if the medical bills send his family spiraling into bankruptcy?"

"Would you prefer that I let him call more officers to the scene? Then I would have to punch them as well!"

The wheels in my head turned furiously to come up with a response to that, but ultimately failed.

"Damn you and your logic," I said begrudgingly. The point

was rendered moot as the sound of more police sirens drifted over to us from the road.

"Run!" I yelled, taking off for the stone steps and veering right between a few trees. My only thought at that point was to get back to the car, which meant going over a concrete wall or through a chain link fence. The latter seemed more probable, especially if the whole area would be swarming with cops. So I hurried across the grounds and over to the guest parking lot, barreling through until I hit trees. I almost slipped on wet leaves more than once, but never quite took a spill. When I got to the tracks for the museum's miniature train ride, I knew we were almost in the clear, so I muttered the words that would turn off the illusion I had cast on us. A hundred more feet or so and we were at the fence. Kurt and I were panting, while Lucas seemed completely unaffected by the run.

"Okay," I said, speaking between inhalations, "I know how we can do this."

"I hope your plan has a distinct lack of burrowing," Lucas sneered.

"Lucas," more panting, "Shut up and take this." I dragged my saber out of its sheath one more time, turning it around so the handle was facing him.

"Ah. I think I begin to see your plan." He wrapped his gloved palm around the sword's handle, pulling it from my grasp as he meandered to the fence. "The sword is unnaturally sharp and durable, but you lack the strength to cut through other metals with it."

"Something like that," I replied. I was just getting my breath back when a noise tugged at my right ear. It was something like a cross between a cat's purr and a big dog growling. I turned around

33

in the direction of the noise, putting me face to face with an otter.

"Um, guys?" I reached over to try and hit one of them, but my hand just met empty air. I kept my eyes locked on the otter's. "Guys, I think we have a problem." Lucas had been practicing some kind of fencing motions with the sword in preparation for his match against the fence. He stopped momentarily to look exasperated in my general direction.

"Foster, what? Did you find another button you need to-" He stopped mid-sentence as the otter came into view. "Is that an otter?"

As though answering Lucas' question, the semiaquatic beast lunged. I yelled something unintelligible and jumped out of the way, but it still latched onto my pant leg as I tried to get away from it. Sure, go ahead and laugh. Those things have teeth like friggin' kitchen knives.

"It's got me!" I screamed, shaking my leg. "It's eating my pants, and then it's going to eat me! Somebody freaking do something!"

"My God." Lucas, seemingly missing the urgency of the situation, walked over and stared at the otter with an intense gaze that even made me more uncomfortable. Lucas' irises were a little too yellow to be brown, falling closer to gold than anything, and his pupils reflected light when it was dark out. I think the otter was justified in being creeped out. It paused in its growling and thrashing to stare back at him in fear. A small screech came from somewhere within the otter, and it slowly released my torn jeans from its jaws. It then skittered to the side before trundling away at full speed into the woods.

"There. The otter is gone, now can we leave before you find something else to distract yourself with?" He went back to the fence and lined up the angle of the sword's curve with the middle of the metal barricade.

"It was going to eat me, Lucas! I really don't see how you can blame me for that." I said as I got back to my feet, brushing off a bunch of wet leaves that had become stuck to my everything. "What, am I too delicious? Do I look too much like a giant crayfish?"

Lucas rolled his eyes but left it at that. The saber swooped sideways through the chain link fence once, then again, and a third time. It made for a square opening just big enough that Kurt and I might be able to get through. Lucas then stuck the sword in the ground and carefully made his way to the other side.

"Alright, just watch out. Make sure your clothes don't get ripped up in the fence." I let Kurt go next so I could pull my saber out of the dirt, wiping it off before sliding it back into its sheath. Once we were all through, it was just a short hike through some more woods before we were back at the school. Police cars were still driving down the road, so we stayed as far back as we could and slipped into the illusionary dirt pile during a break in the sirens. The illusion was see-through from the inside, so once we all got in the car we took to watching the road for a good moment to escape. That moment never really came. Police were already canvassing the area, looking around the woods and even the school parking lot for any sign of a perpetrator. It was going to be a while before we could go anywhere.

"Hey, Lucas."

"What."

"Know how to play rock, paper, scissors?"

"Yes."

"Want to play?"

"No."

Suffice it to say, it was a very long, very quiet wait.

After a few hours, the investigation finally died down enough that we could leave. I stepped out of the car for a second to kick at my dirt array, disrupting it in order to end the spell. The illusionary mound around Kurt's car faded and we drove back to my apartment, where we climbed up the creaky stairs as quietly as we could. I slowly opened the old wooden door into the living room, but it still made an unpleasant chorus of squeaks and groans. For better or for worse, Kaitlin was long passed out on the couch. I looked over to the clock on the DVD player and saw that it was almost three in the morning.

"Kaitlin," I whispered, and I walked over to shake her gently. "Kaitlin, hey. I'm back."

"Mister Foster?" She said, wiping the sleep from her eyes. "What time is- Oh my god. You said you would be back by ten!"

I smiled and shrugged. "Pay you double for overtime?"

She looked at me, her eyes narrowed with rage. Eventually she gave a resigned sigh and held out her hand, palm up. I slid my wallet out from my back pocket and counted out her pay, which she snapped out of my hand.

"My mom is going to kill me," she said as she started for the door. "You're lucky your sister is so cute."

"Have a safe drive," I said, staring at the last twenty I had in my wallet. "I'll call you next week maybe?"

"Don't count on it." She spat before shutting the door behind her. An awkward pause ensued.

"She always says that," I lied.

"Alright," Lucas whispered, "Now that we've broken into a museum, stolen a pseudo-diamond, escaped the police, and almost been caught again by the same police, will you tell us why we've gone to all this trouble?"

"Of course, my good man," I replied quietly. "Kurt, if you would."

Kurt shouldered his backpack off and unzipped the back pocket. He pulled the brilliant gem from within and handed it to me. I took it up as a king might hold his royal scepter.

"This is one of the oldest pieces of arcana in the country, my friends. It has traded hands at least six times since the Hundred Years' War, and is considered by many to be the most beautiful gem in all the world."

"Get on with it," Lucas said. Kurt had already lost interest, choosing instead to clean one of his paintball guns. Jerks.

"The most fascinating thing about the Rouen Diamond is its arcane properties. Once owned by the sorcerer Guizan, he imbued this gem so that when the secret words were uttered in its presence," I held the diamond up above my head and spoke more of the arcane tongue. "Otrius, demar abestus!"

The refracted light from within the crystal grew stronger until its core flickered with a pure white light. The living room was bathed in its soft glow, which was about as strong as a dim lightbulb. I smiled, expecting the others to finally understand my appreciation for the diamond.

37

"That's it, is it?" Lucas said. "You almost killed us all for a medieval flashlight."

"A medieval- How can you say that? This crystal was enchanted by the greatest French wizard who ever lived!"

Lucas shook his head and started for the door. Kurt shrugged and followed suit, at least until a voice came from the bedroom hall.

"Sean?" Zoe called, "Did Kaitlin go home?"

"Oh, hey Zoe! It's way past your bedtime." I moved toward her, but then she noticed Kurt and Lucas by the door.

"Lucas!" she squealed, running over in her pink pajamas to hug him. Lucas smiled and threw his arms open, kneeling down to return the hug. Zoe really liked Lucas, to the point where she would sometimes joke about him being her boyfriend. I think it's because of the accent.

"Have you been good, Zoe? You've been taking care of things here?"

"Mhmm!" She said, nodding with pride. "Because Sean is uncompnetent, right?"

"I think you and Lucas need to have fewer tea parties." I shot Lucas a look of pure contempt. He had a smug grin stretched over his long, thin face.

"Aww," Zoe whined, and she looked disappointed until she saw the Rouen Diamond. "Sean, what's that? It's pretty!" She ambled over to the light source like a pink moth.

"I think so too," I said. "And it's called the Rouen Diamond, from France. Do you know where that is?"

Zoe shook her head and turned in Lucas' direction. "Is that where Lucas is from?" Her eyelids were already starting to droop.

"That's England. France is just South of there, though. In fact, you can take a tunnel under the ocean to get from one to the other!" I kneeled down next to Zoe and rubbed her back a little bit.

"Oh," Zoe's head dipped. I could tell she was going to pass out, so I put my arms behind her back and under her legs and lifted her up off of the beige carpet.

"So, same time next week?" I asked my friends with a smile. Lucas sighed with a little less irritation than usual and shook his head.

"I must be insane to keep doing this. You are going to get me arrested or killed someday, while I could be spending my time lounging at my family's estate."

"Which would be really, really boring for everyone involved," I said with a grin. "Especially you."

"You are probably right about that," Lucas admitted, and he twisted the doorknob. "But next week, we are going to have a plan."

"We had a plan this time!"

"A good plan." Lucas opened the door, but stopped halfway into the hall. "Oh, and I would rather you didn't tell Zoe fairy stories about tunnels and things, you know. Just in case she ever does visit England."

"What?" I blinked. "Lucas, that's a real thing. The Chunnel. You never heard about it?"

"I, erh." He glanced to the side, eyes bulging out. He looked like someone had just shot his butler in the foot. "Well, I must be off. Good bye."

Lucas went, closing the door behind him. I'm pretty sure I heard something about 'the bloody French' through the door. Meanwhile, Kurt stuck the gun he was cleaning back in his bag and nodded at me.

"Seriously, man, what's up with that thing?"

"What do you mean?" I asked. "The diamond?"

"Yeah," Kurt replied simply. He took off his cap, revealing a head of scruffy brown hair. He went about mercilessly bending the brim in his hands. "I trust you, but that rock doesn't look like much. If you say it's really something special, then I'm cool with taking the risks. But if it isn't, then Lucas kind of has a point."

I gave myself a second to mull it over, to consider Kurt's words. He had a much greater capacity for making quiet, thoughtful critique than Lucas. As such, I wasn't quite as dismissive when he gave me some feedback.

"It's worth it, Kurt. Honestly. This thing is going to end up saving our necks, one way or another."

"Alright," Kurt nodded and moved for the door. "That's all I needed to hear. Take it easy." He replaced the cap on his head as he stepped out.

"You too," I replied, shutting the door behind him. Alone again, I looked down at Zoe, at her innocent, heart-shaped face and waves of blond hair. I carried her through the dark hallway to her bedroom, which was the door right after mine. Laying her on the bed, I tucked her under the pink sheets and walked to the door. I turned the knob, then glanced down and realized that I was still holding the diamond. It flickered in my hand.

I looked back to Zoe's small form, a little hill in the sheets, and moved back into the room to place the diamond on her dresser. It thudded quietly against the painted wood.

"Good night, sis," I whispered. I adjusted Zoe's comforter, stroked her hair once and left the room, closing the door behind me.

With that piece of arcana taken care of, I'd have to check my sources for new leads. Right after a nice ten hour nap.

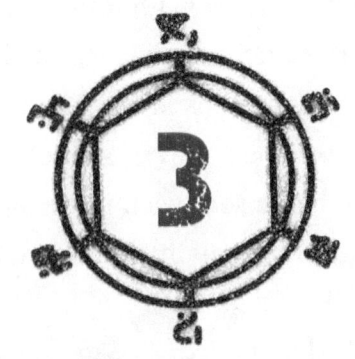

-Angel's Tears-

At least, it would have been a ten hour nap if it weren't for the brain-meltingly catchy theme to one of Zoe's cartoons the following morning. She had the volume turned up high, probably oblivious to the fact that the wall between the living room and my bedroom wasn't all that thick. I writhed around in bed for a while, but I knew I wasn't going to be able to sink back into sleep. I went for yesterday's jeans off the floor, put them on, and immediately slid them back off when I remembered the gash from the otter attack. So I pulled on a t-shirt and another pair of jeans from my clean laundry pile before walking out to grab some breakfast.

"Good morning, sis." I said mid-stretch. "Watching cartoons before school?"

"Yeah," she murmured absently. The colorful ponies on TV had her full attention.

"Got your homework done last night?"

"Uh-huh."

"Did you eat anything yet?" I felt more like a nagging parent than her brother, but somebody had to make sure she wasn't surviving on candy bars and chips alone. I remembered the archaic bartering system that went on during school lunch, and just how easy it was to be out of half a sandwich in exchange for a handful of tiny, second hand muffins. Actually, I kind of missed those days. Those muffins were delicious.

"I had cereal," she replied. "I left the last waffle for you, because I know how much you like them." Best little sister ever.

I smiled and temporarily put my quest for breakfast on hold to go sit next to Zoe on the couch, where we watched the rest of the episode together. It was a cute show with a couple of jokes I could laugh at, so I wasn't about to complain. When it was over, Zoe lunged off of the couch and scampered back to her room.

"Forget something?"

"Almost!" she yelled from her room. "Hold on one second!" When she came back, Zoe had the Rouen Diamond in her hands. It was still sparkling with arcane power, though it was a lot harder to see in the morning light.

"What's up, kiddo? You know you can't bring arcana to school. It's all super secret stuff, just between us."

"I know. I wanted to give it back so you could have it." She put it down on the coffee table before moving to pull on her pink and lilac backpack. "I know I'm not old enough to go help you and Lucas and Kurt find things, so it can go with you instead. It'll be like I'm right there with you!"

A broad smile washed over me. "That sounds perfect. I'll keep it on me all the time, just like mom and dad's book." She

44

nodded happily and went to the door. I jumped up to follow. "Hey, Zoe, want me to walk you to school?"

"Sure!" she beamed. I got up and crammed my feet into my old two-tone loafers and we were off, racing down to the front door of the apartment building. I hoisted her up onto my shoulders once we got out into the chilly morning air. In response, she held a hand horizontally over her brow and started spouting the orders of a grizzled sea captain. A block or two into our voyage and we were both laughing loudly enough to elicit weird looks from people on the other side of the street.

"Hey Sean?" Zoe asked about a third of the way to her school. "I know I can't tell anyone about them, but why are things like the diamond a secret? Why don't magic people just tell everyone else what's going on?"

"Well, they used to. Back in the Middle Ages there were things like court wizards and alchemists, and there were stories about all kinds of magical creatures living in the woods, and people believed in them. But then inquisitions and witch hunts started happening."

"What're those?" Zoe looked suddenly sad, which was a reasonable reaction even if she didn't know it yet. "Did bad people hurt the magical things?"

It took me a moment of mental scrambling to come up with a kid-friendly explanation for the atrocities that happened back then. I didn't want to traumatize her, and I didn't want to pin it all on the Catholic Church. Not yet. It's been my policy to let Zoe come up with her own opinions on religion, and painting the bloody history of Christianity out in full before exposing her to the good aspects of the modern church just didn't seem fair. I had a friend, contact, and long time theological debate opponent who worked as an exorcist for the Armenian Church, and man would I get some disappointed headshakes from him if I accidentally indoctrinated Zoe into my way of thinking.

"Some mean people did really bad things to scare others into thinking the way they did. It became really dangerous to talk about magic, at least in Europe. Since then, people who can do magic have kept it secret." It was a broad simplification of what happened, but still more or less true. "If you tell regular people about the arcana we find, they probably won't believe you, and they might even think you're crazy."

"I promise I won't ever tell." She crossed her heart to back up her claim. "But it's still sad that people who use magic can't just be open about it with everyone."

"I'm with you on that one." I replied. "But for now, it's safer to hide. Maybe someday it'll be different."

"Yeah. And then there'll be unicorns and everybody will be happy!"

"That would be awesome," I agreed. The arcane certainly had the potential to better the human race, but so too could its power corrupt people. While I generally approved of the idea of a society that was open with magic, I knew the issue was more complicated than unicorns versus no unicorns. Still, better to let Zoe come into that realization further down the road. "In the meantime, though, you'll have to keep drawing them. The world needs sparkly unicorns now!"

"I'll draw another one in art today!" She said, giving a little salute. From there, the topic shifted to my favorite kind of unicorn, which we went into great detail about until we reached the school.

After a quick hug, Zoe was off to dive face-first into the hallowed hall of learning that was the first grade. That meant it was time for me to head home, throw a waffle in the toaster, and start looking for a new quarry.

When it comes to finding new pieces of arcana to hunt, I've got a couple of options for sources. One of the most reliable is Matt Hagen, a druid from Sterling. He's another friend from high school, though I don't think he and Kurt knew each other. Like most twenty-somethings right now, he has a degree in Salamander Anthropology or something equally obscure and still lives with his parents. I guess druid-ing doesn't pay that well. Maybe it's for the best. Matt's the kind of guy who's grown into the woods as much as they've grown around him.

I pretty much always have to bum a ride from Kurt to get to Sterling, since it's about twenty minutes from my apartment. It's a comfortable, woodsy town, the kind of place I wish Zoe and I could live. She loves climbing trees and finding little paths that nobody else knows about, but there aren't a lot of those in the middle of the city. At least, none that aren't crawling with rats or fake watch salesmen.

With the Rouen Diamond safely at home and Zoe in school, it was the perfect time to make a trip out and see what Matt might've had lined up for us. I called Kurt, meeting up with him an hour later at a cheap burger joint a few blocks from my apartment. After a painful car ride thanks to the musical stylings of the aptly-named *Thrashcan*, Kurt parked his car, rumbling homemade engine and all in the gravel driveway to Matt's house.

"You coming up with me this time?"

"I'm good," Kurt shrugged, pulling his keys from the ignition and killing the powerful beast. I knew almost nothing about cars, but it couldn't have been necessary for one to be that loud.

"Alright, man, I'll be back soon."

"Yeah, good luck." Kurt munched idly on some overly salty fries.

"I'll let you know if Matt has any magical socket wrenches for us to find."

Kurt grinned at that. "Sweet. Or maybe a monkey wrench that grants wishes."

"A monkey paw wrench?" I stopped, stunned by how glorious that idea was. "Kurt, I knew there was a reason I hang out with you." I laughed and pointed to him as I started to make my way up to Matt's house. Kurt never joined me for these visits, opting instead to hang back and tinker with his car. I think trees made him uncomfortable or something. By the time I got to the top of the long, winding driveway, Matt was already waiting for me. He was built like a birch tree with blue jeans, a flannel shirt, and a mess of blonde hair pulled into a ponytail. If anyone was fit to be a crunchy Earth Science teacher in-training, it was him.

"How are you, mister Foster?" Matt reached out for a handshake-hug, which I returned in an extremely manly fashion.

"Not too bad, sir." I motioned to the trail leading into the woods from his folks' backyard. "Mind if we take a walk?"

"Not at all," he said with a smile. Nature walk-and-talks were our way of maintaining privacy when discussing new leads on arcana. "I have a pine tree that needs some tending, anyway. He's been complaining in my ear all morning."

I grinned, following behind as Matt started for the path. "The one downside to hearing plants talk, huh?"

"One downside? It's like always being in a room full of kids. They're constantly complaining and yelling and asking the strangest questions. I once had an elm tree ask me if I thought she was pretty. What do you say to that?"

"Yeesh. I dunno, I'm terrible when it comes to women." It took me a minute to think of a semi-appropriate response. "It's not you, it's me?"

Matt laughed, nodding and lifting a thick branch out of the way with one hand. When he let it go, the limb remained in an upright position as though it had grown that way. Druidic magic was usually subtle like that; I'm sure if Matt wanted to, he could grow a huge tree from a sapling, or make vines strangle somebody or something similarly cool. From what he's told me, though, the plants still have to draw the materials for that growth from somewhere. So a reckless druid could leave swaths of land barren from the growing of one tree.

"Speaking of women, how is Zoe doing?"

"The usual," I said with a smirk. "Adorable, rambunctious, covered in pink."

"Excellent. Glad to hear it. She's still going to marry your English friend?"

I nodded, looking out at the myriad evergreens and not-so-evergreens on either side of us. Whatever the word for those is.

"Yeah, still waiting on them to set a date. Last time I checked, she wanted it on Christmas. But I think she also said Halloween so everyone could be in costumes and give them candy for presents."

"She's really put a lot of thought into this," Matt replied, a grin holding onto his long face. "And since she ages normally and he'll never really get any older..."

"Yeah, no." I had to nip that little horrific mental image right in the bud. "Ten years from now, Lucas will still be Lucas. He'd have to quit being an uptight jerk about everything way before I let him anywhere near my sister. I don't see that happening in my lifetime or Zoe's."

Matt smiled and shrugged. It was the kind of expression that made you feel like he knew something you didn't, which was pretty much always the case for me. Matt seemed to know everything about, well, everything. He had an old soul, as people describe it.

"What about the diamond?" He asked, pausing to bend at the knees and pick up a hefty looking branch. "I saw the news reports about a museum robbery and some ex-presidents escaping into the woods."

I winced, watching him brush off one end of the downed limb in order to use it as a walking stick. "Uh, yeah. Didn't go all that well. A bunch of cops showed up because of Kurt's EMP machine, which we had to use on the doors."

He blinked, looking to one side. "An EMP? You couldn't have done the thing with a credit card on the lock?"

"I wish. They were electronic, unfortunately."

"Oh. Isn't there an employee entrance around the back of the main building? I could've sworn I saw one last time I volunteered there. It was held shut with a rusty old padlock." Matt also had a way of pointing out obvious things that made you feel kinda dumb. Well, okay, made me feel kinda dumb. But he's not uppity and self righteous about it the way a certain someone always was.

"Yeah, no, it was mostly Lucas' idea. I didn't want to hurt his feelings by deviating from his plan."

Matt arched an eyebrow at that, but seemed to more or less accept it. We started down the path again, past huge old trees as well as groves of little green sprouts. I have to say, I'm a big fan of nature. It's relaxing, quiet, and a little humbling to hang out around things that have been alive for so long. That said, I hate bugs. And not showering. Nature's great, but camping and I don't get along so well.

"But you got the diamond," Matt reasoned.

"Oh, yeah, it's pretty awesome." I couldn't resist the opportunity to gloat just a little bit. Matt was more receptive to the historical aspect of things, anyway. He wouldn't start cleaning a socket wrench or go OCD with a lint brush just to have an excuse to avoid listening.

"Guizan was really amazing, for his time. The core of the crystal has this pure, white light, instead of the blue you usually get from arcane magic. I should've brought it," I lamented. "Zoe was the only one who thought it was at all interesting."

Matt nodded, smiling again. "It's almost like a pattern is starting to emerge there."

"Yeah, maybe I should find a different group of ne'er do-wells to go on wacky adventures with."

"They probably have personals for that somewhere on the internet."

"Probably." I looked up at the sky, noting a cloud that sort of looked like a sheep. Through an admittedly weird, convoluted train of thought, I remembered that I had to get back to Kurt before it got too late and the smell of clean air drove him mad. Plus he had an appointment with a customer about fixing their car, meaning it was probably a good idea to get down to brass tacks.

"So, Matt, since we're out here, have you heard of any promising leads lately?" I took up a spot on the path leaning against what might have been an oak tree. Maybe it was a willow. I should've asked Matt, in retrospect.

"Of course, my friend." He turned to sit on a rock and went about peeling some mossy bark off of his branch. "It's gotten quiet around here, but I know of a rumored cache that might interest you out in New York."

"New York?" I groaned. As much as I loved tracking down arcana, I wasn't sure I was willing to listen to three hours of Kurt's music on the drive over to the Empire State. He played it too loud to make out the genre, but it had to be somewhere between "beating someone to death with a microphone stand" and "metal" of some distinction.

"It's a bit of a haul, but I imagine it would be worth the effort for you." Of course, when Matt says something like that, I always listen to him. Druids generally tend to be very wise and observant. Something to remember next time you meet a big, furry, bearded guy out in the woods. Just make sure it isn't a bear, because bears will eat you. That's two pieces of awesome advice in one paragraph, actually.

Matt glanced to either side, and then up, maybe looking for flying ninja-spies in helicopters. I gave it a shot as well, but didn't see anything. Just lots and lots and lots of trees.

"According to an old story passed down from some friends of mine, there are some caves out that way, North of Albany, that lead to tunnels carved by an underground river." He plucked the last few hunks of bark from his impromptu staff and tossed them to the ground at his feet. "If there's any truth to the tale, there could be a pile of angel's tears sitting there waiting for you."

That was some fantastic news, and I couldn't help grinning about it the way a kid does when they sneak an early look at their birthday presents in their parents' closet. Mind you, this wasn't for nothing. Angel's tears are these amazing crystals that can heal any wound, mental or physical; great for when you've got a magical sword stuck through your chest and don't want to explain it to the receptionist at the hospital.

The problem is that they're incredibly rare, for two reasons: First, they crack and cease to be of any use after doing a certain amount of healing. Second, angels don't tend to poke their heads around our world too much anymore, and when they do, I don't think they'd spend their time sobbing into a bucket. Add that to the fact that everyone who knows anything about arcana wants them, and you've got a commodity people are willing to kill for.

"Alright, so what's the story, Matt? Where did these things come from?" He sighed in response, which couldn't be a good sign. I could already tell that this was the kind of story that weighed you down. He shifted on the rock and let his head hang almost between his knees, and as though moving of its own accord, the walking stick started to draw a wide swirl in the fallen leaves and sticks on the ground.

"The telling begins in one of those darkest moments for this plot of earth," he said, his voice suddenly grim. It was an odd sound, not made for the mouth or the heart of a guy I would call goofy first, and kind hearted after that. Nonetheless, he continued in the dark, foreboding language of the story.

"The people of this colony, those zealots too deep in the texts of God to see their own dark works, fervent and frothing in the blood of their messiah, made war. This was not that war waged by the empire borne of Saxon conquest: That gory, patricidal explosion on the cusp of a new dawn. No, these men gnashed and gnawed at their own, and damned their very daughters and sons to hang as overripe fruit or be crushed to breaking."

The witch trials. Every kid put through the public school system in Massachusetts spent at least a month of their life learning about the horrors committed by the puritans. I vaguely remember the lesson involving a field trip to a museum in Salem, which was pretty cool. That was all before I knew about the actual existence of magic, though. I had to wonder if any of the convincing-to-a-ten-year-old spell components they were selling in the gift shop were actually any good.

"In that moment of deepest despair, among the entrails and the hatred, the smallest hope managed to survive. It was said that a falling star was seen to the West, and that desperate mothers and fathers would follow its fiery trail to a sacred grove, where an angel stood in a pool of flowing silver."

"What, in New Yo-" One of Matt's calloused hands lifted from the branch, demanding silence. The pause that followed was jarring and awkward, but I think we both knew it was necessary to reestablish the heavy narrative. That was the last time I tried to interrupt.

"Word spread of the angel, come down to the ragged bosom of the earth to provide respite in this time of madness. Soon, those who would seek the blood of lambs were drawn to her beacon, and brought with them tests to judge between divinity or malevolent sorcery."

I didn't notice until now, but the methodical turning of the branch in Matt's hand looked to be drawing more than just a circular design. As the story went on, the leaves and thin trenches in the dirt became an eerily detailed image of a winged woman, surrounded by dogs. Maybe wolves. Regardless, the image was another example of Matt's druidic powers. It turns out that druids weren't just a bunch of pagan tree worshipers; they were storytellers and artists. The old medieval traditions of bards and traveling minstrels survived with their order, apparently manifesting in a variety of talents, including stick-drawing.

"The self-titled warriors of God questioned the angel, interrogated her, and when they could not find a way to pierce the golden wall of her benevolence, they tried her body. A sickle found her thigh, and molten platinum flowed from under its blade."

The end of the stick, now caked in dirt and with at least one leaf impaled, drew a gouge in the angel's leg, and then stopped abruptly.

"She bled," Matt stated more softly. Profound sadness welled up in his wiry features, and he looked up, making eye contact with me for the first time since the start of the tale. His expression was one of quiet pleading. I was stopped dead, not knowing what to say or how to react.

It was less than a minute before Matt went back to his previous posture and tone and I was resigned to listening again. The terrible feeling of hollow ineptitude remained long after.

"The angel bled, and thus, by the word of a man with a large wig and a large gut, she could not be of God. Not their God, who was as angry and belligerent as they, who would only send a messenger to this world if it was to wreak terrible destruction upon their sinful households." The narrow end of the staff scratched out the inside of the circle, then redrew a new angel, this time huddled and screaming. "She struggled against these monsters, these men, until she finally broke free, at the cost of one beautiful golden wing."

The branch dug violent scars in the ground, leaving the girl in the drawing crippled and flightless.

"She ran to the West, and ran further, chased endlessly by these ravening beasts. She sought the refuge of a cave, and her innocence itself lit the walls within. In the end, it was her very connection to God that led the men in their tall hats and black cloaks to her bleeding, gasping form." Matt slowed, the momentum of the story grinding toward its inevitable, terrible conclusion. Even the stick, which seemed so adamant in its depiction of the story, drew sickeningly still.

"As a final cruelty to God's messenger, it appeared that the hunters of Lucifer's children had no knowledge of how one kills an angel. They tried every horrific method, failing at each turn. The glorious creature prayed forgiveness for the acts of these humans even as the third day of false killing arrived with an abominable, bloody sunrise."

I don't remember sitting during the story turned ritual, but as we neared this point, I was on the ground, eyes locked on Matt's hunched form.

"It was by simple accident that she died," he murmured.

"Her second wing snapped and was pulled from her as she was drawn and quartered between two sad, emaciated horses. Finally the false witch was silent, and her body turned to glittering sand. The murderers rejoiced, and traveled to their cozy, thatched homes over the Appalachian foothills."

A crushing quiet had fallen over everything else in the woods. I ran a hand through my hair, shaking my head.

"That... Pretty much sucks," I said, and a lame half-chuckle found its way into the mid-morning air. "I wasn't expecting a happy ending or anything, but crap."

Matt finally looked up again and shrugged as he slid off of the rock.

"If it helps, the puritans came home to a town ravaged by Mohawk Indians, and they had to resort to cannibalism to survive the winter. The one who made it went insane and ran into the woods. He was probably eaten by wolves."

I took a second to think about it before nodding. "Yeah, I guess that helps. A little." Jokes aside, I felt awful after that, like I had witnessed the murder in person. I had to work to get to my feet, which were sluggish with the weight of the images tumbling through my mind.

"You think they'll still be there? The tears?"

Matt shook his head, leaning more heavily on the tree branch. "Not really."

"Worth a shot, though."

"Agreed, Mister Foster."

I grinned in spite of the unhappy scenes running through my mind like sludge, and extended a hand for another shake. I had to hope that my listening to the story would help take some of the weight from Matt's shoulders. I'm still waiting to find out if that's the case.

"Think you could find those caves for me, Matt?"

"I sent directions to your Yahoo this morning. Do you check that one?"

"About as much as I check any of my other accounts." I waved to Matt as I started back toward his house. "You gonna be alright with that spruce tree or whatever?"

"I think I'll manage," he said with a smile. "If he finds a way to knock me out and hold me for ransom, you'll be the first to know."

"That sucks," I called back with a laugh. "I'm more or less broke. Think he'll take acorns as currency?"

"Probably." Matt offered a wave before meandering further down the path to tend to his whiney fir.

-Ambush-

The Mass Pike is one of the most prominent highways in Massachusetts. It runs East to West and vice-versa, going all the way from Boston out to Albany. In fact, if you wanted to, I'm pretty sure you could follow it out to Buffalo and skip over to Canada. Which is useful information if you've run out of authentic Canadian maple syrup and really need to find some at any cost. Not that I've made that trip, but I've certainly considered it. I mean, have you ever had waffles with real maple syrup? It's like a tree hugging you from inside your mouth.

Regardless, the Pike is pretty much a straight shot of cracking asphalt, surrounded on two sides by endless trees. Occasionally, you'll drive through what was probably a hill, putting walls of sheer cut rocks on either side of you. Plants will be growing out of the gray crags, which sometimes rise 20 feet above the car. It's beautiful to drive down at any time of year, but I like it most during the spring and winter. Looking out at all those trees and rocks, it makes you want to go hop a guard rail and get lost in the untouched natural beauty. You shouldn't, obviously, because you'd probably get eaten by a badger or fall off a cliff into a nest of bees and hornets, but it really inspires the imagination. For some reason, it always brings me back to the classic fantasy books I'd read as a kid, evoking a sense of undying adventure and wanderlust.

Between Lucas' complaining and Kurt's music, I've never wanted to die quite as much as the night we were driving down that road.

"Look, they have no sense of rhythm, and these lyrics are absolutely atrocious. You cannot simply yell the word 'depravity' again and again and call it song-writing!"

"Dude, shut up."

"This isn't even a chorus! It is screaming, Kurt! They are literally screaming at you, and you pay for that? You pay to be screamed at by these hacks?"

"Dude, shut up!"

"At least turn the despicable racket down! You could have a modicum of respect for the people who have no choice but to ride alongside you in your vehicle!" And then Kurt would turn it up slightly, continuing the cycle. This was the same argument as always, just repeated ad nauseum for three freaking hours. I spent most of the time using the Rouen Diamond to read through my book, and on a related note, I found two separate incantations for causing temporary deafness. If I had been possessed of the forethought to bring a sliver of amber or leather made from bat's skin, I would've been all over that. But that's the biggest problem with using the book: The random stuff you need to carry around just to make a single magical effect happen.

Some of them are easy, like the spell in there that makes you jump really high. All you need are some words in the language of the book and some runes drawn on your feet. Markers work well enough for that one, and then you're jumping all over the place like a superhero with kind of a lame power. I really don't know why some of the incantations require obscure components, and I doubt the book's authors knew either. As far as I can tell, arcane magic was discovered through intense trial and error, though some of my research points to intervention from someone or something that already had access to spells as far back as ancient Egypt.

"They have all of two sounds in their awe-inspiring repertoire: Banging and screeching!"

"I'm gonna punch you in the mouth."

No amber, no bat leather. But I did have a sword. Desperate times and all that.

Fortunately, before I had the chance to test the effectiveness of the saber against my eardrums, we reached our destination. Which happened to be a rest station off the side of the highway. We were in upstate New York, somewhere between Albany and Schenectady, at a spot that was supposed to put us a short distance from the cave. From here, Lucas would be able to find the place easily enough, what with his varied superhuman senses. However, from the minute I got out of the car, something about this rest stop had me on edge. I was like a lion sensing a nearby velociraptor, where the lion has cool sunglasses and a revolver. Or maybe I'd want to be the dinosaur in that situation. I'll have to get back to you on that.

"Hey, guys, check this out." I walked over to the information kiosk and peered into one of the dark windows. It was probably around midnight, so the only light source was a single orange bulb hanging off a telephone pole.

"What is it?" Lucas joined me, followed by Kurt. In that moment, you could have cut the tension in the air with the wrong end of a hairbrush. We were all looking in, but I guess I was the only one who noticed.

"It says there's a gift shop in there."

Lucas' head dropped, pressing the tip of his hat against the window. It was true, though! There was totally a little white placard that said 'Gift Shop Inside!'

"Why is that of any importance, Foster? Honestly, why?"

"What the hell are they gonna have at a gift shop for a rest station? Like, miniature replicas of the crappy benches?" Of course, Mister Holier-Than-Thou was already walking away, nearing the decrepit wooden fence.

"Maybe they have t-shirts." Kurt was at least willing to contribute something to the conversation.

"Oh, yeah! With like, 'I went to this kiosk and all I got was this lousy shirt.'" I looked over for the whiniest member of our elite triumvirate, but only saw the portable bathrooms off to one side. "Hey, where'd he go?"

Another reason Lucas is a jerk is on account of him running off when he knows Kurt and I need him to find what we're looking for. In this case, the two of us were a little lacking in the supernatural ability to hear underground currents, or sniff out cave mold. So while he made it to the caverns in a little less than ten minutes, we were stumbling around the moonlit woods for half an hour. I almost broke an arm trying to scale a tree, and Kurt's guns fell into a foot of water before we finally found the smug mutant. Of course, Lucas showed zero remorse for leaving us to almost certain death, despite the subsequent glare party I threw for him.

"Don't pout, Foster, your face will stick that way." He was adjusting his spats, looking down his nose at us the way he always did when feeling particularly superior. "Of course, almost any change would be an improvement."

"You're hilarious, Lucas. Like watching a puppy on fire rolling down a hill." A pretty apt comparison, if you ask me. Lucas looked up, his expression locked on its 'slightly horrified' setting.

"You know, I sometimes can't tell whether you're being sarcastic, or if you're just a terrible person."

"A little of both, usually." Now that we were standing before the yawning mouth of the cave that stood up from the ground like a half-melted candle, I reached in to dig through my messenger bag and take up the diamond once more.

"Oh, perfect," Lucas muttered in his best impersonation of a pretentious clod. "You brought the night-light we were all nearly imprisoned for."

"Y'know what? Just for that, Lucas, I'm getting you socks for Christmas this year." I repeated the words to make the crystal flicker to life and started into the cave. A decent-sized river flowed down into it, which I had to wade through to get anywhere. It was friggin' freezing. "And not even cool ones with reindeers with googly-eyes on them or anything."

"You could do us all a favor and get me nothing for any holiday ever," Lucas griped. He slogged awkwardly through the greenish, slow-moving water, trying to keep his pant legs dry. It kind of defeated the purpose when he slipped on something and took a dive, leaving him sputtering and thrashing against the lazy current. It was awesome and hilarious until I pretty much did the same thing. To be fair, the bottom of that river must have been covered in some kind of frictionless space-algae, because it was freaking slippery.

With Kurt's help, we made it back up to our feet and continued deeper into the cave. It was spooky, without a doubt, with the sound of dripping water all around and nothing to see except the glimmering of the diamond on the river's surface. Even if there was anything to note, the relative brightness of the light killed whatever night vision we may have had. Lucas sniffed all over the place, whereas Kurt held one of his modified paintball guns out at the ready. We had to keep our collective guard up in case of other arcana hunters or local cops. Sometimes a river or lake in the middle of nowhere would be part of a reservoir, meaning the authorities don't want people walking around them. Or wading through them in search of objects of ancient, mystical power, as the case may be. Matt probably would have warned me if this river was one of those situations. Probably.

It was hard to tell just how much time we spent following the tunnel, but it felt like at least an hour. I looked back and noted that the entrance of the cave was a tiny, slightly less dark circle in the distance, and it was then that I walked into a wall. A big slab of stone literally jutted out from the water, making the end of our little caper seem pretty anticlimactic.

"Foster, wall." Of course Lucas would let me know after I had already gotten a face full of damp cave stone.

"Yeah, thanks." I put a hand up on the rock, which was smooth and cold to the touch. I sloshed along the wall in both directions, mentally creating a map of the chamber, which was roughly circular with only one entrance or exit: The way we came.

"Well, that is rather disappointing, though not unexpected." Lucas folded his arms over his chest and started moving back toward the entrance. Kurt seemed about ready to go as well.

"Wait, c'mon, guys. There has to be something!" I went back to the wall, frantically searching for a crack, or a hole, or anything.

"There isn't, Foster. And if you don't mind, I would like to get out of this miserable cave before you two die of hypothermia. I would rather not drag a pair of soggy, bloated corpses the entire way back to the vehicle."

It really didn't make sense. I mean, I knew that the tears might be gone, but you can't have a river that didn't flow anywhere. I pushed the tip of my shoe against the bottom of the wall every few inches, and bam. Just as I thought, there was a gap between the cave wall and the floor. The water had to be flowing from there into another chamber.

"Lucas! I found it!" I went to my knees, leaning back to keep my face above the water. My arm fit clean through to the other side. "There's more, under the wall! They have to be there!"

"No, they don't!" Lucas argued, his voice bitter and full of his usual pessimism. "You said that the things were put here hundreds of years ago, how can you even begin to imagine that they are still in the same spot?"

He may have had a point. Still, there was one way to check for the angel's tears that didn't involve blowing up a wall or transforming into a herring, even though that would have been way more interesting.

"Venael giserum," I said, standing and holding the Rouen

Diamond up in my palm. The white light within faltered, eventually fading into nothing and leaving us all in the utter darkness of the cavern.

"Oh. Good, now we're freezing *and* blind."

"Lucas, shut up for one second of your freakishly long life."

It took a little while for our eyes to readjust to the shadows of the cave, but once they did, it became clear that there was a light source somewhere under the water. It was shining a royal blue color from behind the wall. I love it when I'm right.

"They're here," I said, smiling from ear to ear. This was fantastic! With the angel's tears, Kurt and I would be able to recover from the occasional run-in with the cops, or gun-toting arcana hunters, or the top of a chain link fence without a trip to the hospital. Actually, there was one time I cut my hand open on a can of tuna, and man, these puppies would've been awesome then. Stitches in your hand are bad enough without Lucas being there to make fun of you when the stupid anesthetic doesn't work.

"Alright, Lucas, can you hold your breath for a long time?"

"What! No! Why would you even begin to think that?"

"You're a werewolf! I dunno, it makes sense!" C'mon, tell me it doesn't make sense. "Wolves are great swimmers! They're like forest-sharks."

Wait, I did mention that Lucas was a werewolf, right? I'm pretty sure I did, like in the first chapter somewhere. Anyway, all the freezing water must have been getting to Lucas. He pinched the bridge of his nose and let out an irritated sigh.

"Forest-sharks. Really?" Some guys just can't take a compliment.

"Yes, forest-sharks. Are you gonna go get the tears, or are we

66

going to have a debate on ichthyology in the middle of a cave at one in the morning?"

He begrudgingly started to slide his wet coats off sleeve by sleeve, grumbling every second. For a guy that was impervious to fire, extreme cold, and being stabbed, he wore a ton of layers. An overcoat, suit-coat, some kind of really fancy vest, and that weird neckerchief thing, all on top of a white button-down shirt and suspenders. As per usual, I ended up being his coat rack while he dove under the surface.

Lo and behold, Lucas swam like a fish. A big, annoying fish in a vest. He worked his way down to the fissure between the wall and the floor, and with a little bit of thrashing from his spindly legs, slid into the next chamber.

"Y'think there's air on that side?" Kurt absently tugged at the ragged sleeves of his long undershirt. They already had thumbholes from him doing that, as all of the sleeves on all of his shirts did.

"I dunno. Maybe." I shrugged.

We both waited, watching the shimmering glow from the other side.

"Dibs on his hat."

"Dibs on his money."

Before I could stake a counter-claim to any bangers and mash Lucas might own, the light from under the wall abruptly shrank, then did so again until the cave was pitch black.

"Huh. Hope those really were the tears, and not a swarm of hungry, man eating angler fish." I couldn't remember at the time whether those lived in our climate or not. It didn't matter in the end, as Lucas reappeared from the break in the wall and we were all bathed in azure fingers of light once again. He burst up from the water and gasped, holding a pile of the biggest angel's tears I'd ever seen. The cores of the things glowed a comforting blue, but whereas they're normally no bigger than a regular tear, they were each about the size of an egg. The outer part was clear and smooth like ice. If I had to guess, I'd say that these things had spent the last few hundred years crystallizing the water around them. I had no idea that angel's tears could even do that. In terms of my own research into arcana, it was a pretty significant discovery. On top of that, there had to be at least twenty of them.

"Oh man, Lucas, that's awesome!" I splashed toward him and held out my arms. If the guy ever deserved a hug, it was then.

"Don't touch me," he stated, his voice flat. Water dripped from him pretty much everywhere. "I'm going to the sodding car." With that, he splooshed back toward the mouth of the tunnel.

"Jeez. I thought it was cats that didn't like getting wet." If he was a wereocelot, I would've understood, but I was pretty sure wolves swam all the time in their natural environment. I had to assume Lucas was just being overdramatic and cranky again.

"There was a waterfall." He growled, looking back at me with those creepy, golden eyes. They reflected what little light there was in the cave, making the stare that much more intimidating. "I almost died for your bloody crystals, and that would be the second time in a month."

"Alright, sorry." It was a semi-sincere apology. "After this, no more crystals or crystalline objects of any kind for at least two weeks, I promise."

Lucas audibly clicked his jaw and made some more threatening sounds, but after that, the walk back up was pure awkward silence. The only noise was the echoed splashing as we trudged up the river.

My feet were pretty numb by the time we finally reached the mouth of the cave, but it was going to be so worth it. I couldn't wait to get home, show them to Zoe, maybe tell her a less depressing version of the angel's story. Earlier that night, I had tucked her in and left her sans babysitter, but with the doors locked and powerful defensive arrays set up all throughout the apartment. It wasn't like we were going to by hiding from the cops for hours on end this time. From the look of things, this caper would go off without any kind of conflict whatsoever.

"Not another step, Herr Foster."

Of course, that was when the Nazis showed up.

Technically, they were from the Thule Society, not the Nazi party itself. It's kind of like a club for obscenely rich Europeans who justify their widespread hatred through mysticism and misinterpreted prophecies. They know way too much about actual arcana for my liking, so we tend to run into them a lot on our capers.

This time, there were six of them. Four guys dressed in gray camouflage, each with machine guns, helmets, and gas masks, and then the two non-faceless-goons. One was an older guy, maybe in his fifties. He had streaks of gray in his long, brown beard, but was otherwise obscured by a medieval cloak and hood. A mantle made of brown animal fur was stretched over his shoulders and held in place by a clasp. It prominently featured a swastika and dagger. Subtle.

Then there was Metzmacher. She was a tall, thin scarecrow of a woman, with high cheekbones and bright blonde hair in a strict, merciless bun. I've only ever seen her in that same black military uniform she was wearing that night, straight out of a World War II movie. If I had to guess, she's probably in her forties. Metz is the type where if she weren't such an effective leader of horrible, over-privileged racists, you know she'd make a very successful evil math teacher.

"You can't be serious," Lucas groaned.

"Very serious," Metzmacher replied, and she pulled a pistol from a holster at her side. Because, y'know, four AK-47s pointed at us wasn't enough.

"Alright, alright. What do you guys want, the tears?" I was already formulating a plan, mostly involving chucking a ball of electricity at them when they tried to fly off in their helicopter. Then after it crashed, I'd have Kurt fix it and we'd have a helicopter. We'd never pay for tolls or parking meters again. It was easily the best plan ever.

"The tears, yes," she said with her bright red lips curled up into a sabertooth tiger smile. "And much more. Der Junge, geben sie mir!"

And on that note, one of the flunkies scurried off to the side of the cave, coming back with someone in tow. Someone with a black bag over their head, wearing a flannel shirt, jeans...

Damn it, Matt.

"I believe you know this person," Metzmacher sneered, and her captive was thrown to his knees. Metz pulled the bag off him, sending a mess of wispy blonde hair everywhere, and jammed the muzzle of her gun up against the side of his head.

Matt looked at me, then at Kurt, over to Lucas, and finally peered up the barrel of the pistol. He blinked.

"Who are you people and what have you done with my underpants!" I would have laughed if he wasn't seconds away from having his brain leaking out into the river. Metzmacher was less amused.

"Speak again, American pig, and I will do worse than kill you." She looked up at me with eyes that were made of ice and hate. "Your idiot friend will die, Herr Foster, unless you do exactly as I say."

"Friend? I've never even met these people!" I don't know if Matt was stalling for time or just trying to get on her nerves. He succeeded at both, I guess. "Also, this is the worst bag-on-the-head safari adventure I've ever been on. The pizza was terrible, and I'm fairly sure at least two of these Nazis are animatronic! I demand a refund!"

Metz promptly thwacked Matt in the face, sending him to the ground like a sack filled with smaller sacks, all of them containing bricks or bowling balls.

"Then again, we can always find less irritating people to hold hostage." She clicked the hammer of her gun back and aimed at the heap of disheveled druid lying on the ground.

"No, wait!" I don't know much about how guns work, but I've seen enough movies to know that when the villain does the gun clicky thingie, they're about to shoot someone. "We'll give you the tears, alright? Just don't hurt him! Apart from the thing where you already hit him in the face, obviously, and I guess we won't count anything you did to rough him up before that point. So, as of right now, no more physical injury to him! Or emotional injury. He's sensitive, y'know?"

"Are you finished?" Metzmacher arched a thin eyebrow in my direction. Her finger sat on the trigger, unmoving.

I shrugged. "Yeah, I think that's about it."

"Good." She nodded briskly at Lucas. "Werewolf. Give him the artifacts."

Lucas looked to me, clearly apprehensive about the exchange. I nodded firmly, giving him the intense "I've got this" look. They had us over a barrel, no question. A big, stupid, swastika-covered barrel. That said, I had no intention of letting them just walk away with our hard earned arcana.

Lucas hesitantly handed the faintly glowing orbs over to me, and I gave him back his Victorian attire. The tears were large enough that I had to cradle them in both arms, close to my chest. For their size, though, they were really light. They made a soft, pleasant sound as they touched and rolled over each other. It vaguely reminded me of wind chimes.

With a grim expression, I trudged toward the Thule lackies. I felt Lucas and Kurt's eyes on me, watching as intently as Metzmacher and her gunmen, all of them just waiting for something to happen.

Suffice it to say, the plan had to be modified slightly.

Halfway there, I broke into a charge and aimed a shoulder check straight for Metzmacher. Her eyes went wide, and I remember smiling about that before the AKs started going off. Fortunately for me, these guys were well trained. Unfortunately, having your torso ripped apart by five or six shots to the chest hurts like hell. I managed to get Metz to the ground before I fell, landing face down on the smooth rocks outside the cave, along with the angel's tears which I had held tightly to my chest on the way down. There was some shouting in German, but I guess Lucas and Kurt managed to keep their cool in spite of me being murdered. Not sure whether I should have been appreciative or insulted.

"The rest of you!" Metzmacher shrieked, "Stay where you are, or the same happens to you!"

To be honest, what came next hurt way more than being shot. The tears started to push hot metal out of my internal organs, healing them as the bullets fell to the rocky ground. The blue cores glowed beautifully over the course of their work, which was incredibly fast since the damage to my chest was split between all twenty of them. I knew I couldn't wait for the excruciating pain to be over before I made my move. I pulled the book from my bag and flipped to the exact page I knew I would need. No components, and an array that was easy enough that I could draw it with some blood on a rock. I quickly did so. The spell only had two words required to activate it.

"Kulutrone-Anvare," I said quietly, trying not to choke despite the holes in my lungs. The bloody rune glowed, then sizzled. I grabbed the stone and held the array so it would face the two closest henchmen.

When historians talk about Greek fire, they're usually referring to what is essentially napalm. But really, over the course of Greece being taken over by Rome, they developed two very effective ways of lighting boats on fire. One was through chemicals, the other was through knowledge of the arcane. But since the average person knew nothing of magic or the techniques associated with it, it was assumed that they were the same thing. The arcane method which I used against the Thule guys was referred to in my book as the Scourge of Ares. Yes, it is as awesome as it sounds.

The symbol on the rock instantly triggered, and a jet of blue fire erupted to engulf two of the gunmen. If this kind of thing happened in a movie, I have no doubt in my mind that it would've elicited like twelve Wilhelm screams. Lucas and Kurt seemed to get the gist of the plan pretty quickly, as I heard more gunshots and yelling.

The tears were doing a great job, all things considered, but I was still feeling crazy sore and more than a little nauseous. I managed to roll over to one side, and saw that Lucas had punched one guy until he was unconscious or dead. The other was in a firefight with Kurt, who was pressed up against one of the cave walls. Metz and the hooded guy were already booking it back to their ride. They're such typical villains that it's almost hard to watch.

"Are you alright?" Matt crawled over to my side, his sky-colored eyes looking over the bleediest areas of my chest.

"As well as can be expected." It wasn't that bad, really. Everything was healed, and the sick feeling in my stomach was fading mercifully quickly. The angel's tears were still a royal blue color that implied they still had a good amount of healing left in them. I gave Matt's face a quick glance. "You knew this was going to happen. The thing about the spruce tree taking you hostage, you knew the Thule guys were coming after you."

The smile that slinked across his face had at least a hint of guilt in it. "I didn't know you would be shot."

"Why didn't you tell me? We could have come up with a plan, fought them off and prevented this whole thing."

"Sometimes it's better to work within your fate than to struggle against it," He replied. "Much like paddling up a river without an oar, one usually ends up in the same place, but exhausted for their efforts."

I nodded, knowing better than to argue with a cryptic druid about divining the future. As if on cue, a cry of pain erupted from the only remaining henchman as Lucas cracked him upside the head. Kurt would be calling him a kill-stealer for about a month after that.

"Alright, sir, let's get you home. It's been a long day for you." Matt helped me up, though I'm sure he wasn't feeling great either, on account of the gash on the side of his head. I offered one of the tears to him, but he declined with an upheld palm.

"The worst part is yet to come," I said with a brief sigh. "Now we have to listen to Kurt's music and Lucas complaining about Kurt's music for another three hours."

Matt gave a knowing smile and held up a scruffy bit of dark brown material between two fingers. It looked like a scrap of rawhide or something.

"I had a feeling we might need some bat leather."

-Break-In-

The ride back was, needless to say, infinitely more relaxing for everyone involved. Lucas was hesitant about the spell, saying that I'd end up making him permanently deaf. I offered the rebuttal that if he was permanently deaf, he wouldn't have to listen to me talk ever again. I guess he found that argument to be less than compelling. That said, if he complained about Kurt's music, I sure as heck didn't hear it.

It was still early morning by the time we got back to the apartment. Zoe wouldn't be waking up to go to school for a couple hours. I'd fallen asleep, waking up to an orange sky and some vocalist screaming about atrophy. Maybe that was the band's name. At any rate, I stumbled out of Kurt's car and into my building with a muttered thanks and an armful of celestial crystals. There was a dull but constant ache in the back of my neck, probably from sleeping on the inside of a car window.

I worked my way up the creaking, ancient staircase to the third floor and finagled with my keys. Zoe was always good about keeping the door locked when she knew I wasn't going to be around. Not that I would just leave her at night undefended. A burglar who was ignorant of the arcane would be incapacitated in seconds from all the arrays I had set up in my place. An arcanist might be able to undo one or two, but they'd never get past them all.

I slid the key in the deadbolt and turned it. It wasn't locked.

A lump built up in my throat as I grabbed the doorknob. The back of my brain tensed up, and I started to hear the sound of my heartbeat deep in my ears. Maybe Zoe got up and unlocked it for some reason after I left and forgot to relock it. It was a stupid explanation, but it sounded better in my head than any of the alternatives. I fell into the apartment with a hand on my saber, trying to tug the stupid thing out of its sheath. The angel's tears ended up on the carpeted floor, rolling behind furniture and under the coffee table.

"Zoe! Zoe, I'm-" The cool, metallic *shiing* noise finally happened, but I was freaking out a little too much at the time to appreciate it. The pit in my stomach dropped out and my head started swimming with thoughts like piranhas. Who could have known enough about magic to get through all those seals? Who else even knew where I lived, and how? Why did my brain always summon the absolute worst case scenario in my imagination when this sort of thing happened? I remember there being a beat of silence before I tore out of the living room and down the hallway.

I passed my room, covered in clothes, random junk, and runes drawn over other runes on the walls. A quick look inside told me that the sentinel arrays were still active. I ran by what used to be my parents' room, where a thick layer of dust had taken up residence. The last time I had been in there, I had torn the room apart in search of clues as to where they went. All I ever found was the book sitting in a drawer in my dad's desk. That was three years ago.

Zoe's room was at the end of the hallway, across from the bathroom. I shoved the door open, barely breathing. My lungs were tense in my chest, heavy and frozen with dread. She wasn't there.

I called out for her, checked under the bed, under the pink sheets and whitewashed furniture. Nothing.

Well, no. There was something. I walked to the window, my mind racing through the divining options I remembered from the spellbook: Scrying, divination. If I could find a piece of Zoe's hair, I could probably narrow down whether she was still in the city or not. My eyes went to the sill, where a note had been jammed under the closed window pane. The glass was shattered. Maybe it wouldn't be that complicated.

I slid the pane open and snatched the sheet of paper before it could blow out into the street. The words were hand written in a sharp, formalized script that hinted at its author.

Herr Foster,

Your Sister is in our hands, now. We will take care for her well. Yet it should be of your note to meet with us in the Auto Garage of your Worcester Train Station, or else she may not remain in such a way for a long time.

Come alone, tomorrow at five o'clock AM. We will kill her, Herr Foster, do not question that.

That was all I needed to know that it was face-stabbing time. Also, I think it deserves to be mentioned that the Thule Society is not populated by grammar Nazis. Not sure whether that's ironic or what.

"Five AM." They even had to be inconsiderate about making other people wake up stupidly early for their hostage situations. I flipped the paper over to see a blank page and promptly crumpled it in my hand. Then I heard a muffled jingling noise from the kitchen.

I crouched and started to sneak back down the hallway, pressing my back against the wall where I could. Ninja-panther mode was engaged. I held my sword at the ready as I crept across the carpet, slowly making my way to the empty doorway between the living room and the kitchen. Peering around the corner, I spied a guy in a dark pinstriped suit crouching in front of the open fridge.

"Alright, hands up!" I jumped out into the kitchen and jabbed the tip of my sword in his direction, grabbing onto the countertop to keep from sliding into the oven. "Who the crap are you and what are you doing in my apartment!"

He didn't react at first, aside from taking a drink from a bottle of cream soda.

"Are you drinking my friggin'- Hey!" I waggled the tip of my sword at him, poking it closer to his face. It was the kind of face that said 'class valedictorian who also scored the big home run and made out with every girl you ever had a crush on.' His slick haircut only helped with that image.

"Yeah. You have good taste, Mister Foster." He started rooting through the cheese drawer with his free hand. "With drinks, at least."

"Dude! I am pointing a sword at you! Freaking pointy, sharp

80

thing!"

The guy turned to look at the weapon, inspected it down the bridge of his nose, and nodded. "That it is. But you've never actually used it, apart from cutting through chain link fences." He casually shut the refrigerator and got to his feet, taking another long guzzle of my damn soda.

For reference, between you and me, I totally did use it once. There was a guy who jumped me and I cut him a new face hole. It was great. You can even ask Kurt. Not Lucas, though. He'd probably say it was a mannequin I spazzed out over. Just because mannequins are creepy and weird when you're alone at night in a warehouse. Regardless, I kept the tip of the saber trained on the guy's fashionably stubbled cheek.

"Okay, so you know who I am and about the Rouen Diamond. Doesn't mean I won't impale the crap out of you."

"Sure, kid." Suit guy leisurely walked past me and into the living room. I followed, though I briefly glanced down the hallway to Zoe's room again.

"You never answered my question," I said, glaring at the back of the guy's stupid fancy haircut. It was a dark brown, like the color of wet earth. "And if you don't start, I'm going to assume you're working for Metzmacher and then stab you really, really hard."

"Relax, Foster." He took to haunting a spot near the TV, next to the doorway out. Every sip he took of that cream soda made me want to punch him in the kidneys that much more. "I'm not with the Thule Society. And for the sake of this interaction, you can call me Evans."

"Great," I said, standing between him and the bedroom

hallway. "Why are you in my apartment?"

"Well, I'm clearly not here to steal your television." He put a hand on the appliance in question and smirked. Sure, the thing was pre-2000 old and sounded awful, but you could still play video games and DVDs on it.

"No, just my soda. My expensive soda."

"Expensive." He raised both carefully groomed eyebrows and peered at the bottle, maybe looking for inlaid rubies. It's like five bucks more to buy the glass bottles, which is just about the only luxury I afford myself. So excuse me, princess.

"To put it simply, I'm here to offer you a job."

"What kind of job?" I had a feeling this was about the arcana, but I couldn't be too outright about it. I didn't trust this guy. Y'know, on account of him breaking into my apartment and everything.

"Something with a steady paycheck and a chance to get in on the good fight."

"The good fight. Only two kinds of people use that phrase to describe what they do: Superheroes and people involved with the government. Superheroes don't sneak into people's houses and steal their drinks, and I don't really think I'm cut out for government work, sorry." I lifted the tip of my saber to the mouth of its gray metal sheath. It'd be better to blast this guy out the door than stab him and have blood all over the carpet, anyway.

"You're more than qualified, Mister Foster." Evans wasn't really as fazed by the refusal as I was hoping he'd be.

"Yeah, and I'm still not interested."

He pursed his lips and looked at me with a pair of cold, gray eyes. "You don't even know what the position entails."

"Something about finding arcana for the government to use against its enemies, whoever you guys decide that is at the moment. Muslims, protestors, immigrants, stop me if I hit the flavor of the week." I always knew the feds were looking into the supernatural. There was too much of it out there for them not to be. I'd never had visits from them before that point, but I was expecting it, and my answer was always going to be the same.

Evans looked past me to one of the dusty windows, mulling over my response. "So you'd rather the artifacts be held by an individual, vulnerable to capture and use by anyone with a lock pick." He lifted a shiny black shoe to tap the front door closed. Smug jerk.

"Better than said artifacts going to the totalitarian regime willing to put up the most cash."

He must have taken my point, as he went quiet for a minute after that. Evans idly swirled the remaining soda in his hand.

"Not a fan of the government, then. Do you vote Tea Party, by any chance?" He asked with a superior smile.

I almost laughed, but not quite. "No."

"Libertarian?"

"I don't vote," I said evenly.

His eyebrows sank, switching to that "Oh, you're one of those people" glare you get whenever you tell someone that you don't vote or that you kick bald eagles down flights of stairs for fun. He finished off the soda and set the clear glass bottle on top of my TV.

"You seem to have a lot of opinions for someone who doesn't want his voice to be heard."

"Yeah, see, I'd speak up, but I'm afraid I'd be drowned out by the sound of all that money being poured into politicians' pockets. I'd rather save my breath, y'know?"

"Funny," Evans put an elbow up on the TV. "I took you for an idealist. Somebody who'd fight for what they believed in."

"And I thought government agents needed warrants to break into somebody's place. Are you going to arrest me, Evans, or just lecture me on why I should take part in the corporate-funded parades you call elections?"

"I could do both, but I'm really just curious why you'd do so much to get a glowing rock, but getting out to vote is too much of a hassle for you." He smirked. "Without the defensive little changes in subject."

"Fine," I replied, looking down toward Zoe's room again. "Voting implies that a person has some kind of confidence in any of the people who're running for office. In my mind, my not-vote is essentially a vote of no confidence in those people and our political system in general. I'd love to actually vote, but there's nobody running on the 'Punch Lobbyists in the Face' ticket."

"Ah." Nothing shuts a civil servant up like complete disdain for the American political system. Evans looked at me like I was a rabid, two-headed moose before moving for the door. "And your disgust is so great that you won't even consider becoming a cog for change within the organization itself."

"Nah. I'll just wait until I have the money and then move to a country with a real economic model. Like Sweden. Then I can wear a Viking helmet and drink mayonnaise by the flagon."

"That's disgusting," he said primly.

"Don't knock it until you've tried it. From what I've heard, it's good for you." I mustered a smile, thoroughly enjoying the opportunity to make this guy uncomfortable, but running out of patience. Some people just won't shut up and leave when all you need is a few hours to divine the location of your kidnapped little sister.

"Foster, it's not a coincidence that I'm coming to you now. Machinations beyond your understanding are beginning to unfold. There will come a time when you need my help."

"Isn't that a little dramatic?" I asked.

"It's not a joke," he replied.

"Well, I'll be sure to set up the Evans-signal on the roof just in case." I folded my arms over my chest and shrugged. "Unless you prefer I call the Evans-phone."

"Very clever," He muttered and finally made his way for the door. Still, there was something bugging me about the whole situation. Apart from Zoe being kidnapped, I mean, and the cream soda thing.

"Hey," I said, catching him halfway into the hallway. He turned back with a brow arched. "You look like the kind of guy who'd be able to break a deadbolt, but how'd you get through all the wards?"

"I didn't," he said simply. "Everything was open when I got here."

"Oh." The Thule Society actually broke in through Zoe's window to avoid setting off my defenses, and then waltzed out through the front door just to spite me. "Those freaking jerks."

"I'll keep an eye out for that signal," he let loose one last haughty grin before stepping outside. The door clicked behind him.

"Yeah, I'll keep an eye out for your stupid face!" I yelled through the door, finally letting out some frustration. It didn't help as much as I would've liked.

"That doesn't even make sense," I sighed. I ended up sitting on the living room floor for a little while, staring up at the huge off-white array I'd painted on the grayish ceiling a few years ago. I thought it was pretty clever, painting it like that so it wouldn't be noticeable. Of course, it only produced its shower of painful electrical sparks on the intruder if they broke in through the front door. My gaze lowered back to the carpet.

"I'm sorry, Zoe," I whispered to the floor. "I'm such an idiot."

After a long pause, I decided that was all the self-loathing I could allow myself right then. Brooding wouldn't save my little sister from the clutches of the Thule Society. I glanced under the couch and noticed the glow of one of the angel's tears. The first step was gathering those back up. The next eight hours would be spent getting in touch with Kurt about a ride, setting up stronger arrays throughout the apartment, and trying to find Zoe through literally every spell in the book.

Unfortunately, that last one proved completely futile. Wherever Metzmacher had taken her, Zoe was hidden from all the arrays I had at my disposal. A very basic spell from the front pages of my book told me that we weren't on the same continent anymore. At the very least, that meant she was still alive, but the Thule Society probably had bases all throughout Europe. I had no way of searching with that kind of range. I had to either come up with a plan or play by their rules.

After a day of drawing circles and runes, along with a night of brainstorming, I still couldn't come up with anything. I'd just have to play along and see what those dirtbags wanted. With two kidnappings in what was essentially one day, it couldn't be about the tears. There had to be something bigger.

The train station was weirdly quiet as we drove around the rotary that led to its grandiose entrance. Normally, droves of people with backpacks and laptop bags would be leaning against the white pillars in front of the doors, each of them waiting for their ride to get through a mile of obscene traffic. It's almost like normal people don't want to wake up at four in the friggin' morning to go do stuff. Of course, Lucas was the only one of us in any kind of conscious, fully functioning state. I contend that it isn't one of his werewolf powers, and that Europeans just have dumb internal clocks.

"You shouldn't be doing this alone." He was sitting in the back this time with his top hat resting in the seat next to him. Without that bit of decorum, he actually looked like a fairly normal person. Apart from the dorky, old-fashioned haircut, anyway. "This is obviously another trap."

"It's a hostage situation. We don't get to choose the specifics." I was on edge, tired, and angry. Not a good combination to add Lucas to. "If one of you two show up next to me, they could have Zoe killed on the spot, and I'm not willing to risk that."

Lucas sighed, but ultimately seemed to accept that. He cared about Zoe too, and in retrospect, that's probably where his anxiety stemmed from. That, and the fact that he saw me as a bumbling idiot who couldn't find his way out of a deflated inner tube.

"Still, we'll be here," Kurt offered. "If you need help or they go back on their word, just call me and we'll drive up and wreck them."

"Thanks." I legitimately tried to sound grateful. Through the early morning haze, it was hard to tell whether I'd pulled it off.

We drove around to the back of the station and trundled through the usual push-button-take-ticket procedure one finds in parking garages. The hourly rates weren't horrendously expensive, which seemed like a small blessing at the time. We'd be spending a buck, assuming that Metzmacher didn't have an hour long evil monologue planned.

It didn't take much to find a spot to park, and as soon as Kurt had stopped the car, I got out and took note of which area we were in. First floor, third space in. Everything in the garage was gray concrete, apart from the yellow lines that marked the parking spaces. Pretty uninspiring, overall.

I walked through the garage itself for a couple of flights, and then took the stairs for the remainder of the trek. The lots up there were empty, which wasn't really surprising, though it managed to be a little eerie. My hand went to my side out of habit. It was where I'd usually have my messenger bag and my book. This time there was nothing but empty air. I had left the bag in the car, along with my sword. To be without them was a lot like missing an arm or a leg, except without the inevitable question of whether to go with a wooden peg or robot prosthetics. I'd bet that Kurt could make an awesome bionic leg for me, but there's something distinctly classy about the old standby. After considering it, I had to go with hoping that I wouldn't need either after this meeting.

Honestly, my usual weapons would be more of a liability

than anything in this scenario. The sword wouldn't do me much good against the gunmen they probably had, and the book would just be at risk of falling into their hands. If they were planning to bargain my sister for my parents' tome, I'd have to regroup with Kurt and Lucas regardless.

That wasn't what they were after, though. If all they wanted was the book, they would have just tried to kill me and taken it. You don't kidnap someone's family unless you want their money or their cooperation. I don't know whether it's obvious yet or not, but I don't have a lot of money to throw around. And if they wanted me to do something for them, the Thule guys couldn't kill me then and there, so I was actually pretty safe.

At least, that was the theory I had buzzing around in my head as I walked up into the topmost floor of the parking garage. It was open to the pre-sunrise sky, meaning everything was stained a quiet purple shade. The two white towers of the train station's main building stood out like big candles on a rectangular cake, and a crane loomed dormant over the rest of the city skyline. A chest height concrete partition ran down the middle of the lot, separating it into two halves. There was an overhang directly across from my position, where a white van was parked so that it's back was facing me. The doors were open. Hanging out within the vehicle was the crowd from yesterday. Or the day before, whatever.

Hooded guy was looming behind Metz again, and they were both flanked by a small army of uniformed flunkies with guns and gas masks. I dunno what it is about these guys and looking creepy as hell, but they sure pulled it off. I wouldn't be surprised if their masks were somehow imbued with magic to protect against illusions or sleeping spells. That'd be a better explanation for having them, considering that I didn't have access to mustard gas. Which was something I really should have talked to Kurt about before that encounter.

I stood there for a while, facing down a crap-ton of automatic weapons and one frigid shrew until she finally decided to step down and out from the shadows of the van.

"Thank you for coming, Herr Foster."

"Where is she," I said, skipping straight to the business at hand. I didn't have any interest in small talk with any of these fascist idiots. Metz did her best impression of a cobra smiling and placed a gloved fist on her hip.

"Somewhere safe," she replied, her voice a menacing purr. "For now." That's villain talk for, 'If we give you any clues, you'll probably find her and take her back, so no dice.'

"What do you want, Metzmacher? What's it going to take to get her back?"

"So impatient," she said with a condescending smirk. "It is like a plague among Americans, and especially the children." I guess she didn't see how referring to a 20 year old as a child could possibly make her seem old. For Zoe's sake, I kept it to myself and focused on glaring. Eventually, she got tired of the silent treatment and actually said something useful.

"We are looking for a piece of arcana, Herr Foster, and have found no trace of it through our methods." I could only guess what those were. Probably torture, maybe involving lederhosen and blood sausage. "We have hired many arcana-hunters. None could find a trace of it. But we know it is here in your country, and we will have it."

That was a pretty decent turn of events, really. If I played my cards right, I could find a way to get whatever this thing was, save Zoe, and bamboozle the Thule chump-ciety all in one day. My mind started racing through a storm of possibilities.

"Fine, what is this thing?"

"A mandrake root," she said, and for the first time I noticed the guy with the long, graying beard looking at me from under his cowl. For a guy his age, his eyes were intense, offering a glimpse into a mind that must have been dedicated to bloody rituals and dark mythos. Shadows flickered across his aged features like lightning as his gaze burned into me from afar.

"What, you really couldn't find one of those on your own?" The root of a mandrake is a pretty freaky looking thing, but not that rare. It's kinda like a long potato, but in the shape of a person. One of those is supposed to be a sort of good luck charm by itself, but the root is also used in countless incantations and spells as a sponge for arcane energy.

"Not any mandrake root," she snapped, apparently insulted. "The one belonging to one man, specifically."

"Adolf Hitler," the bearded man stated. I was surprised equally by the name and the voice saying it, as up until now I had assumed cloak guy was mute. His voice was a brassy baritone, thick with its own accent. It sounded more Nordic than anything.

"Indeed." Metz grinned. I tried to keep my expression neutral in spite of the anger burning a hole in my stomach. "The artifact which saw the Fuhrer's meteoric rise to power seventy years ago."

"The Devil's Mandrake," I said, knowing full well the reaction it was likely to cause. To be fair, that was the name of the thing, at least to those on the winning side of World War II. This

91

particular root was said to be a nexus of dark power, a malignant force which was imbued into it by the sheer malice of the combined Nazi political movement. In that sense, it wasn't just Hitler's mandrake, but a kind of empathic sponge for thousands of people throughout Europe and America over a ten-year period. In fact, it might still be absorbing the hatred from modern day toolboxes who goose step under a swastika.

The weird thing was that I had always heard it was still in the hands of the Thule Society. If they're the ones looking for it, something must have happened, and recently.

"I'm kinda surprised, Metz. You really lost something that powerful? Did somebody get too enthusiastic during spring cleaning and toss it in the recycling with your leftovers?"

"I did not lose anything, Schweinhund!" That really must've pissed her off. The shriek was punctuated by the clicks of her gunmen simultaneously lifting the barrels of their guns. "It was taken from us by men from your country, before my promotion!"

"So, back when you were a second-class racist harpy."

"Be careful," Metz growled. "You come closer to death with every word." In spite of having six or so guns pointed at my face, I wasn't worried about my own safety. Metz was pissed, but she needed my incredible prowess to find her artifact of ultimate evil. Killing me wasn't an option, and wounding me would be counterproductive. The problem was, I wouldn't put it past her to kill a child for kicks.

"Who took the root?"

"Mercenaries," she said, her smile having melted into a bitter scowl. "An elite group. They were Americans, but we do not know beyond that."

I nodded. Good for those guys. I just had to hope that they held onto the thing but didn't know enough about it to become unstoppable embodiments of hatred in the meantime.

"When you find the mandrake, you will call us, and we will return your sister to you. I think you will agree that this is fair."

"Yeah, I guess," I said quickly, preparing to do the dramatic walk away. "How do I contact you once I've got the root?"

"This number," Metz stated, a hint of a smirk curling the corners of her lips. She tossed a sealed envelope on the concrete floor. "You will call it and we will come to you." The heels of her black leather shoes clicked against the concrete as she slipped back behind the line of guns. The hooded guy gave me one last foreboding look before the back doors of the van slammed shut.

So yeah, that time they beat me to the awesome exit. I watched them drive down the ramp, a sick feeling finding purchase in my gut once again. I couldn't help wondering if Zoe had been in the passenger seat of the van. If I could have gotten Lucas close enough to smell for her or something, and then tear through a door panel to rescue her. I had to hope, the way I always did when my mind wasn't racing with something else, that I hadn't failed her as a brother.

As the sound of the van faded, I looked to the brightening skyline and let out a long sigh. I guess I had an evil, man-shaped potato to find.

-At the Spiral-

On the way back from the train station, I decided to have Kurt take a little detour for Kelly Square. It's this horrible intersection in the middle of Worcester where five or six roads come together in the most illogical arrangement possible, and there's no traffic light. It's like you have to break at least two laws just to make a left. The only reason I ever went out there was to visit The Spiral, a little store that's barely noticeable from the street. It's housed on the ground floor of an old, brick building, with less of a storefront and more of a graying brick wall, a thin wooden door, and a couple of small windows. The cracked and faded door had been a mossy green for as long as I could remember, like it had been painted once in the 40s and went untouched since. There wasn't really a sign, just a simple swirling design that had been carved on a polished piece of wood and attached to the wall above the entrance.

"Pull in here," I said, pointing to the alleyway between the shop and the trendy restaurant next to it. The gap was just wide enough to serve as a tiny parking lot which never seemed to be occupied. Kurt's monstrosity thrummed its way into a spot, and the three of us moved purposefully for The Spiral's entrance. It was still early in the day, to the point where most stores were dead to the world. Come to think of it, I don't think I'd ever seen a *Closed* sign on The Spiral's door. I pulled the old, termite-eaten thing open, prompting the jingling of a small brass bell within the store.

"They are actually open," Lucas noted, holding his hat at his side. "That is a bit of a surprise."

"Not if you know Sue," I replied. We took a few steps inside and were immediately greeted by the potent, completely overwhelming smell of incense. Every single time I came to the store, no matter how often, it managed to knock me in the face like a million perfumed steamrollers. Lucas instantly covered his nose and started into a hacking cough. I almost felt bad for the big lug.

Apart from the pungent smell, the store was pretty nice. It was organized, completely devoid of dust, and full of crap I'd buy if I had a ton of extra money or a nice house to put it in. Tall wooden shelves dominated the walls, each one full of stuff that was arranged alphabetically in one way or another. Modern glass display cases contrasted the dark, old world bookshelves and made for a sort of maze in the center of the shop. The merchandise itself was eclectic, to say the least, ranging from old books to candles and semi precious stones. One section of a raw brick wall was dedicated to marble busts and statues of pagan gods, varying in size and subject matter. Of course, those were all mundane objects. The real function of the shop was to serve as a private marketplace for the buying and selling of arcana. From what I had seen, the owner's staples included potions, elixirs, and anything else that you would expect to come out of a witch's cauldron.

The purveyor in question probably did have a cauldron, if I had to guess, though she lacked the hat and nose one usually associates with the profession. So I don't think she really counted as a witch. Her name was Sue, and as far as I could tell, she was the only employee at The Spiral. She was always there, and she always had the same expression: Deadpan neutrality. Sometimes it would waver into chilled disinterest or slight contentment. Overall, I'd say she was the physical personification of that color everyone uses for carpeting. Beige with a hint of gray. That day, when she stepped out from the back room to greet us, she was in perfect Sue-ish form.

"Greetings, Mister Foster. You are not usually here this early." She adjusted her tank top as she spoke, which was a shade of something so pale you couldn't really tell what color it was. Cargo pants in the hue of sandpaper went under that, followed by white, no-name sneakers. To say that Sue was feminine wouldn't really be accurate, but she wasn't masculine either. She must have been my age, but even then, the only thing clearly defining her as female were the subtle curves under her light-something top. Maybe her face, too. That part of her reminded me of an unfinished mannequin. Her high cheek bones, skin the color of aged china, and short brown hair probably had something to do with it.

She drifted over to the glass counter holding her antiquated cash register and scanned the three of us. Her earthy eyes came to rest on Lucas pretty quickly, as he was still hacking out a lung. I briefly wondered how much a werewolf lung would go for at a place like this. I mean, the novelty would be incredible. Why hang a singing bass on the wall of your rumpus room when you could have a real internal organ from a British lycanthrope?

"If your friend wishes, I could extinguish the incense I have been burning." She spoke evenly, seemingly without preference in the matter. She didn't sound especially worried about Lucas' health, either. It was like the offer was just an automated response.

"Actually, Lucas, why don't you and Kurt go stand outside? I just need to talk to Sue, it won't be too long."

Lucas grumbled beneath his glove, "You are aware of how incredibly conspicuous-" he was interrupted by his own violent sneeze, and I decided to take that opportunity to shove him a little toward the door.

"Like I said, it won't be long. You guys need to bond, anyway. Talk about the War of 1812 or something. You were probably in that, right?"

"No, I was not in the thrice-damned War of 1812! I am a Worthing, a member of the upper class!" His indignation was apparently a pretty powerful antihistamine, as he didn't even sniffle throughout that bitter tirade. Regardless, Kurt was happy to clear out, and Mr. Worthing wouldn't tolerate the indecency of exploding sinuses for too much longer. The bell jingled again as they left, leaving Sue and I in the shafts of early morning light that streamed through the small windows of the shop. There were contemporary silver lamps in sconces on the walls, but they must have been set pretty low. It gave a cold ambiance when coupled with the stark white light glowing up from the display cases. Sue stood rigidly behind the register while I started to poke around the colored candle display.

"So, people ever buy any of this stuff?" I picked up a green candle and turned it over. The sticker on the side said that it was made of real beeswax and would promote good health and financial standing. I had no idea bees were so awesome.

"Yes. Typically, they are used by those who are ignorant to the true supernatural as a means of bringing peace of mind, or personally connecting to modern variants of Celtic or Norse gods."

"Fair enough," I said, replacing the candle. Sue didn't talk as though she were a robot so much as she had absolutely no opinion or concern about what she was saying. "Any of them actually do anything?"

"No," she stated flatly. "They are candles, and could thus be used in an arcane ritual, as you know, but are themselves magically inert." I peered over at Sue, trying to get some sense of what she was thinking or feeling. Nada.

"But you didn't visit with the intention of purchasing candles," she went on, making eye contact the way one might with a character in a painting. Even when staring her right in the face, Sue was distant to the extent that it would make me worried about anyone else. It was unusual, but I just took it as part of her overall Sueness. "You could have come at any time, were that the case. If your reason for speaking with me is urgent, it would be to your advantage to be direct in this conversation."

Guess she had a point. I didn't want to just barge in and start demanding information, but then, Zoe's safety took precedence over manners. Sue wasn't the type to get offended by that sort of thing, anyway.

"I need your help," I said, resting my elbows on the glass counter and leaning forward. It helped with the stress that was pressing hard on my shoulder blades. "I need to find a piece of arcana."

"That is what you do," Sue replied. She stood with her hands at her sides, keeping expressionless brown eyes locked on me. "What are you in search of at this juncture?"

"The Devil's Mandrake."

That was enough to create a ripple of emotion within Sue. She blinked, and one eyebrow rose by half a centimeter. After a pause, she cautiously asked, "Why?"

"It's for my sister."

"You're going to give Hitler's mandrake root to your sister?"

"No, I mean, it's for the Thule Society."

"You're going to give it to the Nazis."

"No! I..." My palm met with my face. "The Thule guys kidnapped her, and they're going to kill her if I don't get the thing for them."

Sue's gaze bore down on me. It was clear that she was considering something, weighing the situation in her head.

"You know the potential for destruction the root possesses," she finally said. I nodded. We were talking city-exploding, zombie army creating, super soldier mashing power. I'm not sure why the Thule guys never thought to use it for that in the forty years they had it, but if I had to guess, I'd say the old Nazis knew it was too dangerous. Metzmacher is a neo-toolbox who probably thinks she can steer the end of the world in her favor.

"It is your intention, then, to risk the lives of millions in order to save one."

I looked at Sue. She was cold, emotionless, and strictly factual in everything she did, but I didn't ever realize she was capable of thinking like that. Not about Zoe. Sue had met her, had offered her candy when we came into the store. She politely declined Zoe's constant invites to her tea parties, but I honestly thought Sue liked my sister. I guess she was harder to read than I assumed.

"Yes," I said. Sue's silence prompted me to add, "And if they do go on to threaten everyone and everything, then I'll kick their butts the way I always have, mandrake or no."

"And why do you assume that she is alive at all? Or that they will not simply kill you both once they have the root?" Sue would be really good at hosting a debate or something with the way she was coming up with moral quandaries. That said, I wasn't in the mood for the third degree, especially along that line of questioning.

"Sue, I have to do this, alright? I'm her brother, and it's my fault that they kidnapped her in the first place. I don't have the luxury of contemplating the overarching morality of what I'm doing, because I don't have a choice." I remember my eyes going to a statue of a Greek goddess with a bow and a deer. My voice got stuck in the back of my throat. "And I will do everything I can to save her, as long there's a chance she's still alive."

Sue was quiet after that. I lifted my arms from the display case, fairly sure that I wasn't going to be getting the help I was looking for. I didn't want to involve Matt in another thing so soon after what happened with the tears, but it didn't look like I had a choice there, either.

"I'll ask around," she said quickly. I went to look at Sue, but she had turned and her face was overshadowed in the dim morning light. I smiled. She had a heart after all.

"Thanks," I replied. It was a perfect moment for a big old hug, but I decided against it. Sue didn't seem like the hugging type, even if she did have something resembling a conscience. So instead, I stayed put in front of the register. "In the meantime, any ideas for places I could look?"

The storekeeper gave me a hint of a funny look, shaking her head. "What, without any real information, off the top of my head?"

"Yeah, y'know. Musty warehouses, subterranean catacombs, abandoned construction sites, that sort of thing. Places where people hide stuff." I wasn't positive that Worcester had any underground ruins, but there was a rumor about abandoned subway tunnels that came to mind. That would be cool, and it would totally have given me the chance to use the Rouen Diamond again.

"I- That," she started. You could see the wheels spinning in her head. "You can't just go poking around any building looking for it. Finding the object by sheer happenstance would be extremely unlikely, at best."

"But not impossible," I replied, pointing in order to punctuate my clearly superior logic. "And if I did find it, you wouldn't have to go to the trouble of getting in touch with your contacts."

"The chances of that actually occurring are exceptionally low!" Interesting. It seemed like I was actually getting Sue to emote. Given, she was verging on expressing Lucas-like rage, but progress is progress! "You might as well jump into the Atlantic ocean in search of it. The result would be the same."

"Oh, wait, so you think it'll be on the beach? Kind of a crappy place to hide something, though. What with the tide, not to mention the undertow." It's true. I mean, pirates hid treasure chests on beaches, but this was a plant root. It would suffer all kinds of water damage. Unless it was in a big, watertight chest. That would make it really easy to find, which would be nice, but that defeats the purpose of hiding it altogether.

"No, I didn't say that!" That was definitely rage coming on. "We don't know yet if it's in this state, or this country, or on this continent!"

"Well, yeah, but it's not going to take forever for you to get a lead, right? It'd be stupid to go to Russia or something and then find out that the root is being served as a side for a chocolate chip muffin at a coffee shop in Southern Vermont."

Sue opened her mouth, but no noise escaped. Yeah, okay, that was kind of a dumb example, but I could have really gone for a chocolate chip muffin with cream cheese right about then. It was early and I hadn't eaten yet, don't judge me.

"This entire conversation is completely absurd," Sue said, chopping her arm out in a gesture that seemed to be purely for the purpose of venting her frustration. "It would make infinitely more sense for you to go out and find some other piece of arcana to use against the Thule Society once they have the mandrake root."

"Why, did you have something in mind?" I grinned at Sue, who narrowed her earthen eyes at me. I momentarily questioned whether she could punch as hard as Lucas did, but then it occurred to me that with all her elixirs and junk, it was more likely that she could just shoot laser eye beams at me. In retrospect, trying to make her mad might have been a terrible idea.

"You were arguing that point for the express purpose of getting information on another piece of arcana." Her tone was ice cold, squeezed between tightened jaws.

"Would your admiration of my honesty temporarily outweigh your anger if I said yes?" I smiled and inched toward the door in case of laser related death. Fortunately, I was spared this time. Sue let out a sigh, didn't vaporize me with any kind of beams, and pulled a thick book out from under the cash register. She held it aloft effortlessly, but the tome looked and sounded friggin' heavy when it thudded against the glass countertop.

"There is an object I have been keeping track of since it came to the United States on a museum tour which started in Iran." Sue flipped through the pages, which contained neat, regimented notes on what must have been hundreds of arcane items. There were tons of newspaper clippings and written hyperlinks, too. "And while I do not wish to see such an artifact stolen from a legitimate historical organization, it is the only piece I feel would be powerful enough to assist you in this situation."

"Alright, great!" I leaned over the counter to get a better view of the page in question, almost bumping foreheads with Sue. She took a step back. "What is it? Does it come from the Middle East, like a magical shamshir? Because I already have a sword, but I could replace it if this one shoots lightning or something."

"The piece is an ancient Assyrian rug, dating to roughly 900 BC."

"Oh." Not quite what I was expecting. I tried not to look too disappointed as I peered at Sue's upside down notes. Her handwriting was almost consistent enough to be a type font. "So what, is it alchemically enhanced to gather extra dust bunnies?"

"No," Sue stated, pointing to a line in her notes. "The design woven into it leads me to believe that it is a wishing carpet."

"Wait," I had to stop, putting up my palms. "Wait, wait, wait. Wait. Wait."

Sue stared at me, an eyebrow raised expectantly.

"It's a flying carpet," I said, unable to contain a sudden swell of excitement. "It's an actual flying carpet, like in the books and the movies based loosely on the books and the collectible fantasy card games!"

"A wishing carpet," she corrected. "Flying carpets actually fly to and from their destination. This kind instantly transports the user to their desired location upon the utterance of a phrase secretly inscribed upon it."

"Holy crap, that's amazing! An enchantment like that must have taken some kind of elite team of weavers and alchemists, working together for weeks."

"Each thread is individually enchanted, using elements from all across the Assyrian empire."

"Sennacherib the Elder could have worked on it!" If you don't know who that is, trust me, he's important and really cool, at least as far as ancient arcanists go. To give you an idea, my research points to him as the creator of the first flying ship. It's not too much of a leap to think he'd work on a magic carpet during his travels across the Middle East.

"It would be entirely possible. If I could study the rug, I might even be able to tell exactly where it came from, and who commissioned it."

I looked up at Sue as she looked up at me. We were inches away from each other, nerding over the same piece of arcana. Our noses almost touched.

"That would be, um." It was early, I hadn't gotten a lot of sleep last night, and I guess the whole thing kind of caught up to me right then. Sue just blinked.

"Are you alright?" I never noticed how big her eyes were before that point. "Your face is flushed. Are you becoming embarrassed for any reason? Alternatively, you may have a fever."

Sue had gone back to what sounded like automatic responses. It reminded me of calling the emergency room that one time with the tuna can.

"What? No! No. It's just warm. Y'know, in here."

"Actually, the temperature is between 67 and 69 degrees. It should be optimal in terms of comfort." She must have had a thermometer behind the counter or something. I pulled back from the display case and moved for the door.

"Yeah, it's getting late. In the morning. I gotta go find that magic carpet and stuff."

"Do you want to know where it is, first?"

"Nope! No! I'll find it, I'm good." I'd stumbled out the door into the waking sun and gotten a judgmental glare from Lucas before realizing that yeah, it'd be a lot easier to find the thing if I knew where it was.

"Foster, what in the hell...?"

"I know, wait, hold that snooty observation. Forgot something." I ducked back into the Spiral, inciting another jingle from the bell and almost slamming into a bookshelf. Was it seriously that close before? Cripes. Sue was still hanging out behind the register, but held out a neatly folded piece of paper. She obviously wasn't surprised about my return.

"Actually, can I get-"

"A storage facility in Lowell. It's currently cycled out of an exhibit at the American Textile History Museum." It was almost weird how still her arm was with that folded up note, hovering in place over the counter.

"Oh." I checked the bookshelf to make sure I hadn't knocked anything off, and noticed a book on translated Gaelic incantations.

It was right next to another one on making bread the way ancient Egyptians did. Like I said, eclectic.

I took a few steps over to Sue and nabbed the paper, sticking it in my coat pocket. "Thanks, Sue." I offered a smile in return, which she mostly didn't react to. "I'll be back soon with a priceless artifact to translate!"

I was grinning my way over to the door when the quiet sound of her voice made me stop in my tracks.

"Mister Foster." I looked back and made eye-contact with Sue, who actually looked remorseful. Or disappointed. It was kind of hard to tell. Either way, some kind of emotion was happening there. "You didn't sleep last night."

I can't really say how Sue came to that conclusion. I mean, I was tired, but it's not like I was a shambling mass of eye-bags. I was just occupied with fixing the apartment's defenses and trying to find Zoe. It happens.

I shrugged. Honestly, I couldn't think of a great response, so I just went with a meaningless laugh followed by, "Hey, everybody knows all the best TV is on after four in the morning! I loves me some rotisserie infomercials."

Sue shook her head. She wasn't convinced, but by then I was more or less out the door. Out the door and into the judgment-zone. I had to put on the brakes the second I got outside the shop on account of the well dressed roadblock standing in my way.

"You have the location, I hope." Lucas really wasted no time when it came to getting on my case. "I am already weary of standing here, Foster, as at least one woman over the age of sixty has invited me to go dancing with her. Additionally, two very burly gentlemen with strange facial hair were referring to Kurt as a cigarette, for whatever reason."

"They were talkin' about you, bud." Kurt was leaning against the building, in the middle of reading a magazine. It was probably about cars. He was obviously pretty detached from the whole ordeal.

"Well, either way, it is very odd behavior and I rather dislike it." Lucas adjusted his top hat, followed by the bottom edges of his gloves. "The sooner we can be gone from this particular piece of concrete, the better."

"Okay, so I have good news and bad news." Lucas' expression that followed wasn't entirely unexpected. Regardless of the disgusted glower from my lupine compatriot, I couldn't hold back a smirk. "The good news is that you aren't completely hopeless when it comes to women."

Stuffy Victorian morals aside, I was pretty sure I was about to get punched through a brick wall for that. When the blow never came, I continued.

"Seriously, the good news is that I have the location of an artifact that'll make it way easier for us to get the root, once we figure out where it is." I pulled out the folded note from Sue and waggled it in the dusty city air. "Bad news is that it might take a little while to actually do that."

You could see Lucas biting back his usual negativity. "That is unfortunate. Yet, what is the artifact? And what kind of horrific personal hell are we going to be wading through to find it?"

I grinned. "The pristine linoleum corridors of a storage building, my friends. This one is gonna be easy like putting a kilt on a totem pole." I'm going to tack that particular expression up to sleep deprivation. "All it'll take is an invisibility spell for the cameras and liberal use of an Ares' Scourge on the locks. We'll be in like Ho Chi Minh."

"Foster, you need to stop with those idioms."

"Yeah, seriously, you've got a problem, man." Even Kurt opened his mouth on that one.

"I do not! People say stuff like that all the time."

"No, they really do not." Lucas started to walk for the car with Kurt following close behind. The two Brutuses. Brutii, with daggers dripping my blood all the way to their jerk-chariot. He called back, "Where is this object, and what is it, for the second time?"

"It's in Lowell," I said, unfolding the note recorded in Sue's typewriter penmanship. "And it's a magic carpet."

Lucas paused in half-crouch. His white glove held the car door open, which drew a constant dinging noise from the homebrew vehicle.

"A magic carpet." I nodded at the dumbfounded gent. "With no speakers." He stared at me in disbelief, barely allowing himself to hope for such a thing.

"Not that I know of?" I hadn't seen any notation concerning sound systems on the rug, let alone a port for an MP3 player. "And it's not a flying carpet, I guess it just instantly takes you wherever you want to go."

"Oh." Lucas actually smiled again. "So there is a God."

Kurt decided to start blasting more Thrashcan right about then. Or maybe it was Stigmatasm. Either way, Lucas jumped, but that happy smirk managed to survive. He didn't complain once on the way to Lowell, just staring out the window at the sky the whole time. I like to think that he was imagining himself on a flying carpet, wearing a turban and playing a cello as he soared contentedly to go have tea or whatever it was Lucas did in his spare time. Tea is my guess. And ironing, maybe.

Meanwhile, I kept my eyes on the note, reading off the directions to Kurt. When I fully unfolded the paper, I was surprised to see something written on the bottom, separate from the street names and mileages.

It wasn't your fault, Mr. Foster.

I looked out my own window to the fleeting scenery outside. Namely, rusted guardrails and buildings that looked tired from being endlessly used and repurposed. A lot of New England had that feeling, a sort of weariness from the forced march of time. Right then, I felt it too.

It's weird how Sue always managed to pick up on the littlest things in a conversation. We could talk about a volcano erupting in the middle of Worcester, or a colony of sasquatches petitioning for equal voting rights, and she'd point out that my left eye was squinted a little bit. From that, she'd surmise that I had a migraine because I wasn't drinking enough water. Somehow, she'd always be right.

Her footnote was a kind gesture, but I had to agree to disagree with it. I refolded the note along the creases Sue had made and slipped it back into my pocket.

-Lowell-

In order to get the wishing carpet, we'd need to pull together an invisibility spell. Everyone knows how potentially awesome it is to be invisible, what with the locker room escapades, the automatic membership to any spy organization on the planet, and the free pudding. So why aren't all arcanists invisible all the time? There's more to it than a fondness for one's own reflection, turns out. The process of becoming invisible is much more involved than you might think. It's also a heck of a lot messier, unless you're assuming that it requires jumping in a big pool of mud and pasta sauce. I'd say it's a little worse than that.

The primary component of the spell is water. Which is great, because you can get that from any tap, hose, or lake. Where the water comes from doesn't matter, but what you do to it does. You need to heat the water to boiling, first off, which is a pain if you need enough to make three guys invisible. Then you need a few grains of crushed cinnabar, the ore you get mercury from. Half of the array you draw around the cauldron or whatever is to protect against the poisonous effects of that one stone, so really, don't try any of this at home. Mix up the symbol for dissolution and distillation and you're pretty much cooking your own death sentence.

Once the water is frothing and red, you need at least a few grams of pure silver, which makes this a relatively expensive procedure. On a related note, alchemy has some great solutions for coming up with gold, which can be pawned for money to buy other materials. You just have to make sure you don't go to the same place too often, or else they start to question whether your grandfather really was a grizzled old prospector who hid giant hunks of gold in weird places before his death. Which you're slowly finding with a map he drew on the back of a pizza place kid's menu. Thinking back on it, that was a pretty terrible cover story.

Anyway, back to the recipe. You've got boiling water with quicksilver ore and real silver swirling around inside, and all your runes are drawn correctly, probably in chalk or paint. In a separate container, you need about two cups worth of powdered quartz crystals. Those get dumped in, and then the mixture will start to glisten and glow with a silvery sheen. This is when you need to start stirring, preferably with something you don't mind turning invisible for a while, at least on one end. I use my saber, since it's already resilient against everything and I need it to be invisible whenever I am. While stirring, add a container of cornstarch. After that's all mixed in and the concoction is gooey, you let it cool and you're set to go.

You're probably wondering why you need to add cornstarch

to the casting of a mystical spell, and the answer is surprisingly simple. When ancient Egyptian arcanists first started delving into invisibility, they ran into a ton of problems. Surprisingly, mercury poisoning, finding the right consistency for the quartz, and catching the slaves they tested the mixture on were actually the least of their worries. The biggest concern was the desert sun.

See, when you're done with the concoction, you have to pour it all over whoever's going to be invisible, and the magic wears off as soon as the water dries. With the original recipe, it's much less gross, but your shoulders and arms start to come into view in a matter of hours at most. For the Egyptians, it was way less. The spell would last longer at night, but for some reason, it doesn't work right under the light of the moon. You show up as a stark white silhouette, which is probably the least stealthy thing possible in the middle of the night. In the end, the mixture proved useless to the Egyptians. Either Pharaoh Hatshepsut or Thutmose the First hid the secrets of making the stuff in their burial sites so that other nations couldn't use invisibility against them. The secrets of the spell went forgotten for thousands of years until the tombs of the Pharaohs were excavated. English archaeologists brought clues back from Egypt, and wealthy alchemists bought them up like hot cakes. The original recipe worked a lot better in Britain, and those guys even improved on it by adding thickening agents. These made the solution evaporate even more slowly, extending the length of the invisibility.

Now, you try explaining all that to a werewolf with OCD. We were under a bridge in Lowell, huddled around a fire and a big metal bucket. With Lucas there, we must have looked like the richest homeless people ever.

"You must be joking," he said, deliberately gnashing each word between his teeth. I shook my head and pulled what looked like half a sword out of the impromptu cauldron. "You cannot honestly expect me to cover my suit, my shoes, and my hat in that slop!"

"Afraid so, old chum." In trying to pull that bucket off of the miniature Ares' scourge I'd drawn, I realized just how heavy 10 gallons was. I struggled with the handle for a while before Lucas finally lifted it and placed the invisibility gel next to him on the grass. "Unless you know any magi who'd be willing to cast the spell without components, this is how it goes."

I haven't mentioned it until now, but there are people who can do magic without the aid of components or arrays. They make up about .0001% of the human population, and nowadays, they have to do their best to keep it a secret. If you go around openly flying, shooting lightning out of your face, or turning people into animals, it'll only be a matter of time before you get picked up or shot down by one government agency or another. In that regard, I guess you could say that I was lucky to be completely talentless.

A chorus of grumbles followed from Lucas, which I largely ignored in favor of swinging my half-invisible sword around and poking the array for the scourge until it fizzled out. If I had arcane talent, I could have said a few words, pointed my fingers and made us all invisible without any of the hassle or muck. Unfortunately, as I said, I don't have half an ounce of talent. I can't paint, can't play an instrument, and I definitely can't light people on fire with my mind as the only catalyst. I've tried, believe me. I can't even roller-skate that well. I just had a book and a few pockets full of bottles and chalk which made it really hard to find a place for a wallet.

The concoction was finished, so all it needed to do was cool down. I pulled out some more white chalk to draw a simple array that would suck heat from the bucket, since I didn't feel like getting arrested for suspicious behavior in an underpass while we waited. That's probably an eight-sixteen in cop lingo. Just has that kind of ring to it.

While I was taking care of that, Kurt was sitting against a column and covering some kind of homemade shotgun in plastic wrap. He didn't seem too worked up about the prospect of having this gunk all over him as long as he could still have his toys. Which apparently included a fist-sized plastic ball that was roughly duct taped together and had a single red button on top. He was careful about wrapping that one up.

"That explodes, doesn't it."

"Yep." He didn't even look up from his work.

"If it's invisible, how're you gonna know where the button is?"

Kurt shrugged. Details. I decided to have a seat and toss my sword to the short cut grass behind us. The new rune glowed red as it ripped the warmth from the bucket's contents. I'd have to smear the chalk before the gel got cold enough to freeze, but with the tiny size of the array, that would probably have taken an hour.

I unzipped my messenger bag, slipped a hand between the tome's leather cover and the fabric of the bag, and worked my fingers under its time worn spine. I set the book in my lap to start reading through the pages toward the back, where there were these incredibly complex arrays. They had instructions that had to be translated once just to know which words were being used, and then translated again for content. After finding the book, I'd figured out

115

how to do the first kind of translation more or less by myself, but I ended up needing Sue's help to understand what two *hynt-fvlls, aqva fity* really meant.

Whenever I had a spare minute, I'd sit down and start jotting basic translations in a notepad I kept in one pocket of my book bag. It was less tidy than what Sue had for those arcana, but then, I've seen printed books that were less tidy than Sue's ledger. The particular spell I had been trying to figure out for about a week involved an explosion, but the parts of the array were intertwined so intricately, it couldn't just be a simple arcane blast. The explosion would have to be huge, incredibly destructive, and involve fire, but had seemingly no components. It didn't make any sense when compared to every other procedure in the book.

I wasn't going to make any headway on that particular spell, so I flipped a few pages deeper and came to the end. Several of the aged leather pages had been ripped out, leaving crumpled stubs that barely clung to the binding of the tome. I couldn't help wondering if my mom or dad had done that. If they took the most powerful incantations for themselves and went off to build an underwater utopia, or became immortal and lost their memories, traveling the globe as superheroes until the day they rediscover their long lost kids.

I frowned. Thinking of my folks always brought me back to another possibility: That they were being hunted. Maybe they had to leave to protect us from whatever bad guys were after them. Judging by the incredible stuff in the book, and assuming that my mom or dad knew how to use it, their arch-nemeses were probably worse than the Thule Society. Maybe vampires. Russian vampires, even.

"Hey Lucas?" I looked over to see him towering above the

bucket, sniffing at it derisively.

"What is it, Foster."

"You think you could beat up a Russian vampire?"

He sighed and shook his head. "What kind of question is that?" An awesome one, clearly. "Whether they are Russian or not makes little difference, and regardless, vampires do not exist except in the fevered daydreams of teenage girls."

"Oh, dude, not that kind of vampire. The kind that drinks human blood, has claws and fangs, and bursts into flames in the sunlight."

"Ah." Lucas squinted, leaning back to look up at the sun as it sat in the middle of the otherwise empty sky. "Were that the case, and such a thing existent, I would wait until daybreak and find its place of rest. I would then drag the vampire outside. Does that count as beating it up?"

"No, c'mon, that's dumb. Like if you were in a fight with it." I guess he had never seen any of the hundred movies that depicted vampires and werewolves as mortal enemies, even if he had read the girly vampire books out of morbid curiosity. Which wasn't surprising, considering that he's Lucas.

"I haven't the slightest idea. Or, no, the vampire, because I refuse to be bothered with fighting it." Lucas wasn't any fun when he wasn't angry. I dug my fingers between clumps of strangulating crabgrass before prodding further.

"Lucas, what do you think it would take for you to leave your kids? If you had any, which you should never do, as a note." That might seem cruel, but it's really for the hypothetical kids' sakes. Can you imagine having Lucas as a dad? Getting a top hat as a birthday present, or being lectured every day on the importance of arranging one's silverware correctly? It's a fate worse than death.

Lucas tensed his jaw, but not in the way that usually meant he was envisioning disemboweling me. He looked thoughtful, worried, and maybe even a little hurt. That was the exact moment I started considering the distinct possibility that Lucas ate his parents. I could see it playing out in my head:

"Hello, mumsie, papa! Wonderfully dreary day we're having, toodle-pip and all that!"

"Oh, indeed, lad! I say, is it just me or are your fangs looking particularly acute today?" And then suddenly om nom, no more parents. I watched him carefully from that point on.

"I would not leave my children," he said, carefully mulling over every word. "Not for war, for money, or anything." He was deathly serious, his eyes having fallen from the sky to glare at the river before us.

"What if it was for their own good?" My voice came out quieter than I had intended.

"Never," he stated firmly, bitterness creeping into his tone. "I would die, coat torn and maw full of blood before abandoning my children."

Okay, that was a little dramatic. I was starting to sense-

"Any sensible parent would do the same. Rather than buggering off for some extended holiday, leaving the one they are supposed to be raising in the oddly frigid hands of a maid who helps herself daily to the family wine cellar!"

"Lucas?" As I was going to narrate before being so rudely interrupted, I was starting to sense that I was off about the parent-eating thing. "You okay there?"

"What? Yes! Yes, I am fine. I was simply answering your

118

insipid little inquiry. Is the disgusting sludge you were cooking finished yet? We should go, this sorrowful excuse for grass is embarrassing to stand on."

Geez. Talk about your weird abandonment issues. I ran my fingertips over the torn-out pages at the back of the book one more time before sliding it carefully into my bag.

"Yeah, okay, let me check." Getting to my feet, I made my way over to the bucket and dipped a finger into it. Still a little hot, but not too bad. Of course, the digit I pulled out was invisible, which was pretty cool. I could totally see a cross section of my knuckle, which included pulsing veins and bone marrow.

"Oh, hey, Lucas, check this out!"

"No."

"C'mon, it's awesome!"

"Foster, I am not looking at the inner workings of your hand through your invisible finger."

"No, it's not that! I inadvertently made the perfect cup of Earle Grey." I posit that this was the perfect lie to use on him, even if he did see through it. No pun intended.

"Good lord. Foster, you would not know how to make a proper cup of tea if..." Lucas stopped mid-thought, clearly trying to formulate an insult out of that. I thought I'd help him along.

"If Julia Child rose from her grave as a zombie and taught me how using her incredible undead cooking ability?" That was totally where Lucas was going with that. His vacant stare served as proof enough of that.

Meanwhile, Kurt must have finished up his weapon wrapping. He walked over next to me and unceremoniously dipped his hand in the invisibility gel. His vanished palm then started pouring gunk down the outside of the barrel of his homemade boom-stick. He left the very end uncovered, which made for a dark, quarter-sized hole in the air if you were looking straight at it. Kurt's arms would go next under a slathering of the arcane slime, which gave me an idea for starting Lucas down the same path.

"Hey, Lucas," I said, dunking my arm up to the elbow in the bucket, "Catch!" I whipped a splotch of the stuff straight at his chest, leaving what looked like a clean hole straight through him. In case I haven't mentioned it, I love invisibility spells.

Of course, I wasn't really expecting him to get as angry as he did. I figured it was like diving into a cold pool or pulling off a band-aid, but I guess he wasn't quite ready to get his suit covered in slop. His face twisted into a snarl, and before I knew it, the concoction was knocked over and he was trying to choke me in the puddle it left. Kurt just kind of stood there, half-invisible. I should really look into new friends.

To make a long story short, Lucas ended up drenched in the stuff anyway, and I probably would've died if I hadn't taken his hat hostage. He finally relented, allowing me to cover the outside of some goggles in the gunk that was left in the bucket. Can't cover your eyes in it, after all. We left the rest of the invisibility fluid to dry in the sun, hoping nobody came by and noticed the giant illusionary hole in the ground that seemed to go on forever. Once we established radio-silence, as it were, we walked about a half mile down the road to the storage facility. It was a refurbished brick building with a big parking lot and black metal gates that opened at the beck and call of a keypad just outside. The whole thing was situated on a short side road between a couple of corporate buildings. Fortunately, it was a busy enough day that we didn't have to wait long. The driver of a black pickup truck pulled up and punched their code in right as we got there. The simple, undecorated barricade whirred open, and we followed the truck in as quietly as our squishy shoes would allow.

My original plan had been to use an Ares' Scourge on one of the doors in order to get in, but patience and a bit of improvisation really paid off. A middle aged guy in a white polo shirt got out of the black truck, pulled a big, plastic box out of the back, and walked lazily toward the building. Another entry code at the door, and I couldn't believe my luck: The guy propped the entryway open with his box to go grab more stuff. If I had been able to accurately judge distances from myself, I would've given him a drippy ghost hug for making this so easy. I'd probably do an old man voice and pretend to be his crazy prospector grandfather he never knew he had. It would have been a heartwarming reunion.

Sadly, it was not to be. I rushed for the open door and into a long, wide hallway with those garage door sort of openings on either side. The piece we were looking for was in locker 3-16, which meant the third floor. Lucas and Kurt's footsteps squinched behind me as I hustled for the stairs at the end of the corridor. All in all, the place was nice for a storage building. Air conditioning, clean floors. If I had a ton of excess crap that I couldn't part with, I'd definitely keep it here. Just not my ancient wishing carpets, on account of the ease with which an arcanist could break into the place. Like me. Not that I would steal my own carpet, but you get the idea.

The climb up the stairs was quick, as I took them two at a time and swung around the corners using the banisters and some centrifugal force, and then we were at the third floor. That was when I knew this caper wasn't going to be nearly as easy as I was led to believe by irresponsible box dude.

So, let me take a minute to say that I'm sure it's getting tiresome, being introduced to so many villains like this in so little time. I'm sorry. Really, I wish they hadn't been there either. You should blame them, because they're jerks anyway. Not like Lucas, who only occasionally does something unnecessarily snooty and thinks he's better than me. This is more like jerk-con 5, or Jerkpocalypse 2: The Jerkening.

The first guy was Abercrombie, a muscled, tanned, manly man of an Australian. Out of the jerk brigade, he was probably the one I could tolerate the most, since his motivation was always perfectly clear: Money. At least you could negotiate with someone based on that. He was probably in his mid thirties, and always had his pale blonde hair cut professionally short. That time, he was kneeled over a pile of stuff in a locker with a small circular saw in one hand. 3-16, to be exact. Our locker. As per usual, he was wearing a nice, black leather coat and gloves over a maroon turtleneck and jeans. He always had these nice shoes, too, the kind that you buy in one of those stores that sells suits. I'd hate him more if he weren't so friggin' classy.

Next to him was Seth Michaels, a skinny guy with stringy brown hair and those plastic-rimmed square glasses that are kind of popular among people of the nerdy persuasion. He looked like the sort of guy who really liked indie music, and indie movies, and he was always wearing a t-shirt with a reference on it to something I didn't get. Seth was a mage, the kind with actual talent, and he specialized in creating ice out of thin air. Or thick air, I guess, if he's not on a mountain. He was always scowling and quiet, kind of like Lucas on a bad day. I have to assume he was driven purely by spite for the entire world, with a 20 mile-per-gallon highway rating.

The last one was Ivan. Or Not-Ivan, as he always responded when anybody called him by name. He's unsettling, to say the least. I don't know what happened to him, but Not-Ivan is completely insane. He speaks nonsense, laughs at things that aren't even vaguely funny, and typically responds to anybody but Abercrombie and Seth with screaming or stabbing. I wouldn't ever give that guy anything sharper than a beach ball, but he always seemed to pull a broken pipe or chunk of shattered glass out of somewhere. He was pale, with black hair that didn't look like it had ever been washed. If I had to guess, I'd say he couldn't be older than me.

The worst thing about Not-Ivan, though, was that he was a walking magical dead zone. It wasn't that he drew arcane energy in, magic just ceased to be when he was standing near. I wasn't positive about his annulling range, but as Lucas bumped into me and we went crashing to the floor, it was clear that we were within it.

Abercrombie turned and stood, smirking at us. "Well, now. Good to see you, Foster." Aw, man, he's even wittier than me. 'Good to see you,' after our invisibility spell wore off? What the crap.

"Abercrombie," I growled, pushing up to dislodge myself from my compatriot. "I knew something smelled like shrimp, possibly the variety you cook on the barbie."

Both he and Lucas groaned. Okay, fine, that wasn't my best, but I had to say something! These guys were like our arcana-hunting rivals, and we just stumbled upon them doing something evil. There are rules to these things.

"How do you put up with that?" The Aussie asked, resting the saw on his shoulder. Seth didn't even stop rooting through the locker that they had broken into. "I mean, really, mate, I'd have snapped his neck by now."

"Believe me, it is rather a struggle." Stupid Lucas. "He still answers the telephone with 'ello, guvna' when he knows I am calling."

"Hey! First, that is totally how you sound all the time. Second, I'm trying to help remind you of your home country! Excuse me for being culturally sensitive." I'm such a good friend, and all he ever does is throw it in my face. This was just like the time I covered his bed in dry ice while he was sleeping to give him a taste of London fog.

"Now, do you two wanna go have a meeting of the silly accents club, or are we gonna get down to the hero-villain dialogue?"

Abercrombie sighed, but motioned for me to continue. Lucas did his part in shutting up and shifting so his knee wasn't in my spine.

"Thank you. Now, what are you doing here, Abercrombie? Up to your old tricks again?"

"Yeah? I guess, if my old tricks include taking arcana and selling them to the highest bidder." He shrugged, then pointed in realization. "Oh, and finding them before you do and whisking them right out from under your nose! That's something we do a lot as well."

"Well, not this time!" I leapt to my feet, drew my saber, and ripped the book from my bag in one awesome motion. It was sweet. "We're taking that magic carpet, even if we have to go through you to get it!"

"Magic carpet?" Abercrombie blinked. "There's a magic carpet in there?"

"Carpet!" Not-Ivan repeated with a shaky, erratic laugh. He was sitting against a wall, bumping his head on the bricks with a steady beat. "Carpet, don't get, don't get it. Not in the carpet! Stains, it stains and they'll see! Never, not now, not ever..."

I froze, partially because of the creepiness of Not-Ivan, but also because I might have just told the bad guys what it was we were trying to find.

"You aren't here for the carpet."

"No, not at all! We were looking to get a medieval sewing needle. To my understanding, it's alchemically enhanced to punch through anything. But a magic carpet, that's much better! Good on you, Foster." He nodded over his shoulder to Seth, who shoved a plastic bin to the side and started his search anew.

"Freaking crap." My sword hung low, nicking the floor. Lucas rolled his eyes like he always did when he thought I wasn't looking. "Well, we knew about it first!"

"Finders keepers," Abercrombie said with a grin. "Besides, not only is your magic useless, I've got a gun full of ash bullets."

"Ash bullets? Like, bullets made out of human ashes or something?"

"What? No. That's awfully morbid." It was, I'll admit. Not sure why that's the first place my imagination went. "They're compressed volcanic ash, which is a death sentence for werewolves and other beasties. It gets rid of all those nasty supernatural abilities they possess. Also, you're pretty well outnumbered."

Outnumbered? I looked behind me, and noticed for the first time that Kurt wasn't actually there. Maybe he had fallen behind, or he was still far enough back that Not-Ivan's aura didn't affect his invisibility gel. I had to hope that wherever he was, he was gearing up to help somehow.

Abercrombie pulled the handgun he was talking about from his coat and pointed it at us. With crazypants set up where he was, we'd be no match for these guys. Sure, Seth couldn't use his spells either, but without Lucas' strength or regenerative abilities, we were pretty much up a creek made out of lava without a paddle, boat, or flame retardant swim trunks. Time to stall.

"Alright, fine. You've got us." I slowly went about sheathing my sword and putting the tome away. "But you're going to get caught. We were going to steal the thing while invisible, and you guys are just out in the open for the cameras to see." There were always cameras in places like these.

"We took care of security this morning. Cameras are recording a blank feed, and the guards are already locked in one of these containers downstairs." He rapped on the door to a locker beside him. Man, these guys were good. I was almost jealous. "But I think we'll knock you two out, just in case, and leave you for the proper authorities to find after we're long gone."

"Wait," Lucas said, raising a palm. I looked over, and man was his left eye twitching. "You are saying that the cameras are not functioning."

"That's right."

"And the guards are knocked out in a locker."

Abercrombie looked skyward, thought for a moment, and nodded. "Yes."

"Then my suit is drenched in this revolting, rotten, detestable sludge for absolutely no reason whatsoever."

"Seems to be the case." The Aussie shrugged.

Lucas' head slowly turned in my direction, and the death

glare that he shot at me would level mountains. I pretended there was something really interesting happening on the wall next to me and whistled.

"I despise you. So much," Lucas rasped through his teeth. I glanced at his enraged visage and tried to come up with something to alleviate the situation.

"On the upside, with those goggles and your hat and stuff, you've totally got that steampunk look going on." I gave a reassuring thumbs-up, but it probably didn't help that Lucas had no idea what that was. Or that the goggles were more like the kind you use in a swimming pool.

"Abercrombie," Seth called out from the locker. I was actually kind of glad for the distraction from Lucas' hate, no matter how momentary. The ice mage dragged a decent-sized, rolled up carpet from the storage locker. The thing looked crazy old, but was in perfect condition, which tends to be the case with arcana. That was our wishing carpet.

"Brilliant! And that means it's time for us to be off," Abercrombie stepped forward and flipped the gun over in his hand. "Say g'night, gents."

"Wait!" I put my hands out between us, like that would stop him. The guy was taller, stronger, and all around meaner than I was, and probably had a black belt in gun-fu. "Don't you need to tie us up? Dangle us precariously over something dangerous and time consuming to put together?"

Abercrombie laughed and shook his head. "Nah. I'm just gonna clock you one on the skull and let blunt-force trauma do the work. I give you credit for trying, though."

He walked forward and lifted his gun hand over the opposite

shoulder. I instinctively shut my eyes tight against the incoming concussion, and then briefly imagined invisible Kurt having run off to an auto parts store to steal a backpack full of lug nuts while we were hauled off to the slammer. Fortunately, that wasn't the case.

There was a sudden and violent explosion. My ears were filled with shattering sound and rapidly expanding air. I was thrown onto my back and down toward the stairs, and what felt like Lucas' shoulder ended up behind my head somehow. My ears were ringing, and it took my vision a few seconds to recover from a dizzy haze. Abercrombie was face down on the floor, Seth was laying prone against a bunch of plastic totes in the locker, and Not-Ivan was nowhere to be seen. There was a big hole in the floor where he'd been sitting, like he spontaneously combusted.

I hacked up some powdered brick and struggled to sit up. Though parts of me were covered in dust and obliterated building materials, I was mostly invisible again. Lucas, too. It took a lot to stand, to the point where I fell against a wall more than once in trying to keep my balance.

"Holy crap, Kurt," I groaned, stumbling toward the hole in the floor. "What did you put in that thing?" I waved a hand to dissipate the cloud of dust and peered down through the wreckage. It was pretty clear that Not-Ivan was still alive but unconscious. He was lying in a pile of broken bricks on the second floor, breathing quietly and bleeding out of the head. With the force of that explosion, he probably should have been dead. Maybe his power also worked on mundane energy to an extent. Either way, there wasn't time to contemplate it. There was no telling how long Abercrombie would be out for, and I had to wrench the carpet out of Seth's hands before people started poking around for us.

Avoiding the hole as carefully as I could in my shell-shocked state, I navigated over to the rolled up rug, which was lying atop the ice-mage's feet. As I pulled it off of his blue canvas shoes, he shifted and gasped. It looked like the blast had slammed the heavy rug against Seth's stomach and knocked the wind out of him.

"Foster," he croaked, leaning forward and holding an outstretched palm in my direction. Icy blue smoke started to drift up from his eyes, which glowed with the color of a frozen lake. That wasn't good.

"Seth," I replied, holding the rug firmly between my arms. "Looks like we finally get to have a real mage battle, huh?"

The trendy little jerk shook his head. "No, we don't," he rasped out. "You aren't a mage. You're a crappy treasure hunter with a book."

"Oh yeah?" I dropped the carpet back on his feet. Judging by the face he made, that had to hurt. "And you're just a hipster magic thief who can only cast one kind of spell. Also, I have a sword that I could totally stab you in the organs with. And not like the appendix, either. One of the ones you need." My hand went to the saber's leather wrapped grip.

Seth glared and pointed his open palm at my chest. The only reason he could even see it was because of the particles of dust and shrapnel clinging to the invisibility gunk on my shirt. "Draw that and I will put an icicle through your sternum."

"I don't think you will," I said, grinning, and I pulled a few inches of the blade out of its scabbard, making the telltale unsheathing sound. It's not that I didn't think he would do it. In fact, I knew he would.

"Your funeral," he said through gritted teeth. His irises

glowed brightly, and a bluish-white smoke formed around his arm. In less than a second, the vapor was all sucked into a point just beyond his hand, and a perfectly conical hunk of ice formed. It spun, then the icicle shot forward. It didn't have far to go before it would puncture straight through my chest. It sucked that I was going to have to buy a new shirt after this.

"Kulutrone-Anvare!" I didn't really have to yell the words to activate the Ares' Scourge I had hanging from my neck, but it was friggin' satisfying.

Like I'd said, I was planning to use a Scourge in melting at least one door handle on the way in. To that end, I had painted an array on a piece of wood and threaded a spare shoelace through a hole in the top to make a sort of big, flamethrowing pendant. I didn't think I would get to use it like that, but I was pretty happy about the end result.

A jet of blue fire blasted through the front of my shirt and reduced the incoming icicle to water, then steam in midair. It was really, really cool to watch. Almost as cool as the look of horror on Seth's face. He was pretty much shaking with frustration.

I finished drawing my sword and used it to hack the shoelace off of my neck, allowing me to hold and point the Ares' Scourge right at the ice mage. The column of fire fell just short of his face.

"Alright, now just sit there and your eyebrows will remain intact. For now." I looked back, but didn't see any trace of my werewolf compatriot. Not surprising on account of him being invisible again. "Lucas! Lucas, you awake?"

"Yes," he said, his voice coming from somewhere to my right. "Just move the bloody fire and I'll get the carpet."

"Awesome." I shifted the Scourge up, but kept my sword

130

pointed at Seth's neck. The rug seemed to drag itself away before hoisting into the air. Lucas held the heavy artifact over his shoulder like it was nothing.

"I have the arcana, Foster. We should find Kurt and get out while we are able."

"Hey," Kurt said, apparently a few feet behind me. I jumped, and so did the carpet.

"Dude, where have you been?"

"Saw the crazy guy and went back downstairs. Put the bomb on the ceiling under him." As always, he didn't seem that enthused about the situation.

"That's amazing. On a related note, Kurt, I owe you a million hamburgers."

"Sweet."

Seth let out an irritated sigh. "You three are the biggest morons who ever lived."

"Hey!" I poked his throat with the tip of my saber. "Sword! Neck! No-talky! What is it with bad guys not getting that part lately?"

"They are likely too intimidated by your incredible prowess to think logically," Lucas suggested. Y'know how when you're talking to someone over e-mail or an instant message and you can't really tell if they're being sarcastic or not? Apparently, that also applies to invisible people.

"Lucas, buddy old pal, I think you might be right for once. These jerks are clearly outmatched. In fact, I'll bet-"

It was then that Abercrombie began to stir. By stir, I don't mean to wake up gradually and gently. It was more like spasming under his pile of debris, gritting his teeth and generally looking very

131

upset. I think I was hoping that he would have a concussion, but that seemed less and less likely with each passing moment.

"Well, looks like it's time to go! Take it easy, Seth, give our regards to Freaky McFreakerson, hope to never see you again, bye!" I dropped the still-burning scourge and slashed across its surface with my sword, disrupting the array. The arcane fire flickered, dimmed, and died as Lucas, Kurt and I skedaddled back to the staircase. None of us were completely invisible anymore, covered as we were with patches of dried clothing and dust-covered skin. At that point, though, it didn't matter. We leaped down the stairs until we finally hit the first floor, booking it out the door and ignoring a small crowd of bystanders that was gathered around the base of the building. No cops yet, probably because everyone assumed security was taking care of it, but it wouldn't be long before somebody got the picture and dialed 911.

Fortunately, Lucas was at the front of our partially visible parade, and the mundane folks that had come to gasp and fret over the explosion knew enough to get out of the way of a carpet when it was careening straight for them. Lucas and the rug bounced over to one of the side gates, and then veered straight up as the werewolf started climbing for the alleyway beyond.

"Mom, mom!" a kid in the crowd, probably a few years older than Zoe, called out as Lucas passed, "Look! A flying carpet!"

"It's a wishing-carpet, actually! Very subtle difference!" I ran past the kid and straight for the metal bars, noting the confused expression on his mom's face.

"Mom, it's a *talking* flying carpet!"

Can't win 'em all, I guess. I shook my head and grabbed at the gate, grimacing as I struggled to find a good place to put my foot. The gate wasn't decorative in any way, just straight, metal bars with braces at the ground and about seven feet up. Lucas had jumped straight to the top, which was a little beyond my abilities, not to mention Kurt's. We were both stuck at the foot of this wall with nowhere to go.

Then I heard the *poomf* of compressed air being released, followed by a whirring sound. A grappling hook shot out from a device somewhere on Kurt's person, probably his hand, and found purchase on the top rungs of the gate.

"What, seriously? Since when do you have grappling hooks?" He had never mentioned those to me, and I'm the leader of this operation. What the hell. "Wasn't it, like, a week ago that we couldn't even get glass-cutty things?"

"Glasscutters."

"Yeah, those!"

I saw a vague shrugging motion of some plaster dust, and then Kurt was propelled up to the top of the bars. I really needed a magic cape like in the video games, or some jumping shoes. Or a helicopter.

"Foster, take my hand!" Lucas' voice rang out above me. I guess he had been waiting for me the whole time and I just hadn't noticed. I'd have to look into making Lucas invisible more often. He was way easier to ignore that way.

I waved my arm around in the area above my head until I felt his gloved hand clamp down on my wrist. I then got to experience the joys of having my arm almost ripped out of its socket as Lucas pulled me up, then jumped to the pavement below. For all that Lucas wanted to be dapper and snooty, he clearly didn't know his own stupid strength. I tumbled to the asphalt, barely avoided impaling myself on my own scabbard, and started running between two large brick buildings. Kurt and Lucas were already ahead of me.

"Freaking crap, Lucas! Slow down! Hey!" Of course, he did no such thing. Then, police sirens started blaring from the lot behind me. "Scratch that, go faster! Run!"

We ran, avoiding the main streets and occasionally hiding behind dumpsters to avoid detection. Also because it looked cool. In the end, we made it to the car and started the drive back to The Spiral. I wasn't too sure what would happen to Abercrombie and company, but then, I didn't care that much. We were one artifact closer to saving Zoe, and they were probably on their way to the slammer. Where I come from, we call that karma.

If they happened to get tasered on the way down, that was karma too. Really hilarious karma.

-Translations-

We stopped at a fast food place and got something to eat on the way
back to Worcester. I normally try to avoid the stuff on account of it
being incredibly unhealthy and less than cost effective. Also, the
milkshakes seem to have the same chemical composition as paint.
That said, when you haven't had one of those greasy, recently
microwaved burgers in a few months, they are freaking
scrumptious. It's almost worth the subsequent sick feeling that is
your stomach reminding you that you're murdering yourself a little.
Predictably, Lucas wanted nothing to do with any of it, since the
kids' meal didn't include an option with tea and crumpets. So when
we did get back to the Spiral, I decided to bring the rug in while
Kurt drove the presumably ravenous werewolf to whatever ritzy
apartment he was staying at. I didn't really want to go back to my
place, anyway, and I figured maybe Sue would need help
deciphering the carpet. If it didn't bother the stoic shopkeeper, I'd

just stay overnight and avoid the intolerable stillness of my apartment.

More than anything, I had a sneaking suspicion that Lucas was looking for any excuse to tear me limb from limb for drenching him in the invisibility gunk. Being hungry might have been just reason enough, and I clearly couldn't count on Kurt to do much more than stand and watch, maybe throwing in a disinterested 'yep'.

As I considered the specifics of Lucas' inevitable cannibalistic betrayal, I dragged the carpet across the sidewalk and to the shop's moss colored door. I had to finagle things around a bit to get it open, resulting in a sort of backwards scuttle in order to hold the door open with one foot while bear-hugging the rug. Before that day, I didn't exactly know what an ancient Assyrian carpet smelled, felt, or tasted like. In case you're curious, it's musty with a hint of dust, and it's generally unpleasant.

Considering that my face was having an unfortunate encounter with a gross-smelling floor covering, it probably wasn't surprising that I managed to waddle backwards into the same bookshelf I had run into earlier. Of course, this time there were people in the store, and as I tilted my head as far back as it would go, I realized that I'd caused the thing to wobble precariously. I groaned, which seemed to be the cue for a pile of books to come down on me like a waterfall. Except that a waterfall isn't made out of heavy, non-liquid books with surprisingly hard spines.

I was on the hardwood floor, covered in literature and carpeting when Sue came over. She didn't look particularly upset, though she did kneel down to pick the books up off of my head. "Oh, Mister Foster. Are you alright?" Really, she seemed more concerned with her merchandise, considering the automated tone of her voice.

"Yeah. I'm fine. Just an Asimov-related brain injury, maybe a crushed lung. Nothing too serious." I struggled to get some kind of leverage on the rug that was pressing on my face. If I were making an enchanted carpet, I would have first considered making the thing not weigh a million pounds. That seems like a reasonable advantage to me. I mean, this thing must have been six thousand feet across. I'd have made a wishing beach towel, or hey, why not go with a wishing facecloth?

Without any explanation, Sue abruptly started pressing on various points of my skull and chest. I guess she took my exaggeration seriously, which I probably should have expected. "You do not appear to be suffering from a concussion or damage to your internal organs, though I could call for an ambulance if you are legitimately concerned for your well-being."

I blinked up at Sue, caught in one of those moments where everything seemed to slow down and get fuzzy. Sue's big, brown eyes searched my squished face with some small amount of concern. Her hands felt cool against my ribcage. As weird as it may sound, it was a comforting sensation.

"Mister Foster?"

"Um, no! No, I think I'm good. No worries." I laughed, though there wasn't any reason to, and she went back to poking around for whatever it was a crushed lung felt like.

"Also, Isaac Azimov is a fairly weak example of a Russian author, considering that he was brought to the United States as a young child and never spoke the Russian language."

"What?" I pushed up on the carpet, trying to right myself. It clearly wasn't going to happen. "But wasn't he born there?"

"He was, and that play on words is terrible regardless." Sue punctuated the remark with a firm prod against my ribs, seemingly in subtle vengeance. I couldn't help grinning. She was probably the only person alive who would've picked up on it. I tried to suppress my smile, but it wasn't easy.

"What're you talking about, Sue?" I really just had to hear it come from her. For me, it's the little things that make being crushed alive by a magical floor covering worth it. Sue didn't seem to have the same appreciation, as her eyes rolled to one side of the shop before she finally decided to humor me.

"A Russian concussion, Mister Foster." The deadpan, supremely unpleased delivery she gave only made it that much more perfect. I burst with laughter, and I swear that Sue even smiled a little tiny bit.

It took a second for me to collect myself, at which point I gestured to the rug with my chin. "I got you the carpet to look at, by the way."

"I see that, yes." Sue let go of my upper torso, her expression returning to one of pure neutrality. With a simple hoist, she had the rug standing up on one end. I swear, that thing was heavy as crap! I guess I just have a habit of surrounding myself with hulking supernatural juggernauts. With the rolled up carpet finally off of me, I could get up and help with the rest of the books.

"So, are you going to take a look at that soon? I mean, I know I'm not as good at translating stuff as you, and I'll probably be a distraction..." I trailed off, figuring that Sue already knew the countless other reasons why I wouldn't make much of an assistant for her mystical laboratory. I had gone to Sue when I first needed help with the spellbook, and it was quickly apparent to both of us that our methods were slightly different. To put it simply, I'm a

138

hands on, try stuff until it works kind of guy, while Sue is all about methodical research and rigorous internal problem solving. She likes it quiet when working on a project, and I tend to talk through issues. I like cinnamon buns and chocolate milk, whereas I imagine Sue surviving on a strict cracker and oatmeal diet. Not that I've ever actually seen her eat anything, come to think of it, but you get the idea.

Of course, there are the old clichés about opposites attracting, or different methods culminating to a better result. I'm not sure that applies when one of the people almost kills them both by accidentally drinking a firebreathing potion that one time.

"You wish to assist with the translation." Sue didn't sound happy about the idea, but she didn't exactly sound upset, either. She was seriously harder to read than one of those Magic Eye books.

"Well. Y'know, I figured I could hold up a light for you, or help with any arrays you might need to draw." Fortunately, the couple of people poking around the store didn't seem to notice or care what we were talking about. That's one of the beautiful things about the general populace: You can more or less speak openly about arcane goings-on, and they'll assume you're just a video game nerd. Which works for me, since I'm one of those too.

"I have lights with adjustable necks, and I am more than capable of drawing the circles required for my analysis."

"Oh." I knew those offers were a bit of a stretch, but the simple, emotionless way she went about shutting them down made me feel like kind of an idiot for even suggesting them. "Want someone to keep you company?" Somehow, I knew that was even more unlikely.

"No. Socializing will make the process slower, if anything."

Sue put two slim hands against the middle of the rug and started a considerably more graceful walk toward the door behind the counter. "I'll look over the rug as soon as I lack customers. It will likely be done by tomorrow."

"Okay," I replied, forcing a smile to the best of my ability. No need to make the situation awkward or weird, after all. It's not like I was asking her to prom or something. "If you change your mind, I'll be at home. Do you want my number or anything, just in case?"

"I will not change my mind," Sue stated dismissively, but she paused before carrying the carpet into her expansive stock room. She looked around the carpet at me, one brown eyebrow slightly higher than the other. "Do you have another reason for being so insistent on remaining here, Mister Foster?"

"What? No, of course not!" There she went again, trying to analyze everything I did as though it were some deeply telling psychological episode. "I just figured it might be nice to offer, since we're friends, and I wouldn't want you to have to deal with being in a dark room by yourself, getting lonely and depressed without any distractions to take your mind off of personal issues that might be eating away at you internally."

I noticed that she was staring at me then, along with the two other people in the store. I guess they saw it as weird for a guy to be considerate of someone else's feelings.

Sue nodded slowly, resuming on her path to the back room. "I'll find a light you can hold up, Mister Foster."

I'm not entirely sure what changed her mind, but I'd be lying if I said I didn't appreciate it. I smiled, nodded in return, and set about busying myself with a collection of rings that supposedly aligned energy and relieved stress. They ranged from forty to eighty bucks, which was way beyond my useless nick-knack budget. On the upside, using them to mentally reenact scenes from one of my favorite movies was completely free. It took a while for the two other people to leave. Turned out that one was more of a window shopper than anything, and the other couldn't decide between a rose quartz crystal ball and a selenite one. To her credit, Sue was really honest about her own merchandise. She showed both globes under normal lighting versus lighted stands, and freely mentioned the actual value of each stone. She also talked about the commonly assigned meanings of the two, and while I knew they weren't actually enchanted to do anything, it made for an interesting listen. The guy went with rose quartz in the end, which was the less expensive of the orbs by a few dollars. By the time he left, it was starting to get dark outside. I yawned, an automatic reflex to the coming night, but shook my head against it. I'd rest later. Sue pulled a dusty 'Sorry, We're Closed' sign from behind one of the counters and hung it on the outside of the door.

"I would rather not be disturbed until the translation is finished," she stated, turning toward me and moving for the back room. "Time is of the essence."

"Hey, don't you want this back, first?" I held one of the rings out to her, only smirking a little bit.

"I suppose, yes." Sue gave me a weird look, undoubtedly wracking her brain to figure out what the set up would lead into.

"Well, now that it comes to it, I don't feel like parting with it. It's mine, I found it! It came to me." I like to think that Ian Holme would've been impressed with my little impersonation. Suffice it to say, Sue wasn't buying it, which left me clutching the ring through the awkward silence that followed. I whispered to her, "You're supposed to tell me not to get angry. That's the line, because you're, y'know, Gandalf."

"Give me the ring, or I will leave you to decipher the wishing carpet by yourself." She held out an open palm and glared at me until I handed it over. Spoil sport.

"Fine. Will you at least-"

"No." Sue replaced the copper ring on its stand with all the rest and walked to the back door.

"You don't even know what I was going to say!"

"I am not going to speak or act as any character from that movie, no matter how compelling your argument may have been." The door swung shut behind her. There was no way she was getting out of that one so easily. I jogged to catch up and shouldered my way into the stock room. It was about half the size of the sales floor, with a large, elaborate table in the middle. Turns out Sue was right about the lighting situation, as she had a whole bunch of lamps attached to the tabletop. Just like she said, they all had swiveling heads and fancy bending arms. When coupled with the wooden shelves containing just about every arcane component ever, it made the place look more like a mystical laboratory than the back room of your typical store. Sure, there were carefully labeled cardboard boxes piled here and there, but I could easily imagine Sue using the space to cook up potions or reanimate creatures from beyond the pale to do her bidding. I'm not entirely positive what Sue's bidding would have consisted of, since she seemed to do everything around the store already. Maybe she had an underground well somewhere that she needed buckets of water brought up from. I'd have to warn her about renegade brooms, in that instance.

"Man, Sue, what do you have against epic fantasy movies? I

was letting you be one of the cool characters and everything." I tugged on a particularly bendy looking lamp to test just how far it would go, then made a squiggle with its neck. Meanwhile, Sue picked up the carpet without so much as a grunt, hauling it over to the table.

"I have nothing against the movie, I just haven't seen it." She slammed the rug down onto her worktable as my eyes bulged out in response. "I cannot comment on a movie I have yet to experience."

"Woah, wait, hold on a second." Sue looked up from the rug, pausing in the middle of unrolling it down the length of the ancient-looking tabletop. "No, I mean, you can keep doing that. I'm just expressing surprise at the fact that you haven't seen the biggest, coolest movie ever made."

She shrugged and went back to getting our wishing carpet positioned so that it could be analyzed. It ran lengthwise off the edge of the table, and was wider than our work surface as well. "I haven't seen most movies. It is a considerable waste for me to spend my time sitting and staring at things for hours on end."

"So you just don't like movies in general." I bent the lamp I was holding around itself, creating what kind of looked like a pretzel knot. "What about books, video games, music?"

"I listen to music," Sue stated. She stared at the knot I had made, sighed quietly, and elected to grab hold of a different light source. "It can be both soothing and complex, depending on the genre."

"Not a heavy metal fan?" I smiled, attempting to re-straighten the lamp's neck and fix my own handiwork. It was nice actually talking to Sue. Most of the time I couldn't get anything out of her, no matter what I asked. Heck, I didn't know her favorite color, her last name, or even her preference when it came to brands of peanut butter, and I've hung out with her a few times.

"I listen almost exclusively to orchestral music and chamber choirs. If you don't mind, however, I need to focus," she replied, clicking on the silver lamp in her hand and swiveling it over the middle of the carpet. I guess I never really got around to describing the thing, but that's mostly because I was always seeing the gray, dusty side that was showing when it was rolled up. When it was laid out and put under a light, the carpet really became as impressive as its arcane properties.

The outside border was a rusty red color, mostly, although it had intricate knotwork going up and down the edges in sandy yellow. The middle was really the incredible part. It had scenes woven into four large rectangles, separated by a motif that looked like a blue river bristling with reeds. The top left panel featured two peacocks in brilliant blues and greens standing in front of a mountain. The rectangle next to them had a bunch of ancient warships set against a sunset, and the one below that depicted a palm tree with a bushy, emerald colored canopy. It looked like a golden crown was wrapped around the trunk, which I could only imagine was symbolism for something. I'm not particularly well versed in that kind of stuff. The last panel was really intriguing, at least to me. It contained a gold circle with wings, and inside that was a dude with a bow and an arrow on the string. He was wearing a feathered tunic, which matched the peacocks at the top. Waves of light emanated from him, giving him the appearance of a god or maybe a hero from Assyrian lore.

The level of detail woven into the tapestry was amazing. There were subtle textures in the dirt the birds were standing on, strands of minute color in the archer's feathers, and even traces of light reflecting off of the water. I don't know how you would even begin to make something like that. I mean, I had trouble making key chains out of those plastic beads and cords they have at craft stores. Zoe's always came out awesome by comparison. She made pink kittens and bunnies, as you might expect, while I usually ended up with a green circle. Sometimes it wasn't even a circle, but a weird non-shape with a stubby tail. Of course, she always insisted on keeping the ones I made like they were works of art. It's funny how you can try to protect and encourage someone to the best of your ability, and they end up doing the same for you.

Thinking about Zoe brought me back to reality and had the added bonus of forming a lump of worry in my stomach. As soon as I knew where that mandrake root was, we could take the carpet to it and get her back. I just had to find someone or something that could track it down.

"Any luck? I mean, does any of this stuff mean anything to you?" I winced. It occurred to me the second after I finished talking that I was probably hindering Sue by breaking the silence that had fallen over the room.

"The visible depictions on the carpet are of no real consequence to us, though they seem to indicate it was commissioned by an Assyrian king." Sue craned her neck forward to squint closely at the boat panel. "I don't see the words to activate its arcane properties, but that is typical of an enchanted carpet."

"So if you can't see the code, how are you supposed to use it? I'm awful at guessing games, especially in ancient languages I don't know. Kind of a rough handicap."

"I said that I do not presently see the words, not that they cannot be seen. If you would turn on the light that you are holding, it may rectify the situation." Sue turned her lamp off, leaving us in the dark save for sporadic glistening from her shelved components. I nodded and flicked the switch on the back of my light. A red beam shone out, bathing the room in a creepy, horror movie kind of ambiance.

"Huh. Note to self, don't take any showers back here anytime soon." I twisted around to look at the front of the lamp, tapping on the crimson lens that sat there. "Weird. Why not just get a red light bulb?"

"The lens is made of thinly-carved ruby." I immediately retracted my hand, staring at the simple looking light with a new appreciation. That thing must have cost more than a years' worth of rent. "Magic can often be attuned to crystals, as you know. If I am correct, the code may be sewn into the rug using a thread with just such an enchantment."

Sue reached for the lamp, pulling it closer to the rug. Amid the ruby shade its decorations took on, specks of intense crimson began to show up. They weren't large points of light, and they seemed to be spread randomly across the carpet's weave. It resembled a bloody night sky spread across the table.

"Holy crap." It was definitely impressive, but it didn't do anything to alleviate the knot in my gut. "Does that mean anything to you? I mean, to me it's all random red dots."

"Yes," she said, her tone flat. Sue moved for her shelves and zeroed in on a big, shimmering jar. I figured I'd wait on the predictable question, though I had another that was itching at the back of my skull.

"How did you know it'd be rubies? If you have this one lens, you must have others like it, and it could've been attuned to anything."

"The crown," Sue replied. She came back to the table and extended a finger to the bottom right panel. "It is encrusted with rubies. Sometimes, enchanters left clues such as those in case the original owner was killed or otherwise lost possession of the object."

I hadn't even noticed before, but yeah, there were circular gems at the base of the crown that were red. I guess it was between ruby or garnet, and Sue got it right on the first try. At that point, I contemplated talking to her about joining the team for a caper or two. Those are the kind of results we really could have used more often, though I think she and Lucas would've had to arm wrestle for the position of overly logical person who tries to poke holes in my brilliant schemes.

Sue popped the lid on the jar in her hands and held it up a good distance from the wishing carpet. From there, she tipped the opening away from her and sprinkled some kind of gently glowing dust onto it. It really didn't have a color as a whole, but the individual grains seemed to sparkle with shifting hues as they drifted down to the woven surface of the rug.

"What's that?" I asked, tempted to hold my hand out and catch some of the shimmering dust.

"Crystallized aether," Sue replied. She deliberately shook out some more, until it looked like she would cover the entirety of the carpet. "A solidified form of the driving energy that lies behind all magic. It is pure, elemental chaos."

"Neat." I moved a finger to try and analyze some of the stuff more closely, but Sue immediately stopped pouring and looked at me with muted urgency.

"Do not touch it, Mister Foster."

"Why, what's the worst that'll happen?" It looked harmless enough. Kind of like a cross between falling snow and those fiber optic Christmas trees that continuously change color.

"The pure chaos contained in the crystals will warp the structure of the cells in your hand and give you cancer." And that's when I decided to stop touching anything in Sue's store room forever.

"Holy crap, Sue! That stuff is friggin' radioactive?" I drew my hand back and took a few healthy steps away from the table. "You could warn a guy! Shouldn't we be wearing lead-lined clothes or something?"

"The crystalline shape that each grain is contained within protects us from indirect exposure. Once the crystals are near enough to the aether within the carpet's enchantment, they will be drawn to it and merge with the pre-existing spell. This will simultaneously strengthen the faded enchantment and render the aether harmless as its energy is used as a sort of fuel." Sue said all of that without really thinking or pausing for breath. Her breadth of knowledge was astounding, but so too was her ability to drone on like an instructional video for a retail job.

"But if I touched the crystals, I'd die."

"Potentially. You asked what the worst possible outcome would be." She went on as she finished sprinkling the carpet with crystal dust. "Your hair could also change color, or you could grow any number of extra appendages, or your taste buds could become unbearably sensitive. If the crystals touched your skin, the essence of pure chaos would come to afflict your body. However, as long as they remain on the carpet and off of your person, you will remain unharmed."

Given that revelation, I approached the table again and slipped my hands into my pockets. I had the tendency of doing stuff before I really thought about it, and the last thing I wanted was to accidentally turn my hand into a platypus because I set it down on the table.

Looking back at the carpet, I was surprised to see that what Sue was talking about was actually happening before my eyes. The little particles of glowing dust were gathering around the tiny stars that already populated the rug's surface, lazily drifting toward them and melting into the same crimson shade. The lights added up as they pooled together, and where before there was a really confusing game of connect the dots, several lines and symbols came into focus. It wasn't in English or the language of the book. In fact, I'm pretty sure they were pictographs. Needless to say, I was stumped. I had the feeling that Sue was prepared for it, however.

"It's a beautiful thing," I said with a smile. "You continue to amaze me, Sue. Any idea on the language?"

"It is woven in cuneiform," she stated, looking over the assortment of glowing symbols. On an unrelated note, you have no idea how hard it's been to avoid making a *Scarlet Letter* joke over the course of this scene. It literally took every ounce of my self-restraint to keep my trap shut on that one. "The language itself is likely in Akkadian, though I would imagine that the actual phrase to control the carpet will be in the language of the arcane. Regardless, it will be time consuming to translate, but not impossible."

I nodded, and a yawn forced my jaw open. "Awesome. Do you need help with any books or anything? I could take a half of the pictographs while you take the other half."

"I believe that this part of the process will happen most efficiently if I handle it alone." Sue tugged a small notebook out of one of her back pockets along with a pen. Which made me wonder how the heck she sits down without getting ink all over her butt, but it didn't seem that important at the time.

"Are you sure?" I was going to add something to that, but another yawn stopped me in the middle of my thought.

"I am positive. And given that you still haven't slept, you would likely make mistakes that I would need to correct afterward."

"How do you know I didn't sleep on the ride back here?" It was kind of a moot point, but I felt it was a little presumptuous of Sue to assume things about my sleep schedule.

"Your friend Kurt listens to obscenely loud music, to the point that I can hear it from inside a brick building. You just yawned twice in the span of two minutes, and your posture is terrible. When was Zoe kidnapped?"

Kind of a sore subject, but I decided to play along. "Two days ago. That morning."

"And what were you doing when she was taken?" She didn't seem all that interested, considering that she was just writing stuff in her notepad. I don't know how Sue manages to distance herself from stuff like that, but I couldn't. A hint of irritation might have slipped into my tone, even if I didn't mean for it to.

"Getting a bunch of angel's tears out in New York. Why?"

Her eyes finally lifted from the carpet. "You haven't attained REM sleep in three days, Mister Foster. If you continue to push yourself in a misguided attempt at self-sacrifice, you will begin to lose your eye-hand coordination, short-term memory, and possibly hallucinate. You will be poorly equipped to deal with the Thule society, and Zoe will likely be put in more danger."

"What, are you saying I'm trying to hurt Zoe?" I'll admit that I snapped at Sue. It wasn't intentional, and I know she was just trying to help, but I couldn't take that logic right then, not from anyone. "I'm doing everything I can, Sue! She could be in a trunk or a cell right now, in pain and starving or worse, and it's because of me and my stupid plans! I know that I'm a crappy brother, but I'm trying, even if it's not anywhere near enough!"

I had pulled my hands out of my pockets to make an angry gesture, but stopped everything when I felt a folded piece of paper slip out with them. They were Sue's directions. Her personalized note sat out on the hardwood floor, staring up at me. My voice caught in my throat, and everything went quiet again. Sue was just looking at me, her expression neutral.

"Oh, god. Sue," I covered my eyes with my palms, running them down my face as it sank in that I was really being that much of a whiny, self-pitying jerk. "I'm so sorry. I didn't mean to yell at you. You don't deserve that."

Sue gave a small nod and went back to copying down the lines of glowing cuneiform. "You are suffering from sleep deprivation. It would be best if you rested now. We will use the wishing carpet to find the mandrake in the morning."

At that point, I couldn't argue with her. I clearly wasn't acting like myself, and she was probably right about the loss of coordination and stuff. I looked around for a couch, but didn't see anything of the sort. Come to think of it, that was something Sue's store always seemed to lack.

"Do you have a chair or anything around here? Something to sit on? I feel like it'd be kind of skeezy to ask about your bed."

Sue blinked a few times. "No. I don't tend to use them."

"What, chairs? You don't... Sit often?" That was a little weird, but I guess I shouldn't judge other people for their little idiosyncrasies.

"No. I could purchase a chair, if it would help the situation."

"Don't worry about it." I smiled and bent down to nab Sue's directions from earlier, then walked over to a wall that looked to be the comfiest out of my four options. I slid down against it, looking up at the shelves above me. I would probably have been better off if I went back to the apartment and snoozed in my own laundry covered bed, but I knew I'd never be able to sleep there. My imagination would do a stupid little dance whenever I closed my eyes, producing nothing but images of Zoe in Metzmacher's evil clutches. Here, there was at least the sound of Sue occasionally moving around, reminding me that I wasn't alone.

"Hey Sue?" I murmured, eyes closed and on the verge of tumbling down into the deep, dark pit of sleep.

"Yes?"

"Did you find anything on the mandrake while we were in Lowell?"

She hesitated, and you could hear a hint of remorse in her tone. "I apologize, but no. My contacts are looking into it."

"It's okay," I said, nodding slightly. I was starting to get jumbled thoughts and nonsensical images running through my head, which meant that dreams weren't far off. "We'll find it. You're good at translating and doing things, and making scones. Coconut scones."

The last thing I remember from that night was thinking that I caught Sue smiling again. I don't know if that was my imagination or what, but it seemed real. At least as real as the flying turtle I was riding on at the time.

"Good night, Mister Foster."

-Backtracking-

When I woke up the next day, I was surprised to feel a cushion behind my head and a thin blanket covering my legs. Really, it was one of those sheets people use as wall coverings or curtains. It was purple with a black tribal design splayed over it like a crappy tattoo. I blinked some morning crust out of my eyes and reached for the thing that was supporting my head. It looked like one of the white foam rectangles from Sue's display cases that she kept really expensive merchandise nestled in. I smiled at the makeshift pillow and put it in my lap.

"Thanks, Sue," I whispered into the mid-morning glow that had come to rest in the storeroom. My voice was an unpleasant croak in the back of my throat, but at least my head felt a little clearer. I must have slept for a while. It couldn't have been later than nine when I'd conked out. I still felt like I could sleep for another six hours, but it didn't take long for my brain to start catching up, whirring with memory and purpose again. I looked up to the table, noting that the rug was absent from it and the assorted lamps were shut off.

I stretched my arms and legs until they hurt, but in that awesome way where every joint snaps and it feels like you just expanded your chest cavity by a few inches. With a deep breath, I flipped the sheet off of me and got to my feet. It was a new, glorious day, full of golden sunlight and brimming with hope. Or maybe not hope. Hope was too wishy-washy. I was determined. I was going to find the mandrake, get Zoe back, and kick Metzmacher in the face. Then I was going to get a BLT and kick that in the face too because I don't like BLTs. It was going to be an awesome day.

"Ah, good, you're finally done being completely useless." Lucas. I don't even have anything else to say, just Lucas. Even he couldn't ruin how triumphant everything was going to be that day. I turned around to see him coming through the door in his usual finery, followed by Kurt and Sue.

"It's good to know that being a cynical jerk is still in fashion, even after Labor Day. What're you guys dong here?" I tried to pat down what was probably an awful case of bed-head, or I guess wall-and-display-cushion-head.

"I called them using the numbers in your cell phone." Sue tossed said crappy, old flip phone at me, which I caught.

"Hey whoa, you went through my pockets while I was sleeping?"

"No. The phone fell out due to the angle of your leg and was lying on the floor." Good enough, I guess. I'd have to start watching Sue more carefully. Y'know, while sleeping. "The carpet is translated. I have the code to activate its properties, which I have tested once over the course of the night. I assumed you would want to use it as soon as possible."

"Awesome! Good thinking, Sue." I glanced around for the rug, but then a thought occurred to me. "Where'd you use the rug to go? Out of curiosity."

"To visit my mother," she replied flatly. "The arcana is sitting out on the sales floor. I have already written down the verbal command, which simply has to be uttered while sitting or standing on the carpet's surface. It will take you to the place you visualize most strongly, so it is important to remain focused." She moved to the door as she explained that, ushering us all into the main part of the store. As promised, the wishing carpet was set out and waiting for us between a couple of bookshelves. It looked like it belonged there, actually. I'd say Sue could keep it after all this was over, but I had a feeling we'd be getting a lot more use out of it.

She handed me another piece of paper, this one holding a pretty simple phrase in the arcane tongue. "When you appear at your destination, you will be surrounded by a gray mist that will obscure you to anyone nearby. However, it only lasts for a few moments."

"Gotcha. So you have to pick a good place to appear, or else there'll be a lot of questions. The rug doesn't shrink or become easier to carry or anything?" Again, this is stuff I would've considered when making an enchanted rug. I feel like I would've been a good designer of wishing carpets, apart from my complete lack of knowledge on the subject of weaving and patterns and generally anything to do with carpets.

"No. Such carpets were commonly utilized to travel between palaces, where they would be guarded or stored." As usual, I had no idea where Sue came up with this information, but I found it fascinating. I always love when you can infer bits and pieces about a society and its customs through the history of a piece of arcana.

"We'll be careful about where we take it, then. If we can't be sure of the carpet's safety, we can have one person stay on and bring it back here once we're at the place we need to be." I got a general nod from everyone, which was a good sign. We were all on the same page, now we just needed direction.

"I guess all that's left is to find the stupid root. Sue, any luck on that front?" It was a stretch, given that it had only been nine or so hours since the last time I asked. I wouldn't have kept pestering Sue if she weren't our best bet for finding the root.

"Nothing," she said, her eyes flitting to one side. "Every other arcana dealer I have contact with refuses to touch that kind of merchandise. If it was ever sold to anyone, it would be in the hands of a private collector."

"The guys who took it were mercenaries, if that helps at all. That's what Metzmacher said, anyway. I don't think she'd have any reason to lie about it."

"Mercenaries have loyalty only to coin," Lucas stated. "Even if the mandrake still belongs to them, it is more than likely that they are using it in order to attain further affluence."

"As much as that's unhelpful to our mission, it's true." I looked to the wishing carpet and exhaled my frustration. "But we have to focus on finding the thing in the first place, and I have a plan."

"If it involves becoming invisible or breaking into a museum or both, I want nothing to do with it." Lucas interjected again, folding his arms over his chest. What a team player.

"Technically, the plan doesn't yet. Can I finish before we all jump to conclusions?"

Lucas muttered something under his breath, but seemed ready to cooperate. Which was good, because he was the centerpiece of my grand design.

"Thank you. Now, first things first. Lucas, how far away can you smell stuff?"

"Probably about two kilometers, depending on wind and the environment. Why?" It was clear that Lucas didn't trust my plan by the way he leaned away from me. It's not like I was sending him nose-first into a vat of old fish and gym socks. Mostly because I haven't found one of those yet, but that's not the point.

"Alright. Sue, you must have mandrake root among all those spell components back there. The way I figure it, we can get one of those, Lucas can sniff it to get the scent and then we go tracking it down like in the movies." I paused, trying to figure out exactly how long that would take. "Wait. How many miles are in two kilometers?"

Lucas was riling up to one of his rants, I could tell, but he couldn't even get it out before Sue answered with, "One point two four two seven four two three eight."

We all pretty much stopped right there and stared at her. Sue stared right back, seemingly oblivious as to why we were a little weirded out. I didn't know exactly what was going on with her, but that's when I put figuring it out a little higher on my priority list. It was officially somewhere below getting Zoe back, but above re-watching that mermaid cartoon to spot all the dirty stuff the animators secretly put in.

Before things could get super-awkward, I decided to push

forward with the plan, which suddenly seemed less than ideal. "Only a mile or so, huh? So it would take a pretty long time to go across the continental United States like that."

"That is a bit of an understatement, Foster. Even with the wishing carpet, it would take years." I was about to make some adjustments to the plan that would've undoubtedly made it work, but I was interrupted yet again. "And before you ask, no. No, I do not have some far-fetched wolf-based superpower that allows me to detect certain plants from absurdly long distances. Werewolves also cannot speak to plants! Werewolves cannot turn into plants, nor can they magically create plants! You cannot assume that I am the answer to all of your dilemmas because of my heritage, and in fact, I find that rather offensive!"

"Oh, holy crap. That's it." My arms fell to the side, limp with sudden, overpowering realization.

"What?" Lucas put his diatribe on hold, but its momentum wasn't stopped entirely. "I swear, if this is another crack about my manner of dress, I will put you through a window."

"I can't believe I didn't think of that before. I'm such a friggin' idiot!" I ran onto the wishing carpet, pushing past Lucas and Kurt.

"Mister Foster, what are you talking about?" Sue's brow fell as she attempted to decipher what was admittedly my internal monologue made external.

"Talking to plants!" I gestured at Lucas with outstretched hands and flailed a little for good measure. "Matt! Matt is a druid! If anyone can find a specific plant-related thing, it's going to be him! I was trying so hard not to involve him because of what happened in New York, I didn't even consider that!"

160

"Oh. That makes a certain amount of sense, actually." So Lucas finally agreed with me on something. Awesome. "If your friend can provide us with the location of the root through druidic magic, we could formulate an actual plan and potentially use the wishing carpet to take it without any kind of struggle."

"Exactly. What time is it, Sue?" I looked down at the code she'd written down, mentally preparing myself for whatever weirdness the rug might generate upon use. Sometimes translocation spells can make you nauseous or dizzy for a minute after using them. I had to hope that wasn't the case with the carpet's particular enchantment.

"Nine-seventeen AM." Somehow I wasn't shocked that she knew the time with that kind of precision.

"Then it's time to find us a mandrake." Definitely adding that to my list of possible catch phrases. Of course, my compatriots helped to ruin the adventurous mood by shuffling onto the carpet like they were in line at a high school cafeteria. Is it so much to ask for a little enthusiasm?

"I'll remain here, Mister Foster. Reappearing in the storeroom will be optimal, if you choose to stop here to make preparations. I will also continue the search in case your friend proves unable to find the mandrake root."

"Thanks, Sue." I offered her a smile, and she nodded in return. I'd have to bake her a cake or something when this was all over with. Or maybe croissants. I'm not sure on the appropriate protocol for a "thanks for helping me save my sister from the Thule Society" present. For the time being, I looked down to the paper in my hand and read aloud the words of power.

"Trados mortan, acorum feln. Vortrus!" I closed my eyes and

tried to picture Matt's backyard as firmly as my mind would allow. The big, gray house, a shed that I always figured was full of pod-people or something, and endless woods. I heard a sound vaguely reminiscent of one of those bellows you use to keep a fire going, and for a second it was like being underwater. Not in that it was wet, but there was pressure on every inch of my body, like with the translocation runes I had used at the Ecotarium. The sensation went away as quickly as it came. When I opened my eyes, we were in exactly the spot I had imagined, though a thick, reddish-gray mist had formed all around us. That carpet really was an impressive piece of enchanted decorum. With most of the arrays I knew of, you couldn't go more than a mile in any direction. The carpet seemed able to go anywhere so long as you could imagine it. Sue was right on the money when she had us go after it.

"Hello?" I heard Matt calling from his basement door, though I couldn't really see him. The billowing smoke from the rug must have just come into his line of sight. "Holy cow. Either a very quiet meteorite just found its way to my backyard, or there's a Sean Foster in there testing out a new spell. Or it's a horrible, demonic monstrosity."

"Something like that," I stepped into the dissipating wall of mist and toward his voice. This time, Matt was in a t-shirt the color of faded mustard and plaid pajama pants. "I'm sorry, I didn't mean to wake you up."

"You didn't," he said, extending his hand for a shake before pointing at a plant next to his shed. "I was just about to water an experiment I've been working on."

"Oh, man. It's not some kind of sentient plant-person, is it? That kinda stuff gives me the jibblies." That goes for plant-people,

162

cat-people, and pretty much anything that's not originally human but ends up as a thing with a human body and the wrong head. Early 90s cartoons were a little rough for me.

Matt quickly glanced to either side. "Of course not! No, no. Just regular, non-humanoid plants. Nothing that could astronomically backfire and destroy the human race." He waved a gangly arm at Lucas and Kurt as the fog continued to fade, casually moving to water the experimental flora. It was a bush-looking thing with pink buds and green stems growing out of a terra cotta pot. It seemed pretty harmless.

"I'm going to have to take your word on that. My limit is one evil, world destroying plant per caper." I glanced back at Lucas, who was openly glaring from his vigil atop the carpet. "And in an amazingly seamless little segue, I need to ask for another favor."

"Trying to grow a hamburger tree again?" Matt smiled as he showered the colorful plant with a rusty old watering can that had been left by the shed. The thing had seen better days, to the point where more water came out of the bottom than the actual spout.

"Not exactly. Despite the clear benefits that would have for everyone on the planet, especially impoverished countries and vegetarians."

"I remember the sales pitch. That isn't what you're asking about?" He moved to pour some water on a nearby birch tree as well.

"I need to find the Devil's Mandrake."

Matt blinked in response, moving about as slowly as a tree sloth in reaction to the plant's name. Furrows appeared on his forehead, but otherwise he seemed content to wait for more of an explanation. I obliged, though my eyes turned to focus on a pine tree just to Matt's right.

"It's for Zoe," I started, shuffling a candy wrapper and an old receipt around in my coat pockets. I probably should've seen his reaction coming, but then again, I was still pretty groggy. I'm going to blame it on that.

"You're going to give Hitler's mandrake root to your sister?"

"No, no, I'm sorry. The girl at the Spiral beat you to that one." Once was pretty funny in retrospect, but twice over the course of two days would just be silly.

"Metzmacher and the Thule guys kidnapped Zoe because they want me to find and recover the root from the mercenaries who stole it from them. We can't find the thing on our own, but I figured you might have some way of locating specific plants for us with your druidic hoobie-joob."

Matt nodded slowly. "That makes slightly more sense," he replied, setting the watering can back down. "And you're aware of the underlying issue with the mandrake giving Metzmacher incredible arcane power."

"Yeah, but don't worry about it. I'll figure something out like I always do and everything will be fine!" Apparently, my heroic smile and thumbs up weren't as convincing as I had intended. Matt's expression turned grave, his mouth forming a hard line across his tanned face.

"This isn't a bunch of angel's tears, Sean. It's not a harmless little toy that elicits a chase from the cops. If you give the mandrake to her, or if she takes it from you, you'll be risking the lives of so many people." The druid's eyes dipped toward the ground as he shook his head. "Even if I wanted to help you with this, my magic isn't like yours. I have people I'd have to answer to."

164

"What, is all nature magic everywhere monitored and governed by some group of aloof, haughty guardians or something?"

"Yes." Matt leaned against the shed, almost like he was hiding at the mention of said mystical auditors.

"Oh. Well, crap." I didn't know all the facts about druidism, no, but it's funny how sometimes an imagination inspired by comic books can fill in the blanks. "I'm going to go out on a limb and guess that you'll face dire consequences if you use your powers to find an artifact of ultimate evil."

"You're good at this," he replied, clearly hesitant to say more than he had to. Leave it to an ancient secret society to be all mysterious and stuff.

"Well, c'mon, Matt. There has to be something you can do to keep it under wraps. Druids don't have anything like private browsing?"

"Pardon the intrusion, but could you perform an overarching search for all existing mandrake roots and just happen to glance over the one we need?" I didn't realize Lucas had walked up behind me. I was glad he had done so to help as opposed to whining about the length Matt cut his grass. I nodded, pointing to the upright Brit in agreement. Matt's response was less than positive.

"I could do that, yes," and yet he winced at the thought. "As a druid, I do possess the resources to monitor instances of plant species across the globe."

"Awesome! That's perfect!" It took a few seconds of Matt being silent and morose before it started to dawn on me that he still hadn't offered to do anything. "You'll do it, right? The thing where we figure out where it is and your superiors are none the wiser?"

"Metzmacher already tried to get the location out of me.

Before they dragged me out to New York, they threatened to kill me if I didn't find the mandrake for them. They only got you involved because I refused. I just never thought they would go so far as to kidnap Zoe. I'm sorry."

That came as a weird realization. Of course, it wasn't Matt's fault in the least. I just had a new appreciation for his strength of character. It takes a lot of guts to risk your life in the name of the greater good, especially when you've got a gun to your head.

"Don't worry about it. You did the right thing. It's Metz and her goons that'll have to answer for what they've done."

"It's not just that. I'm sorry, but I can't give you the location either." Matt and his bare feet padded past me and back toward his house. "Not when I know where it would end up."

"Woah, hey! I'm not actually giving it to her to keep! I told you, I'm going to figure it out like I always do!" I jumped to get between him and the door. "I'm just going to get Zoe, then I'll steal it back from them again!"

"It's not good enough." Matt stopped, but his expression was stuck on an overcast glower. "If Metzmacher even touches the root for a moment, there's no guarantee that she wouldn't use it then and there."

"Well, what do you want me to say? I'm not going to give up, Matt. If you won't help, I will find another way. Even if it takes Lucas years of sniffing."

"I am not doing that plan."

"Lucas, I'm just trying to make a point."

"Yes, and I am making it known that I would not participate in that particular scheme, even in the pink candy floss world of your bloated imagination."

166

"Woah, hey! First off, it's called cotton candy. Second, I prefer the blue kind and you know it!"

"Sorry to say it, gentlemen, but this is exactly why I can't say I'm confident about this whole thing." Matt shrugged and tried to shoulder past me, but that was when Kurt decided to finally pipe in.

"I could rig it to blow up." Looking back, it was kind of an obvious solution. I have to give Kurt credit in that department. While everyone else is looking way too hard at a situation, he just looks at the big picture and points out how it could be resolved with explosions.

"Yeah! Yeah, that would totally work, right? You fill that thing up with C-4 or whatever, make a really tiny electronic detonator, and we could blow it up in Metz' face with a cell phone call as soon as we're gone! Kurt, you can do stuff like that, can't you?"

"Yep."

Matt looked down at his driveway, bits of thin, blonde hair blowing over his eyes. Trenches of tanned skin formed across his forehead like tightropes connecting his eyebrows. I could tell he wasn't completely sold on the plastic explosives, so I had to come up with an alternative. A secondary plan in case the technology failed.

"I could draw an array on it, too. Something tiny, barely noticeable. The root is probably covered in symbols and arcane circles, they'd never notice another one without all kinds of equipment!" I wasn't making this stuff up, either. Just like the array I drew on the metal barrel we were making invisibility gunk in, I could draw an explosive circle on the mandrake root. With any luck, it might even be able to tap into the incredible power therein. That would be one heck of a boom.

"Alright, Sean, I understand. It could work." Matt finally agreed. He looked unhappy about the whole ordeal, but still reached for the handle of his basement's screen door with distinct purpose. I let him by, and the plastic parts in the old door clacked as he drew it open. "But after I find the root, I'm going with you."

So even with a brilliant double explosion plan, Matt didn't trust us to destroy the root. I guess it didn't matter in the end, since we'd be getting Zoe back either way. And it would be pretty cool to see Matt in action if it somehow came down to a fight. I shrugged and followed him into the basement, looking back at Kurt and Lucas to indicate that they could come with.

"Fine by me." I instinctively slipped my checkered shoes off once I got inside the carpeted basement. "Never hurts to have more people when you're dealing with the Thule chumps."

"Mmh. You guys stay here, I'll bring the viewing globe." Matt led us in past a bunch of wooden paneling, flicking a lightswitch as we came into the living room area of the basement. It was cramped with an old couch, a computer desk, and a TV surrounded by a forest of cables. A DVD player sat triumphantly atop its prehistoric predecessor, a chunky brown box that could only be for viewing VHS tapes. An N64 was situated under all the hubbub, kept company by a bunch of grey cartridges. I was immediately drawn to them by sheer nostalgia, while Kurt gravitated toward the couch. Lucas had to remove his hat to keep it from bumping into the low ceiling. He stood around like a light post in the middle of the desert: Stick-straight and completely out of place. Meanwhile, Matt ducked into another room past the staircase which led up into the main area of the house. When he returned, he had a large wooden bowl under one arm. The druid's usual saunter was replaced with a more careful, deliberate tip-toe, though I didn't realize why until he set the bowl down on the dirt-colored carpet. It was filled almost to the brim with water.

"Is that a scrying bowl?" I turned from the aging game system to observe Matt's preparations. For the uninitiated, a scrying bowl is a vessel filled with liquid that an arcanist can use to view things from a distance. Throw in a few ingredients, say an incantation, and you can use it to spy on somebody like a true mage. Or you could use it to effectively steal a neighbor's cable. Like a lot of magic, though, scrying does have its limits, like distance. Also, if a skilled arcanist wanted to, it was pretty easy to draw magical wards around an area to protect it from potential spying.

"Not exactly," Matt replied, "But similar in concept. You'll see." He shifted down to sit cross-legged on the floor, and I followed suit. Lucas was watching from his chosen spot, as was Kurt.

What came next was one of the coolest displays of magic I've ever witnessed. Matt began by singing a long, slow note from what must have been the depths of his throat, then produced a chunk of mandrake root from his pocket. It could've been mistaken for a slice of potato if the observer didn't know any better, which would be pretty unfortunate since the whole plant is super poisonous. Matt dropped the pale bit of root into the water, his humming growing louder by the moment. Seemingly of its own accord, the water in the bowl began to swirl around the root, spinning faster and faster. Soon, the water was frothing up above the brim, held together in the shape of a half-sphere. As it spun, the water moved upward and joined at the top, becoming a clear, rippling orb. The hunk of mandrake root sat perfectly still in the middle as the clear ball of water began to hover above the wooden bowl. Its rotation got faster

169

and faster until the ripples smoothed almost completely. By that point, the orb was about the size of a huge pumpkin, but perfectly round in shape. Matt's chant reached a plateau before coming to a sudden halt. Even though the single low note was gone, he was still clearly doing some serious concentrating, at least judging by the way his brow was knotted.

"That's ridiculous," I said, completely in awe. I tried to keep my voice quiet for Matt's sake. "How does that even work? You don't have an array or anything."

"To summon the viewing globe requires practice and training from a master druid. I can't say more than that." Matt closed his eyes and pushed another brassy sound from his throat. In response, the sphere of water shifted and bubbled out in certain places as though the liquid were running over invisible pebbles. The bumps that formed over the surface quickly took the shape of the Earth's continents. As before, Matt quieted once the formation was finished. As much as a lot of my arcane arrays were beautiful in their designs, it was honestly breathtaking to watch a form of magic that was so organic. It only became a more impressive display when a slightly higher note from Matt brought tiny points of light to the whirling sphere. For the most part, the lights were the color of the moon reflected in a frigid lake. A few were green, others possessed shades of purple and blue. Most of the points dotted the shimmering countryside of Europe, but the coastal areas of the United States also had their fair share.

An uneasy excitement welled up around my sternum as a huge red light finally flickered onto the viewing globe. It was just to the East of the Rocky Mountains, probably around Texas. My geography isn't perfect, and the water orb didn't have state lines on it.

"Is that it?" I asked. I didn't want to jump to any crazy conclusions about the ominous glowing light of death, after all.

"It has to be," Matt replied after trailing off with the last note. "The brightness of the light is indicative of the power stored within the individual root. The color tells us the origin of its power."

"Hatred," Lucas stated from behind me. His face was engulfed in the crimson glow, adding an ominous aura to the word. I'll admit that his accent helped too. There's just something about English people that makes them great foreboding narrators.

Matt nodded in agreement, then made some circular gestures with his arms. The surface of the orb rippled all at once, and at first I thought he was clearing it or something. Turns out that he was zooming in on the red light.

"Mister Foster, would you kindly start up my computer on the desk over there?"

"Sure thing." I hustled to my feet and slipped behind Matt. He had a black desktop computer set up on one of those old roll-top kind of desks in one corner of the room, which I plopped down in front of with a certain amount of urgency. I clicked its power button on and was greeted with a quiet whirring sound. The setup didn't look new by any means, but it brought up the operating system quickly enough.

"What am I looking for, Matt?" I swirled the mouse around to bring up the cursor, which he had apparently changed to a leaf. His background image was a panoramic shot of trees. I honestly wasn't sure if Matt just loved trees that much or if it was some kind of self-referential trolling on his part.

"Look up New Mexico. The map should be one of the first

few things to come up."

I nodded and pulled up Matt's browser, entering the state's name into the search engine in the toolbar. Sure enough, there was a map. I switched it to terrain view to help match what the sphere was showing. It took some doing, but I got the image zoomed in to the same area that was showing in the ripples. It was weird trying to synchronize a spherical 3D image with a 2D map, but it ultimately worked out. I watched what was going on with the water and zoomed further with each shift, mostly going by lakes and mountains. As we got closer, lines began to crisscross Matt's watery sphere like flat veins.

"Roads," I said with a smile. "It's all easy from here, guys." After that point, it was a cinch to figure out where the light was coming from. It had pretty much stayed the same size throughout, maybe getting a little smaller with each zoom.

"Looks like we're going outside of Logan, New Mexico. Up route 54 and down what appears to be a dirt road." I clicked over to a satellite view to get more specific. "I guess it's in a little house in the middle of the desert."

"That is rather odd, isn't it?" Lucas asked. "You are quite sure that it isn't on a military base or anything of the sort?"

"Well, I guess it could be some kind of top secret experimental tiny house in the middle of nowhere, but there aren't any landing strips or towers nearby, just farms to the North."

"Are we finished with the viewing globe, gentlemen? It takes a surprising amount of effort to maintain." Matt's voice strained a little, hinting at just how much it took.

"No, that's great, we're good. Thanks a ton, Matt." As soon as those words came out, the sphere of glasslike water collapsed and splashed back into its wooden bowl. The bit of mandrake root bobbed up harmlessly in the center. "I'm just going to go to street view here, and then I should be able to get us within walking distance of the house. If the carpet works that way. Otherwise, we'll have to find somebody who's been to Logan, which would probably be a challenge."

"Could we take a moment to consider the implications of the knowledge we now have?" It wasn't a surprising request from Lucas, but it still rubbed me the wrong way. I had what I needed to get Zoe back right in front of me, and he wanted to take a few more hours mulling over the significance of whether the house had curtains. "The root is likely in the possession of one person who is keeping it far from any largely populated cities. This person either has no idea as to the value of what they hold, or they understand exactly what it is capable of and want to keep it from the hands of people like Metzmacher."

"Yeah. Unfortunately, that really doesn't affect how we're going about this," I replied. I was in the middle of trying to memorize the look of one spot just off of the highway, but I still wanted this little planning session to go faster if at all possible. "No matter what, I'll go up to the house, knock on the front door, and try to reason with whoever's inside."

"Really. That is your plan, to simply walk up and invite yourself in for a little chat."

"Yeah, unless you've got something more interesting in mind." I closed the browser and clicked over to shut the computer off. As I spun out of the rolling chair, Matt also got up. He moved over to a big closet to the side of the cellar door and flicked on another light. "Until we know what the situation is with our friend in New Mexico, we can't assume anything. Maybe it's somebody we can negotiate with. I want to at least try and do this without anyone getting hurt."

"But we'll have to be ready, either way." Matt returned to the middle of the room, holding a six foot long piece of wood with notches on each end. When he looped a line of hemp string around one of the tips, it became a little more apparent that the thing was a longbow. I don't know enough about them to tell if it was authentic to a certain time period, but it looked handmade.

"Holy crap, Matt. You know how to use that?"

"I dabble," he said in reply, slinging a simple leather quiver over his baggy shirt. It was a dusty brown color, bristling with feathers at the opening. He also slipped a necklace over his head, though that seemed less important at the time. It looked to be a simple leather cord wrapped around a quartz crystal.

"Good to know," I looked between Matt, Kurt, and Lucas. I felt like we had a pretty good team between the four of us. "Basically, I'd want you guys to hang back while I go in. If I can, I want to keep whoever's in the building feeling safe. Violence is going to be our last resort."

"That sucks." I don't remember Kurt pulling an explosive out of his bag, but there he was poking one with a screwdriver.

"Sorry, man, but this is way too dangerous and way too important. On the upside, we'll stop by an electronics store for the stuff you need to make the root all explodey. Then we're heading back to Sue's. It can't hurt to have somebody else know where we're going."

That turned out to be agreeable with everyone, and soon enough we were on our way back to Worcester. After Matt put on some jeans and a pair of old work boots, that is. There would be some logistical problems with bamfing around on the rug, especially since it needed to remain out of view of the general public, so we decided to take Matt's van. I'll spare you the details of that shopping trip. It was a lot of Lucas making dumb comments about how useless technology was even though he has a cell phone. I really want to get him an e-reader at some point just to see how pissed he gets at the idea of electronic books. After getting Kurt one of those cheap, temporary cell phones and some wiring, we piled back into Matt's ancient colossus of a vehicle and headed for the Spiral.

-Change of Plans-

Matt expertly pulled the teal van up to the side of the brick building, backing into the vacant alleyway that made up the Spiral's parking lot. It was pretty incredible the way he steered that thing like it wasn't the size of a house. Once that was finished, Lucas and Kurt grabbed the rug out of the back while Matt and I went to hold the door open for them. It was around one PM, so I expected to see some people in the store, but it was completely empty when I pushed the door in. Sue wasn't even around, which struck me as really odd.

"Sue?" I continued on inside. It only took one person to hold a door open, anyway. "Ollie ollie oxen-free! Anybody home?" The lights were even off. Bizarre. I couldn't imagine Sue going somewhere and leaving the door unlocked like that.

"Sorry, Foster," a voice came from the back room. A distinctly male, Australian voice. "Sue's a bit occupied at the moment."

"Abercrombie!" I murmured. He came out from the back room just as Lucas backed into the store. I rushed in, but stopped in my tracks when Abercrombie pulled the handgun from his coat and jabbed it in my direction.

"Don't think so. And these are still ash bullets, wolfie. No funny business from anybody." He waved the barrel of his weapon between the four of us for emphasis. "Bring the carpet in and lay it down peacefully."

"Do it," I said, glancing over my shoulder at Lucas. I turned back to glare at the lowlife in front of us. The bell above the door jingled as it always did when Matt stepped in behind me. "Where's Sue? What did you do to her?"

"She's safe for the time being. And she'll stay that way as long as you cooperate." He smiled as the wishing carpet thudded onto the hardwood floor. We outnumbered this jerk like crazy, but I couldn't make a move knowing that he had a hostage. First Zoe gets kidnapped, now Sue. It was enough to make me want to adopt a secret identity. And a cape. Unfortunately, it was a little late for the adventures of Arcana Man and his sidekicks, Snoot Boy and The Contraption.

"What do you want?" I asked, staring Abercrombie down in the shadows of the unlit store. "It's a bit much to involve Sue like this just for the carpet, don't you think?"

"You're right," he replied, sneering. "And if Sue wasn't already a part of all this, I probably wouldn't have."

"What're you talking about?" My heartbeat was pounding in my ears again, adrenaline making everything about the store seem blurry and fast. It was kind of like being in a scene from a cartoon with all the speed lines and yelling and unnecessary karate moves.

"I wouldn't put it past you to go hunting a wishing carpet just to pop around town, maybe make a grand entrance at some gathering of the geeks, but Sue's a tad more responsible with these things. She wouldn't have told you about it unless you were looking for something even more significant. More valuable." He said that last word with a little too much vigor for my liking. It never occurred to me that Abercrombie might know Sue, but it wasn't all that surprising. She was probably the most legitimate seller of arcana in New England, so it's part of her job to know everybody who knows about the stuff.

"How do you know Sue had anything to do with it? What if we found it on our own?"

"Nah, sorry." Abercrombie's straight, white teeth shone out from under his lips in a cocky grin. "If I didn't know about that rug being there, there's no way you lot stumbled on it. And regardless, Seth's been scrying on your boys since we got out from that storage locker."

"Oh." I couldn't think of a better retort than that. "Well, crap."

"Yeah. So I'm not really in this for just the carpet, you follow? I want whatever it is you're using it to get. I'm hoping it's something big, maybe a faerie gate or a fragment of the Ophanim Array." The former is basically a door into the realm of the fae. If you're not sure what I'm talking about there, skim a plot summary of *Midsummer Night's Dream*. It's like a world of Pucks and Oberons and Titanias, which isn't my thing, but it'd probably be worth a lot to somebody else. The latter is a legendary arcane circle that's supposed to channel the pure creative and destructive

179

properties of the Christian god from the Old Testament. Again, not my dig, but there's a buyer for everything.

"You want to know? Then show me where Sue is."

Abercrombie tilted his head a little. His expression remained smug, but his choppers receded back in the light of my demand. He nodded. "Alright, fair enough. Ivan!"

His call to the back of the shop was met with a crazed, "Not! Ivan!" I was immediately made a thousand million percent less comfortable knowing that he was there. It's odd to think that I'd rather have a gun pointed straight at me than stand in the same room as one guy. When he entered from the back, his bulging eyes poking above Sue's shoulder, I got a lot more angry than worried. The weird thing was that Sue seemed perfectly at ease. Or I guess more accurately, she looked like she always did: Vaguely disinterested in the situation.

"Sue!" I don't know why, but I took a running step toward her. I'd call it a heroic impulse. As one would expect, Matt took hold of one of my arms before I could go any closer and endanger everyone.

"Yes?" Sue asked, standing with her hands at her sides. Not-Ivan's eyes flicked from the ceiling down to the floor, then to something on a wall, one hand pulling hard on his greasy looking hair.

"Are you okay? Did they hurt you?" I tugged at Matt's arm for good measure, at least until I noticed he wasn't holding me back anymore and I was struggling against the air. For all that he had great comedic timing, his dramatic timing could use some work.

"I am unharmed, Mister Foster." Her voice was at its usual stiff monotone.

"You're not just saying that, like Stockholm Syndrome or something? They didn't hypnotize you into thinking you're their best friend?"

Sue blinked, and her brow furrowed slightly. "No. Why are you asking that?"

"I don't know, it's possible. And you always talk like that, so it's hard to tell sometimes..."

"What is wrong with the way I talk?" she asked, still lacking any emotion in her tone.

"It's not that, I just," I shook my head. "Look, you're being held captive against your will, except that you don't seem to care and they don't have you tied up, restrained, anything. April O'Neil got harsher treatment, and that was on a kid's show!"

"I do not know who this person is. I take it she was held hostage often."

"Yeah, every episode or so."

"Are you two about finished with the little reunion?" Abercrombie wiggled his gun to remind us all about the task at hand. "Because I would really like to know what it is I'll be taking from you today, apart from the wishing carpet."

"Yeah, see, that's the thing, Abbie-"

"Call me that again and I'm shooting you in the face."

"Roger that." For reference, I continued to refer to him as Abbie in my head for the next week just to spite him. "But you still aren't much of a hostage taker. Sue could kind of leisurely stroll out of your grasp if she wanted to."

"Not exactly." That must have been a cue, as Not-Ivan refocused on Sue in that exact moment. Without any kind of warning, she started to lose color in her face. At least, it started in her face. A pallid grayness swept across her entire body, even consuming her brown eyes and fading her hair from the root. She looked to be struggling to keep her eyes open, and soon she was losing her ability to stand, too. It was like the psychopath was draining the life directly out of her and she could do nothing to defend herself.

"Stop! Abercrombie, stop him!" My hand went to my sword, but he complied before I got to throw him a stabbing themed 'You're a Jerk' party. A wave of his hand, and Sue's weakness halted. It would be a minute or so before her color would fully return.

"Now, I don't know why my compatriot's talents would have that effect on poor Sue, but it looks like she needs magic in order to be alive." He shrugged his broad shoulders. "As such, I think we can all agree that it would be in her best interests to set out the carpet and start getting us wherever you're going, right?"

Everyone was silent. I didn't have a choice but to give him a begrudging nod and do as he said. The carpet was unrolled, and I did my best to ignore the looks I got from Matt, Kurt, and Lucas. They all wanted to know what the plan was, how I was going to get us all out of this. The truth was, I didn't know. I didn't have a plan. I could bring us somewhere else with the carpet, but I'd be risking Sue's neck with every moment the ruse went on. Plus, I was still on the clock for saving Zoe. Any detours would be another delay and more time she'd have to suffer under Metzmacher's thumb. All I could do was push forward and hope that a plan would present itself in the process.

"Before we go, Foster, you never did tell me what it is we're hunting."

I stared at the designs on the rug, specifically the carefully embroidered peacock in one corner. "The Devil's Mandrake."

If I didn't know better, I would've said that Abercrombie was a little awestruck, or at least impressed. All he said was "Bugger," like he finally understood the weight of what we were doing. It didn't stop him from holding the muzzle of his gun against my spine as we finished the preparations, though.

We all had to stand atop the wishing carpet, as there wouldn't have been enough room to sit, not with all seven of us. Abercrombie decided to stand shoulder to shoulder with me, while Sue and Not-Ivan stood behind us. The rest of the group was clumped in the back.

"Off we go," the Aussie said with a smile. "And no worries. Maybe next time you'll get the jump on us."

I couldn't do much aside from bristling against the gun being pushed into my spine. I sighed my discontent, but went about reciting the words to activate the carpet's enchantment. With the last syllable, we were all flung into that weird moment of darkness and pressure. It was a lot more tolerable when you knew it was coming, which was good, since I had to focus on the composite imaginary photo of this place in New Mexico. I didn't know if it would work or what I'd see when I opened my eyes. I was hoping for a dusty dirt road off of an interstate highway and a tiny house within walking distance.

"Trendaras coreth iln."

You can imagine my surprise when it was Abercrombie being kicked to the ground and Not-Ivan being blasted with a crackling bolt of electricity.

"Woah, woah, what? What?!" It was Sue, and she wasn't just beating the snot out of her captors. A couple of graceful lunges brought her about twenty feet away from the carpet. Seriously, it was like watching a gazelle bounce across the desert if gazelles shot lightning at people. Some stray electricity flickered across Sue's belt buckle as she brought her hands up in a pose that hinted at some kind of martial arts training. I looked back and saw Matt with an arrow on his bowstring. Kurt aimed one of his homemade rifles at Abercrombie, whose shooting arm was being pinned to the ground by a certain werewolf. It occurred to me way too late that I was the only one who wasn't doing anything epic in this situation. I hurried to catch up, yanking at my saber's copper wrapped handle.

"Okay, did you guys plan this behind my back or something?" I tried to be discreet, talking from the side of my mouth at Kurt and Matt. Apparently, Sue heard me as well.

"The carpet produces a momentary stupor in those who are not prepared for it," she said simply. "I seized upon this fact, as it can be assumed that neither of these men have used a wishing carpet before."

"And we had," Lucas added through gritted teeth, though it was clear that Abercrombie wasn't winning their fight. Scrawny as he was, Lucas' sheer physical strength was pretty crazy.

"But what about Matt?" The druid shrugged in response as I looked to him for some support in all this. He hadn't used the rug before, but there he was, bow out and ready for the surprise counterattack.

"I braced myself prior to the spell going off. It seemed like as good an opportunity as any to reverse the situation in our favor."

"Friggin'," I couldn't believe it. This was quite possibly the greatest moment of teamwork in my illustrious career and I missed it. The only thing that pulled me out of my regret was the sound of laughter from the dirt and grit to one side of our group.

"See?" Not-Ivan was sitting up, his hands held up in front of his face. One palm had a patch of blood on it. From where I was standing, it looked like he must've hit his head on a rock as he was thrown backwards by Sue's enchanted belt buckle. "See?! It's on the outside now! All dead, all gone forever and ever, no more!"

There was no way to avoid shuddering at the frenzied laugh that followed his declaration. When he stood and pulled a shattered metal pipe from the back loop of his belt, though, I had to do more than that. The laugh continued, and Not-Ivan went screaming toward Sue. That is, until I shoulder checked the guy back down into the dirt. He flailed and got at least one good swing on my shoulder, but the scuffle didn't get too far before Abercrombie finally said something.

"Ivan! Stop it! They've won."

"Not. Not Ivan," he whined, wriggling once more in defiance. Still, it was amazing how quiet he got simply because of Abercrombie. Whatever was going on in Not-Ivan's bloodied head, there was some amount of trust there. The lunatic stopped squirming, but I held his wrists against the gritty earth regardless.

"So now what?" Abercrombie asked, his hands raised over his head. Lucas had him against the ground with a fist ready to crush his skull in. "Ball's in your court, Foster. I don't imagine you're going to be particularly merciful after our little plot for revenge."

"I probably shouldn't be, no."

"What is it then? A forced march? Execution at the hands of the beastie?" He tilted his head toward Lucas. "Or are you finally going to use that pig sticker of yours?" I assumed he was talking about my sword even though I'd never stabbed a pig with it. I've never been close enough to a pig to try, and if I had been, I don't think I would. They're just so docile and lazy, y'know? I wouldn't call them cute, but definitely not stabworthy.

"How about none of the above?" I slowly pulled my arms away from Not-Ivan, which resulted in a flurry of confused blinks from the grungy maniac. "You're a savvy businessman, right? Why don't we make a deal."

"What kind of deal?" He asked. You could tell from his intonation that I had piqued his interest.

"You guys help me get the mandrake root, and we give you a ride back to the East coast on the wishing carpet. That saves you a walk to the nearest airport and a few hundred bucks."

"Foster, you cannot be serious," Lucas growled. "They would just as soon take the root and stab us in the back at the first opportunity! You are presently doing all of us, especially Sue, a grievous disservice!"

"We'll do it." Abercrombie said, ignoring Lucas and looking right at me. "No tricks, no backstabbing. I'm a thief, yes, but I never go back on my word. I'm guessing we have that much in common." He gave a cocky smile, but it seemed sincere enough.

"I am sorry, but no." Lucas shoved Abercrombie against the ground. "Not after using Sue as a hostage and bringing up that maniac's power to almost kill her for sport! I will send him to the grave myself before I suffer their company!"

I was about to argue the point, but Sue beat me to it. Her arms were down, her posture softened from before. "Their abilities may be useful in procuring the arcana. I am not presently harmed by either man, and I find it unlikely that the pair will be capable of catching me off guard ever again." There was something slightly threatening about that, even though Sue's intonation was flat and dispassionate. Lucas clearly wasn't satisfied with that, and I understood why. I was pissed about the drama in the shop too, but I knew the stakes of what we were about to do. When dealing with an absurdly powerful piece of arcana, it couldn't hurt to have another gunman and a walking magic dead zone.

"I promise I'll make it up to you, Lucas. Let him up and I'll get you a gift certificate to whatever boring store it is you like to shop at. I'm pretty sure there's a discount top hat and antique tea bag emporium somewhere in Shrewsbury."

"This is hardly a joke, Foster." He scowled at me before looking to Sue with concern. After a grumbling sigh, he stood up and let Abercrombie follow suit.

"Thanks," the Aussie grinned, patting dust off his jeans and fancy coat. He moved over toward me as I let Not-Ivan sit up in the dirt. Abercrombie kneeled and checked his partner's head for a sign as to where he was bleeding from. As he examined Not-Ivan's pale scalp, he asked, "What's the plan from here, then?"

"It's pretty simple. We go to that house up the way, and I try talking whoever has the root into giving it to me. If it turns violent, you guys rush in and help me take them down. I don't want anyone to die if we can help it."

"Are you even capable of killing someone, Foster?" Abercrombie asked. I decided it would be best to walk and talk, or else we'd be out in the middle of this desert forever. I looked over my shoulder to see Sue and Lucas rolling up the wishing carpet, which was pretty fortunate considering that I had forgotten about it in the scuffle.

"I'm pretty awesome, yeah. And I totally lit somebody on fire once with a spell. They weren't happy about the whole arrangement, what with the burning skin and stuff."

"Right, but did you kill them?"

"Yeah. Absolutely. They exploded and then died from the trauma one usually suffers from exploding. How about a change of subject, like where your third guy is. Somewhere at the Spiral, waiting behind a box for us to come back?"

"In the hospital." Abercrombie replied. "Your boy's explosion broke one of his ribs."

"Huh. I'd apologize, but to be fair, you guys were either going to leave us for the cops to find or murder us wholesale."

"Don't worry about it, Foster. Comes with the territory. Besides, we'll probably end up on opposite sides again soon, so try not to get too sentimental."

"Noted." We took a few more crunchy steps up to the little house. It had a porch that I guess you'd call quaint, but the yellow siding and shingled roof were faded like they'd been sandblasted by the local weather for thirty years. The front door was dark, overshadowed by the roof of the porch and by the angle of the morning sun. Plain curtains made it impossible to see inside the windows, and the interiors were all unlit. It looked like nobody was home. The whole scene made me think of those houses they built as targets for nuclear bombs, except that I knew there was a real town with people in it a mile or less away.

"Pretty creepy." Kurt chimed in. He and the rest of our small gang gathered around the steps of the front porch, weapons and enchanted rug in our collective hands.

"You are absolutely positive that you wish to enter alone?"

Lucas asked. "Even two of us together would be safer."

"Nah. If whoever owns this house is alone, I don't want to come off as an invader. I want them to think we're on equal footing."

"In reality, you are more likely overmatched. There may be an old woman in there with a frying pan, after all. Or a small family of mice, the largest of which wields a demitasse spoon. Or there could even be a television set inside, in which case we would be unlikely to see you again for several days." I don't know about you, but the mouse wielding a spoon thing just makes me think I'm finally rubbing off on Lucas a little bit.

"Don't worry too much about that. TV has been pretty boring since the internet got good. If I don't come back in twenty minutes, assume I need help. If I don't come back in six hours, I probably found a laptop which I'm using to look at cat pictures and memes." I nodded at my gathered friends and enemies before stepping up onto the first aged wooden stair. I focused on the front door as I approached, trying not to think too much about what might be inside. Best case scenario, it was somebody who had no idea what they were holding onto, so they would be more than happy to part with a creepy old root. Worst case scenario, the root mutated a family of innocent people into misshapen freaks with a singular hunger for human flesh.

The boards that made up the porch were more or less bare of paint, and every other one creaked as I walked across it. On the upside, it was still daytime, with a cloudless blue sky and plenty of sunlight to help push my overactive imagination back into the corner of my mind. If I were doing the same thing at night, I'd be chucking basic light spells into every shady corner until the place looked like Christmas. If any zombies or giant spiders or mutant anteaters showed up to attack, I'd friggin' see them coming.

As it was, the door to the tiny house loomed in front of me. It was terrifyingly normal looking, if that makes any sense. I looked back at the team and got an encouraging thumbs up from Matt. Everybody else seemed pretty unimpressed.

"Go ahead, knock on it." Lucas made it sound easy, of course. He'd never seen *Zombie Martians from Planet 9* at two in the morning when he was seven and hyperactive from eating too much Halloween candy. That lady in the heels never saw it coming when she knocked on the door only to find that it was really an evil robot door.

70s B-movies in mind, I steeled myself for the impending horror. I raised my right hand and rapped my knuckles against the wooden door. I valiantly shielded my eyes in case of impending gamma rays, but nothing happened. I tried knocking again, and there still wasn't any response. Another glance back to the group was less than helpful, as everyone had apparently moved to hide behind the railing of the porch. With the exception of Not-Ivan, who was trying to pull a chunk of siding off of the house.

I exhaled gritty desert air and turned back to the door in search of a bell. When a cursory glance yielded nothing, I wrapped my hand around the doorknob. "Hello? Anybody home?" To my surprise, the mechanisms in the knob turned, and I stumbled a few steps into the house.

The door opened up to a shadowy dining room. To call it Spartan would be a bit of an understatement. There was a simple wooden chair and a similarly nondescript rectangular table, and that was it. No tablecloth, no bowl of plastic fruit, just a thick layer of dust and some wallpaper that looked to be from the 1960s. There wasn't a light on in the place.

"Please don't be full of zombies, please don't be full of zombies." I chanted quietly. It helped cut through the musty silence of the house as I started the trek deeper inside. There was a kitchen to the left, which at least managed to outclass the dining room in terms of furniture. It had an old fridge, an older stove and a sink, though they looked as unused as anything else in the house. Torrents of dust particles danced through the dull beams of daylight that filtered through the curtains. The back end had a door out to what must have been the backyard, meaning I had to turn around and go through the living room on the other side of the building.

At the very least, that section had rugs instead of hardwood floors, meaning I didn't need to listen to my own footfalls as I walked through somebody else's house. The living room was pretty big, containing a decent sized fireplace and a cream colored couch. So far, all of Lucas' predictions were off. No old ladies, no mice, and no TV. Hard to imagine somebody living in that house, unless there was a super swanky basement grotto downstairs. I tried to find a cellar door off of the living room, but instead found what I guess was the master bedroom. I say that because there was a bed and a desk in there, along with the house's only inhabitant.

When I first stepped through the doorway, I was greeted by a quiet gasping sound and a reddish glow. For some reason, my mind automatically dismissed it as the colored light from a computer monitor or something. That is, until I looked to the closet door, where a man was pinned against the wood by chitinous orange tendrils. Red veins pulsed from the center of the formation, snaking all the way out to smaller limbs which covered the man's arms, legs, and face. His head was half obscured, but he looked like he was in his fifties, with long, scraggly hair and a chiseled jaw underneath a scruffy, unkempt beard.

"Holy crap," I exhaled, my legs still trying to decide between running and collapsing like one of those fainting goats. "Hey, are you alright?"

I know. It was a dumb question. Unfortunately, it's the only thing that came to my head upon witnessing that guy's desperate situation.

"You," he said, his voice a raspy echo. It sounded like two people were talking, actually, with one set of vocalizations at a slightly lower pitch. "Why are you here?" He also had a mild Southern accent. Nothing over the top, just enough to hint that he might be from the area.

"You probably know why," I replied. My mind raced as to whether I should have tried to cut him down, yanked the pulsing growth off of him, or gotten Matt in there to help.

"The root." There was almost a smile in those words. He shifted a wrist slightly to gesture at the orange thing holding him up, but the movement was cut short by one of the seething extensions. It curled tighter around his wrist, indicating that this thing was at least mildly aware of its surroundings.

"Wait, this is it? This is Hitler's mandrake?" I'll tell you right now, the plants usually didn't look or behave like that one was. They're more or less magic-absorbing tubers, but the thing wrapped around this guy hissed at the mention of its name. "What happened? How did it get like this?"

"My friends and I," he gasped from beneath the root's hold, "We were hired to take it. From the Thule society." Every sentence

192

he choked out was punctuated with a painful wheeze. "We succeeded, brought it back to the states. The one who hired us killed my men. My friends."

"What?" I shook my head, suddenly grasping how the whole thing had gone down. "Why? What did that accomplish?"

"He didn't want to pay. Or couldn't. I took the root, found out what it was. Kept it here, away from everyone. I've been guarding it." As he spoke, the center of the growth pulsed around his ribcage, drawing out a pained groan. "It's been years. Fighting against it, hiding it. You're the first to come looking. Kind of surprised, thought the Thule Society would send more by now."

"They did," I said quietly, without thinking. Metz had mentioned sending other arcana hunters, but said they had all failed. It was weird to think that others had never gotten this far. "But I'm not really working with them! My friends and I usually kick their butts whenever we come across them, in fact. I just need the root to negotiate a deal with them this one time. They kidnapped my little sister, so I don't really have a choice there. The way I see it, we could kill two birds with one stone. We get you detached from the plant so you're not slowly being crushed to death, and I get my sister back after I rig agent orange there to blow up in the Thule guys' faces. What do you say?"

There was a long moment of extremely uncomfortable silence. At least, it would have been silent except for the pulsing sound of the root's glowing crimson veins.

"I can't let you," he finally responded. "It would overtake you, too."

"No! I promise! Look, I've got a bunch of people who know what they're doing, I'm sure we could make it work somehow," I struggled to figure out how I should refer to this guy. "Buddy, pal, we've got this!"

"My name is Eric Thompson." He responded. Throughout the course of our conversation, his eyes had been closed, but he opened them then. The right was an average brown, while his left eye was submerged beneath the shell of the root. When it opened, the orange chitin split sideways to reveal a glowing red shard, like his eye socket was somehow brimming with lava. The bloody glow from the root intensified with his words. "I am the root's guardian and jailor, and I will not let you return it to them!"

I had no idea where the sudden aggression came from. That is, until I thought about it for about two seconds and realized that he was starting to succumb to what was essentially a battery full of pure hate.

"Eric, I'm not going to! You have my word, I won't let them have it long enough to commit mass genocide or anything! I just need to get my sister back!"

"It isn't that easy!" he snarled. The ex-mercenary's breathing was getting less haggard, probably because the root knew it was finally gaining control. One of his arms started to pull against the restraints, and the tendrils chose to wrap around his muscled limb in response. "You'll kill everyone. I can't allow that!"

"No! For the love of crap, calm down!" I reached over to grab at the biggest hunk of plant I could wrap my fingers around and yanked, to which the mandrake responded with a shrill hiss. "Can't you see the damn plant is getting to you? I just want to help!"

"Help?" he repeated, pulling his entire right arm off of the wall. "I've fought this thing for years, and you think you can just walk in here and blow it up?!"

"Well. Yeah, pretty much!"

"Have you even thought about the kind of energy this thing still possesses? The size of the crater it would leave?" Eric's hand shot down to clamp onto my wrist, and a spike of pain ricocheted up my arm in response. It was kind of like the feeling I imagine you'd get if someone drove over your hand with their car. "You'll need to work on your story, friend. I'm not nearly as stupid as you think I am!"

I remember shouting from the pain in my wrist, but then everything suddenly went fuzzy and slow as Eric's other arm detached from the wall. The hard surface of the root covering his fist worked more or less like brass knuckles, which connected hard with the side of my head. Next thing I remembered, I was laying on the floor with him looming over me. Eric was completely freed from the wall, the orange tendrils writhing around his body like snakes. There was wind, too, a red wind that cut into my clothes and skin like a hurricane made of razor blades. Looking up, I saw that both of Eric's eyes were glowing red. The part of his mouth that I could see was moving, but there was a ringing in my ears that I couldn't hear past. Without warning, the walls of the bedroom began to shudder. The miniature tornado surrounding us was literally tearing the house apart. Wooden beams, tiles, and shredded curtains became a vertical wave of flying shrapnel. There wasn't any way out, and Eric was way beyond reasoning. Couldn't say I blame the guy. It's pretty incredible that he held out as long as he did against the root's influence. All I could do was hope that the guys could find a way to take him out without killing him.

The guys. I had to focus and regroup with the others, or else I'd end up impaled on a curtain rod. While Eric yelled some more and commanded the bloody winds, I dug around in my bag for one of my little glass vials. Specifically, I was looking for one that contained silver oxide and a few teaspoons worth of melted snow. The black powder made the clear water brackish and gross, but I wasn't going to be drinking it. In honor of Seth and his broken rib, I touched the tiny array I had carved into the top of the cork and whispered, "Emrizen fadra antures," before tossing the vial at the edge of the crimson wind. White smoke fizzled out as the glass shattered, which the mini hurricane picked up and spun. Suddenly, the smoke expanded, crackled, and turned into continuous hunks of ice roughly in the shape of a giant frozen helix. That stopped the wind long enough for me to crawl away from the root-possessed Eric and back toward the front of the house.

In the good news department, half of the walls were torn down by the wind, making it easy to navigate back to the front door. I stumbled through and fell onto the porch, where the gang had apparently gathered for what had become a late rescue mission.

"Good lord, Foster! What happened?" I guess my hearing had come back by then. Also, I guess I was bleeding all over Lucas' shoes. Which would have been fine except that it was a lot of friggin' blood, and I needed some of that for my internal organs.

"Remember how I said we might have to resort to violence?" My question was punctuated by a snapped support beam plunging about five feet deep into the scrub-covered front yard. "Yeah. That."

-The Fight Scene-

Here's hoping that title isn't too much of a giveaway. I mean, we're pretty much getting to the tail end of the book here, so I'm guessing it's not much of a surprise. It had to get to a grotesque display of physical violence eventually.

"Kurt! He needs an angel's tear!" Lucas pulled me off of the porch and over his shoulder before dumping me back onto the dirt further away from the house.

"I got it," Kurt replied from somewhere to my left. There was a crashing sound from the house, and something that sounded almost like the howl of an animal. Then, there was a calming blue light as Kurt waved one of our healing crystals over my gashes.

"Good. I think it is roughly time to go punch whatever that thing is until it learns some manners." Lucas threw his top hat and gloves to the ground, then ran up into the half collapsed house.

I took a few woozy glances around to check on the others.

Matt was kneeling on the ground over one of his arrows. From the looks of it, he was tying a couple of small feathers at the base of its sharpened tip. I could only imagine it being part of a druidic spell. Sue was also doing some preparations, pulling a sharpie and some bandages from the back pocket of her jeans. She drew arrays on the strips of cloth like lightning or maybe a laser printer, then tied a bandage around each of her ankles. Another went around her midsection like a loose belt.

To the other side, Abercrombie was loading a new clip into his gun. It came as a bit of a surprise when I noticed that there was an array on the side of the handle, which he touched before pointing the weapon toward the house. He muttered a quick chant and blue flames flared up along the barrel. I don't know why it never occurred to me that Abercrombie would have an enchanted gun, except that he never used it on us.

Meanwhile, Not-Ivan was still trying to rip that siding off of the house. He was determined, I'll give him that. A real trooper.

It didn't take long for the angel's tear to repair the damage Eric had done. In a matter of moments, I was back at the top of my game. No cuts, bruises, or possible brain damage to speak of.

"Thanks for the help, Kurt." I nodded at him, he nodded back, and I pushed myself up into a sitting position. "I don't really know what will work against this guy and what won't, but at least the ice elixir stopped the hatenado."

Of course, fate loves to make a liar out of me. That was when the ice helix fractured. The murdergusts started again, picking up the frozen chunks and hurling them outward in every direction. An ice block the size of a minifridge landed a few feet behind me, narrowly missing both Kurt and I.

"Or not." I grimaced and got to my feet just as Lucas came crashing through the living room window. Parts of his suit were slashed to ribbons, and a massive cut tore across his face. I could already tell this situation was going to get on his few remaining nerves. No matter how quickly he healed, his swanky clothes didn't share that superpower.

Next into the house was Sue. She spoke a few words and patted herself down with some grayish powder first, touching each of the arrays on her bandages in order. Her skin quickly gained a silvery sheen which flowed out from her center like molten metal. An ironskin spell. It would render her impervious to pretty much anything, but it'd also slow her down immensely. At least, it normally would.

Instead of a slow, stomping advance, Sue leaped straight up and into the heart of the vortex. The arrays around her ankles must have enhanced her strength like crazy, or else she'd never have been able to move like that with so much weight. The spell effectively creates a dynamic mesh of metal and pure force over the user's skin. It feels a lot like wearing a suit of armor because you kind of are at that point. Sue's landing was appropriately loud, as were the sounds of combat that followed. I remember wishing that more of the house was destroyed so I could watch Sue kicking butt.

"Bloody hell!" Lucas roared, rolling onto his side. The gash in his face had closed up, but blood was still dripping onto the scrub grass from tons of smaller cuts in his arms and torso. "What did you *do*, Foster?!"

"Before I answer that, how's it look in there?"

"Like a sodding abattoir, what do you think!" Okay, fair enough, even if that was less than helpful. "There is a man covered in seething, red, living armor of some kind levitating in the middle of a cyclone!"

"Friggin' crap. It's red now? That can't be good."

"What's going on?" Kurt asked. He was loading the hopper on one of his guns with little metal spheres. They looked like they might explode on impact. "Where's the root?"

"Well, turns out it's kind of sentient." I decided to join Kurt and Abercrombie in arming myself and tugged my saber out of its sheath. "And it kind of took over a guy's mind and body to keep me from getting it."

"Are you saying that the mandrake root is the thing that man is covered in?" Lucas asked, obviously perturbed.

"A little bit, yeah."

That was when Sue reappeared through the front wall of the house. She careened out and bounced once against the dirt, then left a trench down the front yard as she was dragged toward the road by sheer momentum.

"Oh man, Sue!" The ironskin probably protected her from whatever hit sent her flying, but it wouldn't do anything to keep her neck from snapping. I took a few steps toward her and slid my saber back in its sheath, but not before a thundering crack came from the house. I turned back to see the whole thing lifting up on either side, creasing in the middle like a giant pop-up book. Except that the walls and furnishings smashed together and shredded as if in the middle of a food processor. The storm surrounding Eric was getting bigger and more destructive by the second.

"I am fine, mister Foster." I whipped back around to find Sue standing behind me. Her face looked smooth and flat, kind of like the visor of one of those full face motorcycle helmets. So I couldn't tell anything about her emotional state under the ironskin, but she looked unharmed. "However, we are not going to be able to subdue the mandrake through conventional violence. The plant has developed a sort of exoskeleton that appears to be impervious to concussive force, and the vortex will make it impossible for you, Kurt, the druid, or Abercrombie to draw near without significant risk."

"What about Not-Ivan? Do you think he'd stand a chance if he threw up his dead zone and attacked the root up close?" As it was, the guy was presently trying to jam a shard of broken glass onto the end of a snapped dowel. It was good that he was staying busy in all this.

"While the winds are likely arcane in nature, the shrapnel moving through the air is mundane. A stray nail alone could injure him to the point of death."

"I can do something about the wind, I think." Matt said as he was finishing up with his feathered arrow. "Couldn't tell you for how long, though, and I probably won't have time to make another one of these."

"There's another problem," Kurt added. He pointed his sleeve-covered hand up and toward the former house. More specifically, he was pointing at Eric. He was almost completely covered by the burning red tendrils of the mandrake by that point, which makes me think I should probably start calling him something else. Mandrake Man sounds pretty redundant. Maybe The Red Monger? It's tough, especially considering that Eric wasn't even a bad guy. I admired what he did, it just sucks that he had to lose control before I could do something to help him.

At any rate, he was floating twenty feet above the ground,

still surrounded by the crimson tornado of debris. That was going to make it a lot harder to even get near him, on account of our combined lack of wings or jetpacks. The red slivers of light that were his eyes were still shining through the storm, glaring down on us with unquestionable contempt. If nothing else, the sheer power that thing held was incredible.

"So the thing finally shows its face," Abercrombie said with a predatorial smirk. He aimed the arcane handgun at Eric, holding the weapon in both hands. "And that means we can bag this ornery shrub." The flames around the barrel of Abercrombie's gun flared as he fired, sending what looked like tiny comets streaking toward the mandrake's stolen form. He fired three shots that way, two of which exploded in blue fire as they struck the whirlwind of debris. The final shot made it through, striking Eric in the chest. He was pushed back a few feet, but the arcane fire seemed less than effective against the root's armor. Seething red liquid dripped from the wound for a few seconds before the writhing tangle grew back to cover it. The veins running through the mandrake began to glow white from beneath its crimson flesh. Somehow, it looked more angry than hurt.

"That's no good," Abercrombie said. "Foster, is there anything you can do about the rubbish flying around him? I can account for the wind, but I can barely get a clean shot in through the wreckage."

"Can't hurt to try, I guess." I pulled my book out and flipped the pages open in search of a solution. I was fighting the wind, which made it a bit of a hassle, but it didn't take long for an idea to present itself.

"Sue! Do you know the array for a Scourge of Ares?"

"Yes, Mister Foster," her voice echoed slightly behind her protective spell's mask.

"And you've got a strength enchantment on, right? For the ironskin spell?"

Sue paused momentarily before responding. "I have enhanced physical strength, yes."

"Perfect. Can I borrow your marker? Lucas, Kurt, Abercrombie, and Matt, I need you guys to try and distract him while we do something."

"Distract the mandrake root? How do you propose we accomplish that, exactly?" Lucas griped. "It is a plant, for Christ's sake!"

"Just borrow one of Kurt's guns and shoot at it! Or find a big rock and chuck it!" Sue obliged me the use of her sharpie, which I used to start drawing arrays on my hands. "Or just start complaining at it. That always manages to tick me off." Lucas grumbled in response before heading over with the others to help.

"What is your plan, Mister Foster?"

"It's elementary, my dear Sue." I jogged over to the wooden support beam that was lodged deep into the ground, ducking under a wooden door as it flew through the air. "We make a giant Ares' Scourge and lure the mandrake over to it, then activate the array. The debris burns away, leaving just the hate-wind so Abercrombie and Kurt can start laying down some firepower. It also might let Not-Ivan do something useful."

"Your logic seems sound," she stated in return. "Do you believe that the Scourge would do anything to weaken the mandrake?"

"I'm not counting on it." Sue got on one side of the support

203

beam and pulled, while I pushed from the other side. It would've been way easier to make the array with a can of spray paint than to carve it into the dirt, but we didn't have those options at the time. "Judging by the effect Abercrombie's bullets had, the thing can regenerate pretty easily."

Sue paused. Without her help, I stumbled forward a bit, falling against the support beam. It must have been pretty happy about fulfilling its purpose one last time. "If Abercrombie's bullets have little effect on the mandrake, then what is the purpose of doing this?"

"For funzies?" I shrugged and gave a short lived chuckle. "It's the best plan I can think of, honestly. It might buy me another minute to think of something better."

"Hm," was Sue's only reply. With that, she went back to dragging the beam through the ground like a blunt knife through cold, gravelly butter. I wouldn't say she was doing more work than I was, but the outside circle of the array would've been way less circular if it weren't for her steering. The shape ended up being pretty huge, maybe twenty feet across. Then Sue and I had to pull our giant chisel out of the ground and draw kind of a big check mark that went from outside the circle to its center. A few arcane symbols around the inside edge, and we were ready to go. Which was fortunate, considering that Lucas apparently throws like a chinchilla with a broken wrist.

"Okay, Lucas! Kurt! We need to draw him over here!"

"How?" Lucas yelled. He hurled one of the giant chunks of ice back at the red tornado, but it missed the mark pretty badly.

"Well, first you might want to work on your aim." I took up my book again in search of a spell I could lob at the mandrake. "Sue, go with him and attack from inside the vortex again. I'll throw something at it with Kurt, Matt, and Abercrombie."

Sue nodded and rushed back toward the tornado, calling out for Lucas as she went. He stumbled after, and the two soon disappeared behind the wall of spinning debris.

"Alright, guys, pull towards me and light him up!" Man, it was ridiculously awesome to actually say that, especially since this was a real fight and not Kurt and I playing an on-rails shooter at an arcade. The three long range guys let bullets and arrows fly, with Abercrombie using his magic pistol, Kurt switching to a long, rifle-looking thing, and Matt loading up his bowstring with three projectiles at a time. The feathery arrow had been stuffed under his belt for later use.

For my part, I flipped through the leather pages of my book, inevitably coming to the explosion described toward the back. If I could figure out what the components were, I had no doubt it would be enough to rip Eric and the mandrake apart. Barring a long research session with Sue, though, it wasn't going to happen.

I shook my head and flipped back a few spells. Fortunately, there was another really damaging one that was kind of like the Ares' Scourge: A sunlance. It took a bit more preparation to pull off, requiring a mirror made of polished brass and a specifically faceted prism. Fortunately, I always came prepared. Those two components were in a side pocket of my bag. After replacing the book, I grabbed the mirror and held it up to the sky, positioning the crystal in front of its reflective face.

"Turan, adreth coren tem! Virulen kadres!" A single beam of light shot down from the sky to the prism and bounced off of the mirror. That beam reflected back and forth again and again, intensifying each time until the high pitched whine of plasma filled my ears. "Anvare!"

Upon uttering the final part of the incantation, a white hot beam of pure sunlight shot from the prism. My aim wasn't perfect, so I had to swing the beam right across the sky until it hit the center of the tornado.

I honestly didn't expect the plan to work so perfectly, but when Sue and Lucas both came flying back out, a high-pitched, alien shriek erupted from within. The storm of energy and imploded house parts lurched toward us.

"It's working! It's actually working!" I was elated for a minute, until it occurred to me that I was going to die horribly if I didn't get out of the way. "Wait. It's working. Crap, crap, crap!"

I ran back, throwing the prism and the brass mirror into my bag and kneeling on the outside of the giant array. Kurt, Abercrombie, and Matt scattered as the cutting wind drew close, but I had to hang out longer. Shattered glass and broken planks started whipping by. Looking up, I could see the glowing eyes and veins of the mandrake hovering in the middle of the storm.

"Sorry, Eric." I put a hand down before the trench that made up the outside of the circle and spoke the words to activate the Scourge. "Kulutron anvare!"

I barely got the chance to roll away before a huge wall of blue fire erupted out of the ground. The heat was incredible. I wasn't even engulfed in the fire and I came away from the whole thing with burns on one side of my back. I kept tumbling for my life at that point, but when I was able to turn around, the flames were already swirling up the entirety of the windstorm. Another pained shriek came from the root, and then there was an explosion directly beneath it. I was thrown back even further, as was everybody else. I don't know how long it took to get my vision and hearing back, but when I looked up the mandrake-possessed Eric was completely visible. Anything that remained of the house was scattered or burnt to ash, leaving a thin layer of magical wind between us and the root. To top it off, the thing's tendrils were blackened and charred, sizzling as its glowing lifeblood poured out of its many burns. I still couldn't see Eric himself, which left me hopeful that maybe the root had protected its host.

"Guys?" I looked around. Most of the group was up and moving, but Matt and Kurt didn't exactly look conscious. "Guys, now would be a good time to start punching it and stuff again!"

A section of the root around Eric's chest folded outward, almost like a mouth, and it let out a painful screech. Then one of the sizzling, charred hands rose toward me. Red electricity crackled around writhing tendrils that resembled thick talons more than fingers.

"Oh, dude, lightning hands? Are you friggin' kidding me?" If it weren't for Lucas running through the red wind and latching onto the mandrake's back, the crimson bolt that struck the ground right in front of me would've been fatal. Of course, Lucas then took a blast to the chest, sending him reeling back to the ground. The mandrake screeched and levitated higher, slowly healing from the giant, fiery array. The regrowth of the plant could only be compared to watching giant red slugs or leeches piling on top of one another to cover a third degree burn.

"Lucas, are you okay?" I started moving toward Kurt in the hopes of finding that angel's tear he had from earlier.

"Yes, fine," he groaned, clutching his chest. "I think my heart stopped beating for a second or two, but that really isn't anything to be overly worried about."

"Great!" The mandrake decided to start throwing bolts down with impunity then, which left the conscious people to run as erratically as they could around the cyclone to throw the thing's aim off. "Y'know, I'm starting to think that this fight is getting a little unfair, don't you?"

"Fairness is not something I would imagine a Nazi artifact would be particularly concerned with, if I am perfectly honest!" Lucas dodged to one side just as a streak of red lightning blasted the ground where he was standing. "The more important question is really what you plan to do from here, as I imagine we will all be dead after a few more minutes of this!"

"You have a point," I admitted, rifling through Kurt's backpack in search of the tear. After a lucky guess of the front pocket, I grabbed the blue crystal and waved it over Kurt. "I've got a plan forming, I just need a second to think!"

"What?" Kurt murmured groggily. "It needs transmission fluid."

"Yeah, that's awesome, but we've got to move!" I did my best to grab Kurt's shoulders and pull him away from an incoming spear of electricity as he started coming to.

"The thing's got lightning hands?"

"Yeah," I said, moving to get us both up off of the ground.

"That's cheap."

"Foster, the root is healing! If we are going to do something, it has to be now!" Lucas was being a pain as usual, but he was right. If anyone other than him and maybe Sue got hit with one of those bolts, they wouldn't survive. Abercrombie was doing well enough strafing around and shooting at the mandrake with his fiery bullets, but Kurt wasn't in great shape, and Matt was just starting to get up from the explosion. And then there was Not-Ivan, who was just standing there and staring at the root like it was a big Christmas tree ornament. I watched as a streak of red lightning came close to hitting him straight on, but then the whole bolt just disappeared. Not-Ivan was completely unaffected.

That's when it finally dawned on me. He was the key to stopping the root. I couldn't believe I didn't see it sooner. I looked at the marker still on my hands from the strength spell, then at Lucas, then at Kurt's backpack. In an instant of clarity, everything came together.

"Sue!" I started running around the tornado in Matt's direction, angel's tear in hand. "I need to borrow your bandages! I have another plan!" She nodded in response and circled back to me just as I reached Matt. The tear was running out, I could tell, as the blue portion was turning clear. We were just lucky enough for it to bring Matt back up to speed before fracturing, disintegrating into tiny fragments that slipped easily into the wind.

"Think you can still fire that arrow for me?" I nodded toward the one still wedged between Matt's belt and his jeans.

"That I can, mister Foster." He clapped a hand on my shoulder for support, scavenging his bow off of the dusty, tortured ground. "Just say the word."

"Alright." I turned to Sue and took the white cloth, quickly scribbling the strength array twice more with the marker I had borrowed. I only got halfway through the process before being forced to dodge another blast of electricity, but Abercrombie and Kurt managed to do a good job holding the root's attention otherwise. Once finished with the two arrays, I ripped the two strips of cloth apart and gave the rest back to Sue.

"What can I do to aid in this situation?" She asked. I paused mid step on my way back to Lucas and turned to her.

"Well, y'know, there's a long standing tradition in really over the top action sequences where the male protagonist gets a kiss from the female protagonist for good luck." Before you go making any judgements, tell me you wouldn't at least try for it in my situation. Sure, her face was completely obscured by the ironskin spell, but she was pretty under that façade of molten metal!

"I do not believe that would actually improve the chances of our success," she replied, lacking any emotion whatsoever. "If anything, it would waste time that could be spent attacking the root or formulating another strategy."

Cold, Sue. Real cold. I would've been way more sulky and upset if that wasn't exactly how she acted all the time, so it was kind of my fault for thinking that angle would've worked in the first place.

"Right. Yes. Good point. You should probably shoot lightning at him. From your belt. That would help." I continued the jog back to Lucas, calling over my shoulder, "Does that mean like it would never happen, or...?" By then, she was too busy blasting thunderbolts back at the root to hear me. I decided it was better to cut my losses and deal with romantic endeavors another time.

"Lucas, real quick! I need to borrow your feet."

"What?! What the hell are you talking about?"

"I need to wrap these around your feet or your ankles or something, because I'm assuming you can't currently jump high enough to get to the root." I held up the bandages before kneeling and starting to tie one around his ankle. He stared up at the floating menace, shrugging his agreement.

"Well, no. I likely could not. But what is the point? Every time I get close enough to attack it, I am flung off like so many dirty linens!"

I paused for a second to process that. The above idiom would eventually become number sixteen on my list of things that Lucas has said that makes him completely pretentious. "You're not attacking it, Not-Ivan is."

"How? If I am the one leaping up to," Lucas stopped, realization hitting him like a million pounds. Am I talking about weight or English currency? You decide! "Oh no. I am not giving that maniac a ride on my shoulders!"

"No, you aren't. You'll be carrying him in one arm and one of Kurt's bombs in the other. And before you argue with me on this, save it. It's the only plan you're going to get, and I don't care if you're uncomfortable with the idea of getting cooties from touching a human being."

"Well, I never!"

"Good, so you've been keeping up with your cootie shots. Kurt! I need a bomb that sticks to things! A big one!" Fortunately, Kurt was more than happy to oblige. I was just finishing tying the second array around Lucas' torn pantleg as Kurt trotted over with a two-chambered sphere. One side was plastic and spray painted yellow, while the other side was metal and blue. There was a single homemade button on the metal side.

"Smash the yellow side to stick it, hit the button to make it blow." Short and sweet, just the way it should be with explosives. And pastry.

"Awesome. Lucas, you heard the man." The bomb was tossed to said werewolf, who almost dropped it before nervously cradling it in both arms. "Hey Not-Ivan! I've got a thing for you to do!"

He turned in my direction, but made no move to go anywhere or do anything. Mostly he just stared at me with cold, dead eyes that kind of made me question using him in my plan at all.

"You'll get to make something blow up!" Apart from telling him I was throwing him a pizza party, that was the best offer I could make. Fortunately, it worked. Not-Ivan smiled a creepy, emotionally hollow smile and slowly walked over to us.

"Okay! So, I don't know how much control you have over your power, but I need you to turn it off, turn it on when I say so, then turn it back off again. Is that cool?"

"They'll never find you. Not now. They're coming for you, but they can't! It stains, the blood, not yours! Not now! Not ever." He scratched at his own forearm as he spoke, leaving long, white lines in his already pale flesh.

"I'm going to take that as a yes?" I desperately looked to Abercrombie for some kind of help interpreting the fevered nonsense.

"I've got it, Foster! Just do what you're going to do!" He yelled over the sounds of wind, thunder, and gunshots, sending a thumbs up my way.

"Okay, let's do this. Not-Ivan, I need you to put your aura-thingie down right now." As soon as he gave a slight nod, I touched the two arrays tied around Lucas' tattered ankles and said the verbal components. "Now, Lucas, pick him up and jump for the root."

212

Lucas appeared nauseous about the idea. "Is there no way you could perform this particular task in my stead? I am unfamiliar with explosives, and with the particular brand of madness this young man suffers from."

"Suffer!" Not-Ivan cackled. The laugh abruptly cut off, however, and soon he was back to breathing raggedly and watching as Sue and Abercrombie threw arcane fire and lightning at the mandrake.

"Yes, see? That is what I am referring to." Lucas said. One of his eyes was squinched up uncomfortably. "You are much more versed in mental psychosis, on account of your close personal experience with it."

"That's a long way to go to say that I'm crazy." I replied, an eyebrow raised.

"Yes, well! It seems rather odd that you would require I do this!"

"Think about it, Lucas. You're stronger than me even before those strength runes. I can't say if they'd give me the ability to jump that high and hold Not-Ivan up at the same time. Plus, if you fall too far and break your legs, they'd heal without a trip to the hospital."

"You know, if you ever consider a career in motivational speeches, you may want to stop immediately."

"Are you going to do this and save the day like a hero, or do you want me to find a way to tell all of England and parts of Scotland that you're the wussiest werewolf who ever lived?" I'd do it, too. Not that I knew anyone East of Cape Cod, but that's what the internet is for!

"Fine!" Lucas finally shifted the explosive sphere under one arm and approached Not-Ivan. There was a weird pause as he puzzled over the appropriate way to carry someone with one hand. In what I can only describe as an incredible display of his complete lack of compassion, he roughly yanked on the back of Not-Ivan's shirt and jumped.

"Dude!" It was too late to try and correct him. His leap was almost completely vertical. "Whatever works, I guess. Matt!" I pointed at the druid and mimicked the action of drawing and firing a bow. He nodded and set the feathery arrow onto the string. A quick flex of his arm sent it flying skyward and toward the center of the crimson wind. Matt let out a high-pitched note, which must have been the somatic part of the spell. Blue-green streaks of light swirled out from the spinning arrow's head. As it breezed by Lucas and the mandrake and struck the ground, the glowing streaks quickened until they became similar to the crimson tornado. A burst of emerald light erupted from the point of impact, resulting in a shockwave that stopped the red wind completely. The twirling beams from the arrow somehow turned to water in the process, spattering the ground with dark spots and evoking a momentary rainbow.

Without the tornado to guard it, Lucas continued his freefall and latched onto the mandrake. He dragged the thing down a few feet, but it remained floating even as it bore the weight of both werewolf and psychopath. Its many tendrils rose to crush them, each one with inset veins that beamed fiercely in white-hot anger.

"Ivan! Now!" Abercrombie yelled up at his partner in crime, which elicited a bitter, frustrated shriek from him in response.

"Not! Ivan!"

Lucas took that as his cue to shove Not-Ivan at the mandrake. The field went up, and the results were incredible. Any tendrils within a three-foot sphere of him simply vanished, and the ones that intersected the area were suddenly cut off. A screech echoed out, and Eric reappeared from under the piles of corrupted plant-matter. The mandrake itself reverted to its natural form: A long potato with four limbs and what looked kind of like a head. It was still latched onto Eric's chest, but any evil glow it possessed was immediately extinguished.

As per the plan, Lucas slammed the yellow side of Kurt's bomb against the mandrake. The plastic dome shattered and yellow goop poured out, probably a fast-acting adhesive of some kind. It adhered to the root and a portion of Eric's chest almost instantly. Lucas growled and slapped the button on the blue side before letting go of Eric's shoulder.

The two fell, and as soon as Not-Ivan was far enough away, the mandrake surged back to its former strength. A wave of chitinous tendrils swooped out to smother the bomb as it had Eric, but too late. The explosion went off regardless, resulting in a huge, reddish-black cloud and blasts of scarlet fire. Chunks of root came tumbling down from the sky, followed by trails of brackish gore. The mandrake thudded next to Abercrombie. It was whole and in its brown, mundane form, except for its ominously glowing red veins.

"And that, my friends, is how you do it." I said. I was admittedly basking in the glow of victory at that point, so I didn't even bother questioning where Eric had gone.

"Mister Foster," Sue interjected, "There is a hand on your foot."

I blinked and looked down. Yep, there was totally a severed human hand sitting on my shoe. I promptly kicked it into the air, fell over and vomited. It took a minute for me to get any kind of composure back, and even then, I threw up a second time on attempting to get back up.

"Hail the conquering hero," Lucas said, pinching the bridge of his nose.

"Oh god, he's dead? He's dead." I shook my head and wiped the side of my mouth with my sleeve. "We killed him." It was my first time seeing a dead body, or at least parts of one. It was also the first time where I was partially responsible for it. I remember my whole body shaking pretty badly. I didn't get why I was the only one freaking out. Was I seriously the only one that wasn't okay with that?

"I would probably file him under really, really dead," Abercrombie said. He had the mandrake in his hand, examining it like you would a jewel-encrusted baguette. "But you got what you wanted, right? Or I did, anyway." The smile he gave after that statement was pure avarice given form.

"Don't even think about it," I said with a grimace.

"Why do you even want this thing, Foster? I wouldn't say it's exactly your style. Always took you for a fan of magic swords or sparkly, shiny things."

"I need it to get my sister back. The Thule Society will kill her if I don't give it to them." I was getting sick of explaining that, but it was a necessary annoyance.

"Your sister," he replied. I nodded, and Abercrombie looked to be in deep thought for a moment. Then, he gave a shrug and tossed the root at me. "Nobody in their right mind would buy it, anyway."

"The man has a point," Matt said. He approached the mandrake with a foggy white stone in one hand. An uncut quartz crystal. It was hanging from a leather strap that hinted at its prior use as a necklace. "Maybe moreso than he realizes." I pushed myself back up into a standing position, my legs faltering at first.

"What's up, Matt? What do you mean?" The druid picked the root up and held his rock against its smoking flesh. The crystal glowed a faint red color, probably with a weaker light than the Rouen Diamond.

"It's drained, Mister Foster. That last fight used up whatever power it had stored up."

"What? How? What about the city destroying, zombie army creating power it was supposed to have?" One of my eyes was squinting weirdly at the sudden development. "I mean, you said it yourself! That thing is supposed to give the Thule guys enough juice to destroy the world!"

"Well, from what I understand, it drew power from the hate held by members of the Nazi party, which has been in fairly sharp decline since the 1940s. Back then, it might have had that kind of arcane energy. Not so anymore."

"Does that mean I don't get to blow it up?" Kurt already had a soldering iron in one hand and the temporary cell phone in the other. It was kind of sad, like a puppy staring at a chew toy that had been taken away.

"It would certainly be more of a risk to do so, all things considered." Matt replied as gently as possible.

"Tell you what, Kurt, we'll blow up something else, and it'll be even more awesome. The sooner we can get Zoe back, the better." I wouldn't get the satisfaction of blowing the root up either, but I was okay with it overall. It meant a little less stress on me in terms of timing, and hey, giving the Thule guys a dud mandrake was just as good as it blowing up in their faces.

"Yeah, alright." Kurt shrugged and put the tools away.

"Great." I held out my hand to Matt, taking up the mandrake. It pulsed weirdly in my palm. "Then we need to set up and call them in."

-Showdown-

Before calling the number Metzmacher had given me in the sealed envelope, and before doing anything else, I gathered up any big rocks I could find in the sandy ground around the ruins of the house. I wasn't religious, of course, and I'm still not, but I believe in universal respect for the dead. Lucas and the others more or less watched as I built a crude funerary mound for Eric, though Kurt helped. I couldn't bring myself to look for any other body parts that might have been left from the explosion, but I had to do something.

"I'm sorry," I whispered to the pile of rocks. The apology felt inept and futile in my throat. "I didn't think it would..." I couldn't go on after that. I spent a while staring at those rocks. Kurt stood next to me, offering his brand of silent condolences. He clapped a hand down on my shoulder at one point. Eventually all I could do was shake my head and walk away.

"Foster," Lucas said, less irritably than usual, "You did what you had to do. No one would fault you for that." I turned and looked to him, taking in his concerned expression along with those of Kurt and Matt.

"Thanks, Lucas." I forced a smile and started the walk away from the house. "Let's get somewhere a little more remote. I don't want the Thule idiots to find this place and start looking for stuff."

Lucas nodded, and with that we were off. We walked in silence, going into the scrub grass until the ruined house was indistinguishable from the bristly plants in the distance. There wasn't much to see besides parched dirt and sand. Even the highway had disappeared into the horizon.

"I guess this is as good a spot as any." We were standing on a decent sized mound of rocky dirt, surrounded by sand. I didn't know too much about tactical maneuvery stuff, but that seemed to be a defensible place to be. I looked up at the sun. We were getting into the afternoon, meaning it would be night before we were finished with all the preparations I had in mind. Sue and I spent a while drawing more arrays, refreshing strength runes, and doing everything we could in case Metzmacher's goons decided to go back on their deal, which seemed pretty likely, all things considered. But they weren't getting their root until I had my sister, even if that meant going Rambo on them.

Stars were just melting into the sky when we finished the final steps. The whole thing would've made a great montage, though it would've been better if we had old mine carts to mount flamethrowers onto. Montages are always cooler with blowtorches and snappy orchestral music.

"Everybody ready?" We were all standing in a tight circle as I pulled my phone from my pocket. The group gave a collective nod, and so I dialed the number that would let the Thule Society know we had the root. I held the phone to my ear, expecting to hear someone's voice after a few rings. Someone did pick up on the other line, but only for a moment before hanging up.

"Man, that's just rude." I replaced the phone in my pocket and drew the Rouen Diamond out of my bag. "Hope they gave me the right number. I'm pretty sure numbers are different in German, and Metz' English isn't perfect."

"The Thule Society has members throughout Europe, Asia, and the United States," Lucas replied with an eye roll. "I have no doubt that she could have cross-referenced them with someone."

Lucas was proven right that time as the air around us started to crackle with arcane energy. The atmosphere wavered between quivering silver veins that died in chaotic bursts, all while shadows of people and vehicles slowly burned into view. I wasn't sure how Metzmacher was able to translocate all that equipment, barring a really powerful array that I didn't have in my book. They faded into view all around us, surrounding our little spot of dirt with a line of gas-masked gunmen and gray jeeps. We had a decent distance between us, but I wouldn't bet on us being out of range for their guns. Metz had clearly been planning this for a while. I glanced around for some sign of her, or Zoe, or anything to indicate that we weren't all about to be gunned down in a blaze of really predictable betrayal.

"Herr Foster," I heard her call. I immediately whipped around to face Metz, who was standing on a bit of a dune, looking down at us with her arms crossed victoriously. "You have called?"

"Yeah," I replied. I hadn't noticed that I was gritting my teeth together until right then. "I've got the mandrake, just like you wanted."

"Really? So quickly?" Her thin eyebrows moved toward her pale hairline. "I would hope that this is not a trick, since you have found it so soon."

"No tricks. The other guys you hired probably didn't have the same connections I did. Or maybe they just sucked."

"I see," Metz said. She looked to Matt and smiled, maybe enjoying the thought of him finally using his druidic powers for evil. If only she knew. "Show it to me."

"I want to see Zoe first." I was trying not to sound angry, but it didn't work all that well. She glared into my eyes, looking for weakness to exploit. I'm sure she wouldn't have conceded to anything unless she knew she had to.

"Bring her forward." The men behind her wasted no time in parting. My heart almost imploded in my chest at the sight of her as she was brought forward by the cloaked, bearded man. She looked unhurt, for what that was worth. Her long hair even appeared to be brushed recently, which raised a few questions, but she was still in her pink pajamas. A white cloth was tied around her face to prevent her from speaking, but I could hear a quiet cry leap forward from her anyway.

"You see?" Metzmacher stated, as though I was somehow inconveniencing her and wasting everyone's time. "She is here. Now, the mandrake."

"Fine," I replied, pulling the root from my messenger bag. It seethed slightly in my hand, wriggling in what I could only guess was an attempt to be free. The glowing red lines that crisscrossed its brown flesh looked a little more impressive in the dark, which I hoped would work in our favor. Metzmacher turned to the hooded man, who nodded slightly at the sight of the thing. She couldn't contain the reptilian smile that followed.

"Wunderbar," she said, just loud enough to be heard. "Bring it to me."

"No friggin' way, scumbag." I enjoyed watching her smile deflate into a scowl of disbelief. "You bring Zoe halfway, I bring the root halfway. You do something stupid and evil, and I throw the root to the werewolf, who makes it into an after tea snack!"

"It is far too late for tea," Lucas grumbled. "And further, I am not your personal garbage disposal."

"Just this once?" I asked, whispering to him through one side of my mouth. "Just pretend, for Zoe's sake?"

Lucas sighed. He must have been feeling generous that time, growling quietly and making vague clawing motions in the air to emphasize his voracious appetite, I guess.

"Very well," Metz bitterly agreed. "Do it." She nodded at her cloaked associate once more, who placed a hand on Zoe's shoulder. Her big, blue eyes glanced up at him, then quickly turned back to us. The pair walked forward, so I did the same. We each trudged over prickly brush and through the sand for what felt like forever until we were standing face to face.

"So how's that whole 'being a Nazi' thing working out for you?" I held the root out, but didn't release it into his hand until he lifted his from Zoe. She ran to my side and grabbed at the bottom of my shirt, pulling the white cloth off of her face with one hand.

I don't know if the guy in the cloak spoke terrible English or what, but he didn't respond. He simply pulled the mandrake from me with surprising strength and turned to walk back into the assembled line of goons. He probably didn't appreciate the comment, though, judging by his countenance. The guy was perpetually stuck with the face of somebody whose computer just lit on fire for no reason.

"Sean," Zoe whispered, "I missed you so much." She buried her face in my coat, hiding from the dark circle of guns and vehicles surrounding us.

I kneeled down and wrapped her in a tight hug. "I missed you too, Zoe. I'm sorry it took so long to get you back."

"It's okay. You did your best, I know you did." Zoe pressed a tiny smile to my shoulder. "You always do."

I squeezed Zoe once and picked her up the way I had the night I came back with the Rouen Diamond. There might have been manly tears involved, I really don't remember that well. I ran her back to the group, where she immediately reached out to hug Lucas. Meanwhile, Metz and her bearded advisor examined the root more closely. The shadows that were the gunmen and their jeeps became darker by the moment as the night deepened.

"You have done surprisingly well, Herr Foster." The root disappeared behind the folds of the man's cloak as Metz spoke. "You have found the root in very small time, and without tricks. You are honorable, and you love your sister."

"Yeah, and you guys are a bunch of kidnappers and horrible racists. What's your point?"

"If you were willing to change your attitude, I would say that we would consider not killing you along with the rest of the world. You have the features of the chosen people." Metzmacher shook her head. "Such a waste."

"Yeah, well, I'm going to go out on a limb and guess that a lot of blonde people don't really agree with genocide based on ethnicity. Just a guess, though." The last thing I wanted was to be associated with the Thule Society just because of my hair and eye color.

"True. Many will die unnecessarily, I am afraid. But in its wake, the Fuhrer's mandrake will leave a utopia for those who embrace the true word of God." The two things I hate discussing over dinner and also in the middle of a desert: Politics and religion. That said, I couldn't deny that she was at least passionate about her completely nutbag theory. As she spoke, her arms lifted up from her sides until her gloved fingertips reached skyward. It didn't take long for her to return to her stick straight posture, though. "In honor of your service to the Thule Society, I think we will end your miserable lives first."

"Raise your hand if you saw that coming," I said. Literally everyone in our group did so, including Zoe. I think one of the thugs in the firing line even did.

"What about us?" Abercrombie asked. "You don't even know who we are! What if we were captive Thule operatives?"

"Are you?" Metzmacher asked, lifting her nose a few degrees in the air.

"Well, no."

"Then it is irrelevant." She unholstered a handgun from her side and pointed it at our group. The rest of the gunmen followed suit, taking aim at us with a completely unreasonable number of barrels. "Do you have any other pointless comments before your blood paints this horrible desert?"

"As a matter of fact, yes!" I replied, thrusting the Rouen Diamond from my coat pocket into the night air. "Check this out! Otrius, demar abestus!" The crystal twinkled with pure light, creating white lines in the sand and dirt to match its faceted surface.

"What is that, a medieval flashlight?" Metzmacher turned to her hooded advisor, who didn't bother to respond. I scowled over at Lucas, who was smiling slightly. The moment we made eye contact, he went back to a serious expression.

"No, it's not a medieval flashlight! You friggin' jerks." I tapped Kurt's shoulder, which elicited a knowing nod. I watched as his thumb slipped onto the send button on the temporary cell phone. "A flashlight only has two settings: On and off."

My confidence probably tipped them off, explaining why Metzmacher would shout the order to fire just as I gave the verbal component that would ramp the diamond into a blinding strobe. I shut my eyes and yelled the mystic language into the night.

"Aetra, aetra aetra aetra!" Each utterance of the phrase exponentially increased the amount of light from the crystal until I could see every blood vessel inside my eyelids. There was shouting from the gunmen, but nobody was firing anything yet. It must have only gotten worse for the Thule guys when Kurt detonated the explosives we had buried in a wide ring under the sand. I'd say the minions were pretty much standing on top of them, judging by what I heard when Kurt set off the chain reaction.

Shots started going off then, but Sue was right on cue with the incantation for the wishing carpet. We'd buried it in a layer of sand beneath our feet, meaning we'd be back in Worcester before the Thule Society knew what hit them. Before the whoosh of arcane power flowed over me, though, I remember hearing something above us. I'd figure out later that it was the sound of jet engines, something Metz probably didn't have access to. Then the world went dark, and the sounds of gunfire were muffled and drowned in silence.

After a moment, the underwater feeling receded and left us on the sales floor of the Spiral. I was dumb enough to open my eyes the minute we reappeared, which resulted in a black and red cloud that pulsed in the center of my vision for the next hour.

"Friggin'! Venael giserum." The light winked out instantly, returning the shop to complete darkness. "Holy crap that thing is bright."

"What happened?" Zoe asked. I felt her hand reaching blindly for my shoulder, so I reached up to hold onto it. "Sean, where are we?"

"We're safe," I replied. After days of worrying and bearing the weight of Zoe's kidnapping directly on my shoulders, I could finally relax. I smiled. "We're safe. Do you remember Sue's shop?"

"The Spiral? We're almost home!" I shared her enthusiasm about that, definitely. "But how did we get here?"

"A wishing carpet," Sue answered. From the sound of her voice, she must have stepped off the carpet to go turn on some lights. "A piece of arcana which instantly transports those atop it to whatever location they visualize."

"Cool!" Zoe exclaimed. The lights came on then, revealing that the carpet had brought along the sand we had gathered on top of it as well, leaving a bit of a mess on Sue's polished wooden floors. I was too busy hugging Zoe again to care too much, but Lucas went ahead and asked Sue for a dustpan to help clean up. I'm not sure whether he was being polite or obsessive compulsive. Meanwhile, Abercrombie guided Not-Ivan off of the rug and toward the door.

"Hey, Abercrombie," I said. He paused in mid step and looked back over his shoulder. "Thanks. Not for trying to hold Sue hostage or doing your best to beat the snot out of us in Lowell, but with the mandrake."

"I had a vague idea that's what you meant, yeah."

"We worked pretty well together. I'd say we should tackle some arcana again sometime if you weren't in it solely for profit. And if you didn't subscribe to the ends justifying the means." I let Zoe down so she could scramble around the shop, happily bouncing around Sue's feet and thanking her for helping.

"Considering what happened to the guy with the mandrake, I'd say we aren't all that different in that regard." He smirked, knowing full well that I wasn't exactly done coping with that aspect of the adventure. My gaze dipped to the floor.

"I never said it was right, or that it was even worth it. I thought the root would protect him. If I had known," I trailed off, which gave Abercrombie the moment he needed to land a last verbal punch to the kidneys.

"You would have done the same thing, because you love your sister more than a guy you knew for all of ten minutes. Welcome to the real world, Foster." The bell above the door jingled as he opened the shop up to vibrant midnight air.

"Do you think we'll still be enemies?" I had to ask. The question came out stilted and weak. "Next time we see each other?"

"Oh, yeah. No question. Unless you're just going to start lying down and giving us whatever arcana we'd normally fight over. And that would just be a kick in the teeth for Seth. He still wants to impale you on an icicle pretty badly." With that, Abercrombie lifted a hand to casually offer a backwards wave as he and Not-Ivan strolled out.

"Okay, yeah. I guess that's fair. But hey, I wanted to thank

Not-Ivan, too!"

"In the walls! Screaming! Screaming and it hurts, hurts to see! Never again," Not-Ivan howled. The door swung shut, cutting off any further ramblings.

"I'm going to go ahead and take that as a 'you're welcome' and leave it at that." The rest of the group had scattered themselves across the sales floor, with Lucas aggressively sweeping up sand, Kurt looking at a book on Buddhism, and Matt perusing a glass jar full of long, swooping, multicolored feathers. Sue had apparently given Zoe one of those root beer barrel candies before taking up her spot behind the register. It was almost like nothing had happened and we were back at square one. The only notable exception was that I was still dreading going back to our old apartment.

"I guess all that's left is to say thanks to you guys." I pulled away from the carpet to make Lucas' self appointed task a little easier. "I know I inconvenienced you all a lot, and I'm sorry for that."

"Now isn't the time for apologies, Mister Foster." Matt said. He had selected a green and blue feather from the jar and was holding it up to look at it through the light of one of the wall sconces. Subtle silvery daubs shimmered along the edge of the feather. "Now is the time to celebrate a very unlikely victory, drink some wine, and relax."

As soon as Matt finished that statement, Kurt clicked a can of beer open. I still have no idea where he got it. I guess he just kept one in his backpack in case of emergencies.

"I would find myself hard-pressed to ignore a glass of fine liquor," Lucas agreed. "I should still have a bottle of Castell Coch at my hotel room, which I could fetch easily enough using the wishing carpet."

"My store may not be an ideal location for such a celebration, considering that I have few chairs and keep little food here." Sue stated flatly from behind the counter. "Additionally, Zoe should likely be sleeping at this point in the night."

"Aw, but Sue! I'm not even tired!" Zoe proclaimed around the candy in her mouth. Of course, she yawned immediately after, which didn't help her case any.

"Well, we could always just hang out on the floor and set up some pillows and stuff for Zoe. Unless you'd rather we didn't." I looked to Sue, who stared back with her usual expression.

"I have no preference in the matter," she replied.

"So, is that a yes?"

"I have no preference."

"So we can hang out here, then, and you're cool with it."

"You could hang out here, yes. However, I have no preference as to whether you do so."

That was my breaking point. I mean, if anyone else was acting like that, I'd call them out for being passive aggressive like nobody's business, but I think Sue was being honest. Which reminded me about the thing with Not-Ivan.

"Sue, who the heck are you?" I asked. Matt and Lucas turned, uncomfortable with that particular line of questioning. Kurt sipped his drink and flipped to the next page in the Buddhist book.

"Perhaps it would be best if we took Zoe to see Lucas' hotel and picked up refreshments there," Matt said, walking back onto the wishing carpet. "How does that sound, Zoe?" She seemed receptive to the idea, nodding and running next to the druid. Lucas did the same, seeing fit to drag Kurt on as well in spite of a lazy grunt.

"Can I do it?" Zoe asked. She tugged at one of the heavily embellished corners of the carpet. "What do you have to say to make it go?"

"You need to be able to see the location you want to go to in your mind, Zoe. Which means that Lucas has to do it this time." Matt offered a warm smile as a consolation. "But if you want, you can do it on the way back." That appeased her eagerness, and after a couple of attempts, Lucas successfully repeated the words. With a burst of reddish smoke, they were gone, leaving just Sue and myself in the store.

"To answer your previous question, I am Sue," she explained simply.

"Yeah, but I mean, why did Not-Ivan's magic-negating field almost kill you? Are you a lich?" For those who don't keep up with their necromancy, that's somebody who places their consciousness in an object and then continues to control their ageless, unfeeling body through some creepy ritual.

"I am not a lich."

"A vampire? Lucas told me those don't exist, but I'm pretty sure he's lying about that."

"I am not a vampire."

"Are you a chupacabra?"

There was a brief pause after that one, and Sue looked at me with a hint of disbelief. "I am not a chupacabra."

"Then I'm pretty much out of ideas." I paused, slowly looked up to the ceiling, then blurted out, "Are you a mummy?"

"I thought you said you were out of ideas." Glancing back to Sue, she didn't even seem flustered.

"Yeah, I thought maybe I'd catch you off guard with that

231

one."

"You did not. And I am not a mummy."

"I kind of figured. Too much skin, not enough rotting bandages. So what's really going on?" I was about two seconds from trying to grab her hand in an impassioned moment just to see if she had a pulse.

"I am not going to tell you," she answered. "It is not yet necessary for you to know." I was a little dumbfounded by that. I guess I knew we weren't really close friends or anything, but it wasn't like I had given Sue any reason not to trust me. Still, if she didn't think it was any of my business, that was her right. It didn't mean I'd stop wondering or prodding her about it, but I imagine she knew that at the time.

"You do realize, of course, that I'll probably have a curiosity-induced aneurysm because of this." I smiled to indicate that I was joking, but Sue responded exactly how you'd probably expect her to.

"Aneurysms are not known to be caused by excess curiosity." However, she did give the slightest bit of a smile in return. "But I will call an ambulance if you appear to be suffering their symptoms."

"I appreciate that, thanks." I leaned against the display case and shook my head with a laugh. "On an unrelated note, what are your plans for the wishing carpet? Going to return it to the museum circuit?"

"I have not yet decided," she replied. "It is in some ways the rightful property of the public. However, there is also responsibility to be considered if it were to be stolen again by another arcana hunter, especially now that it has been restored."

"Plus, you could use it to take really cheap vacations. I've always wanted to see the Arctic Circle, or Japan, or New Jersey."

Before Sue could ask why on Earth I'd want to go see New Jersey, the wishing carpet returned with its passengers. Matt had grabbed some pillows and blankets, while Lucas had an ancient looking bottle of wine in one hand and a few wine glasses in the other. Kurt had somehow materialized a second tall can of beer, and Zoe was holding tight to a two liter bottle of root beer.

"I did it!" Zoe squealed. She bounced on her heels before running over to me. "I did it! It took a few tries and I think we went to Vermont a little bit, but we're here now!"

"That's awesome!" I gave Zoe a broad grin and reached down to pick her up from under the arms. She giggled happily, especially as I proceeded to spin her around.

"Sean, the soda! You'll make it explode!" she cried out between exuberant laughing fits. "Sue will be so mad at you!"

"Oh, man, you're right." I slowly drew the spin to a halt, letting Zoe back down in the process. I grinned at Sue, who was just barely smiling again.

"As long as the bottle remains unopened, the contents within will not burst from the bottle," she stated. "The carbonation within the soda will not create sufficient pressure to burst the plastic bottle, except in extreme environments."

"Oh." Zoe blinked and looked at the floor, and then back up at Sue. "But if it did explode, you'd be super mad, right?"

"No. I would clean the mess, and that would be the end of the situation."

"Really?" Zoe turned her head at a funny angle and set the bottle of root beer on the dark stained floor. "Because if I was you, I'd be super mad and be like, I'm gonna get you raaahhhh!" To illustrate her point, she threw her hands in the air, fingers crooked like menacing talons, and started attacking my legs with harmless swats.

"Oh no!" I cried out, collapsing to the floor under the fury of Zoe's assault. "Sue, why would you do this?!"

"I would not do that," Sue tried to explain, but Zoe wouldn't hear of it. She continued to roar and growl as she stepped up onto my sternum, drowning out Sue's objection.

"I'm Sue and I'm so mad! I hate soda, and bottles, and seagulls!"

"Seagulls?" I lamented from the floor, "Sue, why would you hate seagulls?!"

"I do not." The fact that she didn't seem to get at all annoyed with the game only encouraged more rounds of growling mixed with juvenile giggles. On the sidelines, Matt, Kurt, and Lucas all started cracking into their drinks. They took up seats on the floor, resting their backs against the main display case. Lucas shook his head as he watched the shenanigans unfold.

"You know, Zoe is very sweet now, but I fear that when she grows up we will just have another Sean Foster on our hands." He swirled his wine and gave it a sip before continuing. "It is rather a terrifying prospect."

"Not just another Sean Foster, but one who has a crush on you, apparently." Matt added between gulps of British red.

"Aw, Matt, really?" I opened my mouth and stuck my tongue out in disapproval. "You know Sue's probably going to wait until we leave and then write crazy fanfiction about that now, right?"

"I do not write fanfiction," Sue stated with just a hint of bitterness.

"Sean, what's that?" Zoe paused in her stomping and rampaging to ask.

"I'll explain it when you're older," I said. "When you're thirteen and just getting into anime. Seems to be the appropriate time for that kind of thing."

"I think I will consider myself fortunate to have no idea what either of you are talking about." Lucas said as he poured some more wine into his glass. "I may also go so far as to suggest a new line of conversation."

"Don't mind if I do, actually." I crawled to my hands and knees, then slid back until I was sitting against a tall bookshelf. "Hey Zoe, I don't mean to bring up any scary memories, but what happened when you were with those guys? Did they do anything bad?" That question had been gnawing at me since Metz had first kidnapped her.

Zoe shook her head and walked over to my side. She sat Indian style before letting out a yawn and leaning down so her head sat against my leg. I guess she was finally starting to get sleepy. "At first they were really mean and they said something about taking me to a cell. They drew one of your circles on the ground and then we were somewhere else. It was outside a really big, really old looking building. There were creepy, metal bars all around the outside, and there was a statue of an angel. I couldn't tell if it was a boy or a girl, though."

"Might be their headquarters," I supposed. "Sounds pretty serious."

"I don't know," Zoe replied. "It was really big and it looked nice on the outside, but inside it was all dark and scary. The evil lady went to go do something, and then we went down a hallway and there was a really pretty lady. She talked to the other ones in the uniforms. She sounded really mad, so they let me go."

"A pretty lady?" I glanced around at everyone else, but it was clear that they were as stumped as I was about this person's identity. "What did she look like?"

"She had hair like mine and a red sweater and a white skirt. I kind of want to look like her when I grow up. She had pretty red shoes, too." Zoe nodded and stretched out onto the floor, which prompted Matt to toss a pillow my way. I caught it and placed it between her head and my lap.

"How old do you think she was?"

"I'm not sure. She looked like your age, Sean. She talked to the men some more and they ran off, so she held my hand and led me to another room. It was amazing. The bed was so big and soft, and the room was so fancy. There were paintings on the ceiling and everything!"

"Wow, that sounds really nice!" I felt it would be best to mask my distrust of this person for now. "Was that where you stayed for a few days?"

"Mhmm!" Zoe turned so that she was looking up at me with her big, blue eyes. "It was really fun! I don't think that lady spoke English, but we played with dolls and painted our nails. She brushed my hair for me, too. I feel bad for her."

"Really?" I asked, trying to keep a positive tone. "Why's that?"

"Because she was sad," Zoe said softly. "Even though she was pretty and her room was nice. I think she was too nice to live with the rest of the mean people."

"That's too bad," I said slowly. I wanted to tell Zoe that

everything would be alright, and that the woman who took care of her would find a way out, but I hate lying to her like that. I didn't know who this mysterious girl was or why she was living with the Thule Society, and I probably never would.

"Another hostage?" Lucas asked, staring into his cup of deep red wine.

"Why would they keep a hostage in the lap of luxury?" Matt said. "It seems to me like she's a higher ranking member of the organization who simply has an aversion to harming children."

"Maybe." I wasn't entirely convinced of that, but it was a possible explanation. "Either way, I'm glad she took care of my little sister." The little scamp had fallen asleep on me, so I grabbed the blanket from Lucas' hotel room and did my best to drape it over her.

"It could have been much worse, certainly." Lucas stated. "I think luck has been kind to you both, despite the kidnapping."

"You have a weird definition of luck, but I can't exactly disagree with you." I let the back of my head thud against the intricately carved wooden shelving behind me. "Hey Matt, can you pass me the root beer? I'm a little stuck here."

The rest of the night was spent chatting about nothing in particular. The rest of the guys drank until their combined buzz was palpable, while I finished about a third of the soda. Sue kept a silent vigil at the cash register. Orange sunlight was creeping up on the tiny, round windows of the store when we started dropping off into floor-sleep. It was the kind of slumber that felt so right at the time, but would be murder on every bone in your body when you finally woke up.

-Epilogue-

The next day started around noon, when we all woke up in a haze and stumbled out of the Spiral. I still didn't feel like going back to the apartment, but there wasn't much else to do besides heading to Dunkie's for lunch. We thanked Sue on the way out, receiving a predictably mild response. I had to hope we didn't accidentally overstay our welcome.

The cheap coffee and the egg sandwich I got didn't exactly sit right in my stomach. I ended up feeling pretty sick for the rest of the day, which I should have expected. Zoe and Kurt got donuts. We sat in Kurt's car in the parking lot for a while, eating and working through the midday slump, but we had to get back to the apartment at some point. Zoe would need to go back to school, and all her stuff was there. I'd need to figure out what we were going to do next.

At that point, the apartment was brimming with runic circles and protection arrays. Even if the Thule Society wanted to attack us again, we would be well protected. That didn't account for Zoe's route to school, though. And I couldn't extend my arrays into the hallway outside our apartment, or the building in general. They could still be watching us as long as we lived there. Zoe didn't seem worried when we got back home; she bounded into the living room with an enthusiasm I wish I could have shared. Instead, I felt anxious. I checked every corner of the house like I was robbing another museum or an ancient temple. Fortunately, neither snakes nor poison darts came pouring from the walls. We settled back in for a few days, but I knew we couldn't stay there.

That Friday, I started packing. Zoe was tentative about the idea of moving, especially when I told her that I didn't exactly know where we were going. I promised her a room that was just as cool as the one she had now, which seemed to help a little. We talked about colors we would paint things, and furniture we would look for at Goodwill and yard sales. She wanted me to try and paint things on the ceiling, which I agreed to. Not that I can paint castles or dragons, but I could probably manage clouds.

By the end of that week, everything was in boxes, with the exception of the stuff in my parents' room. It was going to be hard going through it again. I'd probably have to sell the furniture, but I wasn't sure about all the rest of their stuff. The closet was still full of clothes, books, and everything else they had left behind. I waited until Monday to box it all up while Zoe was at school.

The process took a lot longer than I had thought. I think I was hoping to throw a lot of it in the trash, but I ended up folding most of the clothes and almost all of their nick-knacks into carefully arranged boxes. I decided to move the dresser over to a different wall to get at the carpet with our crappy old vacuum, but I stopped when a slip of paper fell to the floor. It must have been wedged between the dresser and the wall for years, and I never noticed.

My hands shook a bit as I ran my fingers along the carefully folded creases. The paper was still crisp and white. As soon as I tugged on one of the edges, the whole thing opened up, revealing two simple lines hand-written in black ink. The first read, 'Prophecy of Saint Alban', followed by 'Verulamium'. It looked like my dad's handwriting.

Before I could think on the meaning of the note, there was a knock on the main door of the apartment. It wasn't something that happened often, so I was immediately put on edge. I stopped over in my room to grab my saber before pulling the door open just wide enough to see the visitor's face. His smug, just slightly stubbled face.

"Mister Foster," Agent Evans said. He tried to prop the door open with his overbearing smile. "Nice to see you again."

"Wish I could say the same." I held the door tight in one hand and my sword in the other. "What do you want?"

"Can I come in? It's less than polite to discuss things through a doorway like this."

"Do you have a warrant?"

Evans sighed, but flashed a folded piece of paper for a second before stuffing it back in his pocket. Still, it was out long enough for me to read a line or two.

"That's not a warrant, it's a pay stub. And you were holding it sideways."

"Do you have any idea how long it takes to get a warrant? Especially when it involves the supernatural."

"I don't, no," I said before trying to shut the door on his face. "But I'll start timing you from right now if you want."

"I just wanted to extend my thanks, Foster." The arm of his fancy suit poked into the doorway to keep it open. "For bringing the Thule Society onto American soil. It was much easier to take them down here than it would be in Europe, I'll tell you that."

That gave me a reason to pause. I even stopped trying to crunch his arm off like an alligator with the door. "You guys took down Metzmacher?"

"Not her, no. She and about half of their goons made a hasty escape with some kind of translocation spell. But the rest are on their way to an interrogation room as we speak." He seemed pretty happy with himself over that. Me, I don't get too excited about the prospect of someone being hooked up to a car battery, no matter who they are.

"Congratulations. You managed to beat up and arrest some guys who aren't peaceful protestors. Do you want a medal?"

"It would be a nice gesture if you had one." Evans grinned through the slim opening. "Really, I was hoping you'd reconsider the offer to work with us. There's a significant paycheck in it for you. Who knows, maybe you can be less bitter about the whole military-industrial complex when you're on the profitable side."

"Yeah, I don't think so." I was about to shove hard against the door when Evans finally retracted his arm.

"I'm not doing this for my benefit, Foster. There are things going on that are over your head. The entire world might be at stake." After all that repartee, the sudden dark change in Evans' tone managed to be sufficiently foreboding. "If we don't start working together, then I'm going to have to start working against you."

"Y'know what, Evans?" I quickly stepped back from the door,

letting it swing wide open. "Go ahead. Try and arrest me. It'll set off protective wards that are so big, so destructive, you'll need to be scraped off sidewalks from here to New York."

He stood in the open doorway and glared, his perfectly sculpted skull clenched tight. His eyes scanned the living room, which was populated almost exclusively by my couch and a forest of cardboard boxes.

"Somebody's been packing. Moving to Sweden already?"

"Well, I've got this problem with jerks randomly showing up here. They start demanding stuff or kidnapping my family members, it's becoming kind of a pain." I set the tip of my saber on the carpet and rested a bit of weight on it. "So are we fighting, or what?"

"Not here, and not now," He said. "But soon, we will end up on opposite sides in your little escapades."

"I'll look forward to kicking your butt when that happens." I probably didn't need to be that confrontational, but I was honestly still mad at him about the cream soda from before. The front worked, anyway, sending Evans walking back and down the stairs like a prowling cat. Just in time, too. I wanted to leave early to pick Zoe up from school. I shut the door and decided to use a simple translocation array. It'd help avoid an awkward situation where I'd somehow be walking right behind Evans for a block and a half, and we'd both be trying to avoid eye contact so we wouldn't have to talk to each other. I friggin' hate that.

I was waiting for about twenty minutes before the elementary school kids were let out, but I was fortunate enough for there to be a playground near the entrance. The swings were a little low for someone my size, but I made due. The bells within the school went off soon enough, echoing over to me on a gentle spring breeze. I jumped off of the swing set as far as my momentum would carry me, which was a little pathetic compared to how I remember it from my childhood. Zoe came running out with all the crazy energy a kid should. I was glad. She seemed relatively unfazed by the kidnapping, whereas I was still shaken up by it. I smiled as she made a b-line for me off of the paved walkway. She came in with her hands up, eyes bright with anticipation for a spinning, flying hug. I wasn't about to disappoint her.

After a gaggle of laughs and a little happy squeaking, I set Zoe down on the grass so we could start walking back home.

"Man, kiddo, you are getting big! I think in a few more days, you'll be taller than Lucas."

"Really?" Zoe asked with a grin that almost stretched off her round face.

"Definitely. I'll have to call you in anytime the ceiling fan needs dusting, or if a flock of geese start attacking from above."

"Aw, but I like geese! They're cute."

"Vicious animals, Zoe. They're your best friends as long as you have some bread or leftover herring in your pocket, but the minute you're out, they'll be nipping and honking at your heels."

"Then I'll train one to be my guard animal, and I'll teach it to bite anybody 'cept you and me and Lucas. Oh, and Kurt, and Matt, and Sue, too."

"You'll be completely unstoppable. Zoe, Queen of the Geese!" She bubbled over with giggles, but overall seemed to like the idea. It was then that I stuffed a hand in one of my pockets and felt the folded up note I had deposited there earlier. I pulled it out between two fingertips and stared at the paper.

"Hey, Zoe, I found this earlier today. I think it's from mom and dad." I offered it to her, and she took it up with wide, curious eyes.

"What's it mean, Sean?" She asked. Her little eyebrows drew together in confusion. "What's a Vermamalum?"

"I'm not sure yet. Do you want to help me look it up online when we get home?"

"Yes! Maybe it'll help us figure out where they are!"

"Maybe!" I didn't want to get her hopes up too much. It might have been nothing, just a random scrap accidentally knocked off the dresser.

"Oh, and I forgot something!" Zoe said, digging through her own pockets. "I mean, I found it in my pajama pants pocket, but then I forgot about it, but I remembered it because you reminded me!"

"Okay," I wasn't entirely sure where she was going with that until she produced a piece of rose-colored stationary from her backpack. It was covered with elegant script written in black ink.

"It looks like a letter, but I can't read it at all. Can you?" She got on her toes to try and hold the message up to my face. It looked like the writing was in German or something similar.

"Afraid not, sis. Looks like German."

"That's too bad," Zoe said. She pouted ever so slightly. "Two notes, and we don't know what either of them mean."

"Not yet. But with some help, I'm willing to bet we'll find somebody who can translate the pants off of that note." I purposefully mussed up the hair on top of Zoe's head and grabbed the cell phone out of my pocket. She was elated.

"Does that mean Kurt and Lucas are coming over again

tonight?"

"If they don't, I'll tell them there'll be a very sad little girl in Worcester, and it'll be all their fault. And that they'll probably be mauled by a goose."

"Yay!" Zoe bounced with joy before spinning and upping her pace to a run. "And I'll make cupcakes, too!"

I hurried to catch up, an unwavering smile on my lips. "Hey, Lucas! What are you up to? Yeah, that's fascinating- I think it's time for another caper."

-Epi-Epilogue-

What? Of course that's a thing. It happens all the time in books. What are you, the epilogue police?

I heard about this happening a while after I got Zoe back from the Thule Society, but I thought it'd be perfect to include here. I have it from a very reputable source that the following events happened in the frigid mountains of the German Alps. I'm paraphrasing, of course, but it went a little something like this:

A line of bundled forms marched up the incline of a mountain path in the middle of a raging snowstorm. At the front was a woman in a black winter coat, her face obscured by sunglasses and the furry edges of her hood. A bearded man in a dark brown cloak followed behind, holding a writhing mandrake root in his gloved hand. After him was a procession of thin, pale men and women, all of them dressed in bulging coats to protect against the wind. They moved with slow determination toward a gray, stone building at the peak that jutted from the mountain like a frostbitten finger pointing to the bleak sky above.

They eventually reached their destination, pulling open the heavy door to the frozen tower and stepping inside its sterile walls. They peeled their layers of coats off, all except the bearded man who let his cloak drip with melted snow. Metzmacher slid her sunglasses into the inner pocket of her winter coat and motioned toward the giant machine at the building's core.

It looked somewhat like an evil microscope, with numerous onyx columns reaching from the high ceiling and hiding within them unknown horrors of modern science. There was no exposed wiring, no gears visible to the naked eye, only glossy black and silver and a humming noise that originated from an unseen power source. It was clear that the singular purpose of the gray building set so far from anyone was to house this machine. Its black cylinders turned slowly as the Thule Society's greatest scientific minds moved toward a platform at its base.

Metzmacher took the mandrake from her cowled subordinate. Once the entirety of the group was gathered upon the platform, she pressed a button on a control panel, and they were lifted to a comparatively small interface halfway up one of the black columns. Keys were pushed, a thin metal lever was pulled, and a mouth opened on the side of the huge cylinder. The woman placed the mandrake within, then clicked the lever back in place, closing the mouth. Whirring began all throughout the facility.

The black machine came to life, with its many columns splitting in the middle, dancing around one another in an intricate pattern, and ending up in a stance that housed the mandrake in a tube of light at the center of one of the cylinders. The lights all throughout the rest of the building shut off one by one until only the mandrake was illuminated. A wicked thrum began and the other parts of the machine spun like a centrifuge around the plant. They became blurry to the spectators, who watched from their raised platform with the reserved awe only scientists could maintain.

The blonde woman who commanded them, on the other hand, smiled with all the cruelty that possessed her aging form.

The tornado of glistening metal continued until the orange veins of the plant root within its clutches started to glow once more. The hate that still lingered within started to bleed into the pure white light around it. Glowing red lines appeared in the black cylinder, starting at the middle and moving in both directions. Crimson electricity shot from the machine like a plasma ball.

"Gut," Metzmacher whispered, apparently to the root. Her fingers curled around the top rungs of safety rail around the platform. "Sehr gut..."

Then, the orange glow subsided. The Devil's Mandrake went dead, and the red lines that had run up the central part of the machine flickered off. The spinning columns even slowed in their mechanical dance in response to the lack of energy. After a few moments, the room was still once more, and the mandrake root looked to be as common as any other. Metzmacher's hands tightened until she threatened to tear her gloves on the railing. The scientists dared not move nor speak, though their eyes glanced to the exit that was so far away.

"Foster," she hissed quietly. Metzmacher's body shuddered with sudden, uncontrollable rage, her breath ragged. Her second annunciation was a shrill scream to the heavens that echoed through the freezing air of the facility.

"Foster!"

At least, that's what I was told happened. I wouldn't make that kind of stuff up.

www.ingramcontent.com/pod-product-compliance
Lightning Source LLC
Chambersburg PA
CBHW050503260626
47157CB00004B/1171